RISEN FROM ASHES

CASSIE QUINN
BOOK 9

L.T. RYAN

with
K.M. ROUGHT

LIQUID MIND MEDIA

THE CASSIE QUINN SERIES

Path of Bones

Whisper of Bones

Symphony of Bones

Etched in Shadow

Concealed in Shadow

Betrayed in Shadow

Born from Ashes

Return from Ashes

Risen from Ashes

Into the Light

1

Every piece of equipment in the sterile examination room was as familiar to Cassie as an old friend. The only sounds were the thumping of her own heart and the rustle of the doctor's coat as she moved around the room. Outside the window, the lush treetops swayed in the silent breeze.

Dr. Chen's gaze landed on Cassie's face like the white-hot spotlight of an interrogation lamp. This was her final checkup after three months of recovery following a gunshot wound to the chest, and her future depended on the other woman's assessment. Cassie refused to meet the doctor's eyes, fearful that she'd see some reason to deny her the outcome she desperately wanted.

It took all Cassie's concentration to remain expressionless while the doctor lifted her arm and rotated it this way and that. The skin along her chest pulled taut in mild discomfort. The deep ache inside her chest caused more pain, though that was more phantasm than physical. Even three months later, her mind still spun from what had occurred in that parking garage back in April.

"Anything?" the doctor asked.

"The skin's a little tight there." Cassie couldn't get away with saying everything was fine. "But otherwise, it feels good. Better than last time."

"Good." Dr. Chen let go of Cassie's arm but didn't step back. "Do you mind pulling your shirt down so I can look?"

Cassie did as she was told, diverting her gaze from the mirror on the other side of the room. Everything in here triggered an onslaught of unwanted memories. The machines to her left reminded her of those first few days of recovery, and the nausea bubbling within the confines of her stomach made her unsteady even though she was sitting down. The verdant forest pressed against the cerulean sky reminded her of their isolation. They were located somewhere in Virginia, but she didn't know anything more than that.

Movement from the corner of the room begged for her attention.

She closed her eyes, but Cassie found no solace in the darkness. Her mind's eye conjured the faces of the people she loved. The subsequent ache in her chest had nothing to do with her injury. It was also a thousand times more painful. She'd rather get shot again than continue this hidden existence where everyone, other than a handful of strangers, believed she was dead.

Dr. Chen finished checking her front before she circled around back to check the exit wound. "It's normal to feel some tightness, but it's healing nicely. Your doctor did a fantastic job."

Cassie rolled her eyes, and for the first time in days, she had the urge to smile. "My doctor is a lot of things, but never modest."

Dr. Chen let go of Cassie's collar and walked back around to stand in front of her. This time, Cassie forced herself to look the other woman in the eyes. Her physician was petite in every physical sense of the word—just over five feet tall with a thin waist and delicate features—but she was no pushover.

Today, Dr. Chen had pulled her long black hair into a ponytail that revealed three pairs of diamond studs in her ears and the hint of a tattoo along her neck. Cassie wondered, not for the first time, who this woman was and how she knew Omega. Better yet, what did Dr. Chen know about *her*?

"Physically, you're doing great. There will be stiffness for a long time. If you continue your exercises, you'll get used to the sensation. It's important to keep those muscles in your chest and shoulder loose and strong. Otherwise, you'll experience mild discomfort. Much easier to avoid that altogether."

"I understand."

Dr. Chen pushed her large glasses up her thin nose while she studied Cassie. The other woman's eyes were golden brown, and the unusual color always caught Cassie off-guard. Or maybe it was the sharpness of her stare and the intelligence behind it. "Cassie?"

"Yes?"

"How are you doing mentally?"

Cassie tried to hold back her sigh of frustration, but it forced its way out of her mouth anyway. In addition to Dr. Chen, Omega had set her up with a psychologist to monitor her mental health after the *incident*, as everyone called it. It had been frustrating at first because no part of her wanted to rehash her backstory with someone new—especially someone she wouldn't see again after she left Virginia.

But Dr. Bower had worn her down with his argyle sweaters and the promise of a new book to read each week. Or maybe Cassie had realized she'd never get out of this place if she didn't show some progress. Omega refused to tell her anything other than the bare minimum about what was happening in the outside world until both her doctors had agreed she was recovered enough to join him in taking down Apex Publicity.

The physical rehabilitation had been the easy part. Her wound had been the best-case scenario for the situation—a through-and-through that missed any major organs or arteries. It didn't even shatter any bones. Omega had told her she'd been shot in the chest, but her shoulder had taken most of the damage, and that's where she'd feel the mild discomfort for the rest of her life.

It had still been a serious injury. If she'd been alone with Chris, there was a one-hundred percent chance she would've bled out on the concrete floor of that parking garage. It was only because Omega had administered first aid and called an ambulance that she'd survived long enough to make it to the hospital.

Those first few days of physical therapy had been tough, but she'd fallen into a routine. The physical exercise was a welcome distraction from the monotony of her day-to-day life, and she felt stronger than ever.

Her mental recovery, however, had been an uphill battle. The isolation was suffocating, despite the fresh air that filled her lungs every time she stepped outside. No matter where she went, her skin prickled with the sensation of being watched. And not just by the people around her. Those other watchful eyes had been on her for the past three months, though she'd become an expert at ignoring them.

"Cassie?" Dr. Chen repeated, her brows pinched in concern.

Cassie took a deep breath, knowing she'd have to be more honest about this part. Dr. Chen and Dr. Bower were in cahoots, she was sure of it.

"I'm doing okay." It was hard not to let her voice fall into a robotic rhythm. Cassie had repeated these words so often, she couldn't tell if she believed them or if she said them to get everyone off her back. "Dr. Bower and I have talked about the incident ad nauseum. I don't know why Chris did what he did, but I understand that he was backed into a corner. As difficult as it is to believe, I don't think he meant to kill me."

Dr. Chen nodded but said nothing.

"The worst part has been feeling trapped." Cassie's voice wavered. "I miss my friends and family. I'm worried I might never see them again. And if I do"—Cassie cleared her throat twice before she could finish her thought—"I'm afraid they'll never forgive me for not telling them I'm alive."

Dr. Chen's golden eyes filled with sympathy. "These are all normal feelings. It's good you're not ignoring them. Dr. Bower said you've come a long way." She paused, as though deciding how to phrase her next question. "I've heard your daily walks have gotten longer. Are you experiencing any pain, or—"

Cassie shook her head. "No. I enjoy being outside." She looked to the window again. It was midday, and fluffy white clouds filled the sky. She imagined lying back on the grass and soaking in the sun while she looked for meaning in their shapes. "I'm getting stronger, so it's not as difficult as before. It helps with the restlessness."

Dr. Chen nodded her approval. "Sometimes we forget physical activity is as good for our minds as it is for our bodies."

"Trust me, no one here will let me forget it."

Dr. Chen laughed, high and clear and full of the kind of good humor Cassie hadn't felt in some time. When the laughter died out, the doctor picked up a clipboard and flipped through a couple pages while she chewed on the inside of her cheek.

"Well, that's all I needed to hear. You're in good health and your scars look neat enough to put in a textbook." She looked up at Cassie and winked. "I can't speak for Dr. Bower, but as far as I'm concerned, you're all set to be discharged."

Cassie sat up straight. "You think so?"

"Not to be modest or anything, but—I *know* so."

A wave of hope crashed over Cassie, sweeping her up into a maelstrom of unbridled excitement. She might not be able to go home yet, but she'd taken the first step.

2

THE EXAM ROOM DOOR SWUNG SHUT BEHIND DR. CHEN'S RETREATING figure. Murmuring voices came from the other side of the wall. A moment later, Omega slipped inside with nothing more than the squeak of his boots against the tile floor.

Cassie's mood dimmed. It hadn't taken long for her to stop thinking of the man as Robert, the stoic driver she'd met on her first day in Tennessee. When she'd encountered him at the airport, she hadn't known what to make of his impassive nature, but she'd come to enjoy his calm, steady presence. Out of everyone she'd met at Apex, he'd seemed the least caught up in Apex's machinations.

Of course, he'd been a traitor to them the entire time.

"Morning," Omega said, letting the door click shut behind him. He swept his gaze around the room before landing on Cassie. "Dr. Chen gave me the good news."

"Apparently, the scars from my surgery are textbook worthy." Her upbeat delivery of the information sounded saccharine. She wondered if Omega had picked up on it. "Now I just need Dr. Bower's approval."

Omega crossed the room to lean against the opposite wall, crossing his arms over his broad chest. He didn't smile, but there was a twinkle in his dark eyes. The silver along his temples and the dusting of a beard and mustache reminded Cassie of her father, and the thought was like a punch to the gut. She could hardly breathe at the sudden sensation, and it took all her willpower to focus on Omega's next words.

"I ran into Dr. Bower earlier this morning. He and Dr. Chen are in agreement."

Cassie studied the man across from her, trying to discern the thoughts behind his eyes. To most, he would look like some sort of farmhand, dressed in a fitted blue t-shirt and boot-cut jeans. He was old enough that his experience showed in the lines of his face, but no one would think him anything less than formidable. He'd spent months, if not years, hiding in plain sight as Anastasia's driver, and he'd killed Agent Chris Viotto without a second's hesitation. And then saved Cassie's life.

Cassie wanted to flick her gaze to the corner of the room, but she resisted. It was better to focus on the tangible.

She wasn't afraid of Omega—he'd blown his cover to save her life, after all—but she didn't know what he wanted from her. Even though he'd given her no reason to distrust him, she'd seen what he was capable of. And something told her she'd just scratched the surface of his skill set.

"Good to go," Cassie repeated, failing to keep her voice light. "But not home."

"No, not home." Omega raised both eyebrows in an expression caught somewhere between exasperation and sympathy. "But you knew that. This is what you signed up for."

Cassie looked down at the floor, not wanting him to see the regret in her eyes. Not only had Omega saved her life, but he'd also pulled strings at the hospital so the doctors would pronounce her dead on arrival. Then he'd whisked her off to Virginia to complete her recovery in secret. Upon regaining consciousness, her first thought had been about taking revenge on Apex. She'd let anger lead the charge, but she couldn't deny she'd been in her right mind when she'd agreed to continue the ruse Omega had devised.

"What now?" Cassie only glanced up once she'd gotten her emotions under control. "You said you needed my help, but I don't understand why you think I'm the only one who can help you."

"You're not the only one," Omega said, pushing off the wall, "but the best one."

A spot of discoloration caught Cassie's attention, and her gaze drifted down to Omega's ribs. His shirt was dark, but she could still see the stain. She'd seen similar injuries over the past few months. "You're hurt."

Omega followed her gaze and lifted his arm to get a better look. Grunting, he walked over to the sink in the corner and rummaged through the top drawer for gauze and tape. Turning his back to her, he lifted his shirt and cleaned the wound with quick, practiced movements.

When it was clear he wouldn't offer up the information on his own, Cassie asked, "What happened?"

"Knife wound." He said it the way someone would observe a ketchup stain on their pants. "It'll clean up easy enough."

Cassie knew that was all the explanation she'd get. It'd been like this for months. After the first few weeks went by with little information, Cassie had changed tactics and tried to find out more about her enigmatic savior. At the very least, she'd wanted to know the identity of the man who'd pretended to be Omega outside the Parthenon in Nashville. So far, she'd only learned he'd been Omega's old military buddy. Someone who'd known the risks of the mission and had accepted anyway.

Omega's expression had conveyed his lack of interest in sharing more than that.

Hovering over the chrome sink on the other side of the room, Omega finished patching himself up and tugged his shirt down over the bandage before tossing a few pieces of bloody gauze in the trash. The whoosh of the swinging cover underscored his next words. "You don't seem too excited about getting the green light."

"I've learned to be cautiously optimistic when dealing with Apex."

Omega's lips pinched together. "The good doctors signed off on you getting back into the field, but I'm not about to drag you out there by your hair. It has to be your decision, just like last time. I'm not interested in teaming up with someone who doesn't have their head in the game. That's a good way for both of us to get killed."

Cassie winced at his harsh words, but he wasn't wrong. "What did you have in mind?"

"What do you remember about Pearl Everly?"

It felt like years had passed since she'd first heard that name. Omega had promised to tell Cassie and Jason everything he knew about Apex if they provided him with more information on Pearl. Chris Viotto had gathered the information from Apex's own files, but at the time, she'd had bigger problems to deal with than trying to figure out who this person was and why she might be important.

"She was a young girl who went missing years ago," Cassie said, dredging up the memory like she was pulling a net through sludge. "The case remains unsolved."

"Apex, and specifically Anastasia, has been interested in her case for several years now. To the point of obsession."

"Who is she?" Cassie asked, feeling yet another unsolved mystery digging its claws into her skin. "Why is she so important?"

"That's what I want to find out."

Realization dawned on Cassie like the warm glow of a sunrise. "That's why you need me. You're hoping I can find her."

Omega nodded. "Apex doesn't take interest in people unless they're at the top of their game."

"Mine isn't exactly a common industry."

"You'd be surprised." Omega didn't crack a smile. "I've been on this earth a good long while, and I've seen a lot of things I can't explain. You, Miss Quinn, defy the odds."

Cassie sobered. He'd meant it as a compliment, but she felt like an aberration. The urge to crawl out of her own skin was overwhelming. Omega's eyes turned sympathetic at the shift in her demeanor, but it looked too close to pity to comfort her.

"Apex had good reason to go out of their way to recruit you," he said.

"You mean blackmail me."

"Fair enough." He paused, rubbing a hand along his beard like he was unfamiliar with the sensation. "They've spent immeasurable resources keeping Pearl out of the spotlight. Dead or alive, she knows something Apex is desperate to find. Or keep hidden. If we get there first, we may just find the key to bringing them down."

Cassie liked the sound of that, but it was rarely that simple.

"I'll help you," Cassie said, "on one condition."

Omega raised an eyebrow, but she couldn't tell if it was in interest or condemnation.

"We rescue Christina and her kids first." Cassie had been thinking about Chris' sister and his niece and nephew nonstop since the moment she woke up in her hospital bed. When Omega opened his mouth to argue, she cut him off. "Once they're safe, I'm all yours. I'll do whatever it takes to bring Apex down."

The sunlight filtering through the window glinted off the silver in Omega's beard as he worked his jaw back and forth. He was as tired of hearing this argument as she was of making it. After asking him to ensure her friends and family were safe, Cassie had begged him to find out what had happened to Christina and her kids. He'd relented, hoping the answer would satisfy her.

Apex still held Christina and her children prisoner, and they'd been too well-guarded for Omega to mount a rescue alone. But after three months, he'd still done nothing to get them out of the situation.

Standing in front of her now, Omega gave the same answer he'd given every time she'd asked the question. "No."

"Please—"

"You know it's a trap." Omega said this through clenched teeth, as though it took every ounce of willpower not to shout at her. "If Apex wanted them dead, they would've killed all three of them the minute they were no longer useful, which was the minute Agent Viotto died."

In other words, the minute you killed him.

Cassie didn't say it out loud. They'd had no other option. And dead didn't always mean gone.

"They're only alive," Omega continued, "to draw you out."

"You said they were pretty convinced I was dead."

"Apex didn't become who they are by being impulsive. The more time we give it, the better chance we have of getting away with a rescue mission without drawing suspicion."

"And the better chance they have of ending up dead. Think of those kids—"

"I have. I'm not a monster, Cassie, but I have to keep an eye on the bigger picture. I can't let this ruin everything I've worked so hard for."

As Cassie looked away, a tear tracked down her right cheek. She didn't bother wiping it away.

Omega sighed, softening. "The longer Apex thinks you're dead and I'm in the wind, the more room we have to do what needs to be done with minimal distraction and risk. Once we figure out why they're so interested in Pearl, I'll make sure Chris' family gets home safe."

Cassie nodded but still didn't meet his eyes. "What's the plan?"

If Omega noticed how quiet her voice had become, he didn't acknowledge it. "Pearl's parents waited two years before they buried an empty casket. I have the location of her gravestone. I've got some business to take care of in the morning, but we'll make it by nightfall if we leave after lunch. If she's there, we may get our answers sooner rather than later."

"And if she's not?"

"Let me worry about Plan B. You just make sure you're in the right state of mind to communicate with her if she shows up."

Cassie nodded, her gaze locked onto the spotted tile floor. After a moment of weighty silence, Omega turned with another squeak of his boots and left her alone in the exam room.

As alone as she ever got these days.

Because three months ago, David Klein's spirit had hovered at the edges of her vision, encouraging her to stay strong while she fought for her life. His voice had been a salve against the blaze of pain in her chest. In the end, she'd recovered.

The next day, she'd seen a different spirit manifest out of the corner of her eye. It remained on the other side of the room, ever-present and ever-silent. When she moved toward it, the specter would fade away and reappear opposite her. There was no hiding from his pale green gaze and no mistaking the three holes in his chest for anything other than bullet wounds.

Chris Viotto was dead, but he was far from gone.

3

ASSISTANT CHIEF OF POLICE ADELAIDE HARRIS COULD BE FOUND IN HER usual spot—hunkered over a keyboard in her office. The building was quiet except for the hum of the air conditioning and the occasional honk of a horn from the street outside her window. The soft glow of the desk lamp offered enough illumination to type, though it left the corners of her room shrouded in shadows.

Her hips were stiff from sitting for so long, and the knot in her shoulder throbbed in time with her heartbeat. She pushed down the pain until it was nothing more than an errant thought in the back of her mind. Tomorrow she'd go to the gym and stretch her legs, or maybe make an appointment with her masseuse.

Tonight, she'd given in to the nagging voice in her head that told her she was a failure, that she'd missed a vital clue, that maybe if she watched the video one more time, she'd find the answer to a question she hadn't thought to ask.

The voice was a liar, but that didn't stop her from pulling up the security footage from the parking garage in Nashville to watch Cassie die for the hundredth time. The feed was dark and grainy, and the camera had a smudge of dirt in the bottom righthand corner, but she could envision the moment as though it were in technicolor.

The way Chris had killed Emma Bannerman, then turned his gun on Cassie.

How an older man had approached without either of them knowing, pointing his own weapon at Agent Viotto in return.

The manner in which all three of them had exchanged words before the inconceivable happened.

How Cassie had collapsed to the ground milliseconds before Chris, blood pooling beneath her.

The older man—Harris had confirmed he was an Apex employee by the name of Robert Callahan—had administered first aid to Cassie and called an ambulance. They'd arrived in record time, hoisting her onto a stretcher and into the back of the vehicle. The stranger had climbed inside without hesitation, as though he had every right to witness Cassie's final moments on earth. Then the ambulance peeled out of there.

They'd pronounced her dead at the hospital.

The police had arrived inside the parking garage a minute or two later, inspecting Chris' body and roping off the crime scene. Harris could still smell the coppery blood in the air like she'd been there just moments before. She could hear horns honking and tires screeching from the street below. Feel the warm breeze on her face that did nothing to dispel the ice-cold dread that had clawed its way up through the concrete, taken root in the soles of her shoes, and overwhelmed all her senses until she was numb with pain.

Harris stopped the video and rewound it, pausing when the stranger had stepped out of the shadows. When Harris had first seen him, she'd thought he'd been the one to put a bullet in Cassie's chest. It'd been a surprise, then, to see that he'd defended her. Even more of a surprise to learn he worked for Apex.

Had worked, she corrected. When Harris had inquired with the company as to his whereabouts, she'd expected lies and secrets. What she got, however, was a harried employee who'd informed her that he hadn't been to work in three days and therefore was no longer a part of their company. Harris had visited the man's home address, though it had been nothing more than a vague imprint of what a home should be.

She'd hit a dead end.

Pressing play on the video, Harris watched the three figures exchange words. She paused it again before Chris pulled the trigger, studying each of their faces in turn. Cassie looked shocked and betrayed. Callahan appeared resigned to his next action. From this angle, Harris couldn't read the expression on Chris' face.

She hadn't known Agent Viotto well, but Cassie had described him as a good man who had been working to take down Apex just like Cassie. Harris had gotten the sense that he'd had stronger feelings for Cassie than she had for him, but he didn't seem like the kind of person to go off the rails about it.

It made no sense why he'd chosen to kill her.

A lump of emotion rose in Harris' throat. With no one to witness her tears, she let them cascade down her face. The screen blurred before her, but she didn't need to rewatch the video to know what happened next. She could describe every micro-expression on their faces and each movement of their bodies. When the bullet hit Cassie's chest, an invisible one had pierced Harris' heart at the same time.

A sob escaped her. Harris muffled it with her hand in the hopes of holding back the rest of the sounds building in her throat. It had been three months, and yet the emotional wound was as fresh as if it had happened yesterday. Each morning, Cassie was the first person Harris thought about. Every night, she worked through every conceivable theory as she fell asleep, each more ridiculous than the last. When she dreamed, Cassie was centerstage in every single one.

Deep in her gut, Harris couldn't believe Cassie was dead. Every day, she tried to move on from this moment, to accept what had happened to her friend and learn to live without the other woman's shining presence. And each day, she failed to rid herself of the hope that Cassie was out there somewhere.

In all her days as a police officer, Harris had witnessed the best and worst humanity had to offer. She'd seen people die for less, but she'd also seen them survive far worse. Cassie's will to live had been put to the test time and again, and she'd always come out the other side.

The hospital had no explanation as to where Cassie's body was, either. Her first instinct was that Apex had a hand in that. But for what reason? Were they covering up yet another murder, or had they wanted to use her body for science? Harris shuddered at the thought of them experimenting on her, cutting open her brain and taking a peek inside to see how it worked.

Harris' sobs had subsided for the moment, and she wiped her cheeks with the backs of her hands. When she blew her nose, it sounded like a horn piercing the silence of the building. She stared into the dark corners of her office for so long that when she turned back to her computer, she had to squint against its harsh light.

That voice in her mind rang out again. *You're missing something.*

Hitting play on the video again, Harris watched as Cassie collapsed to the ground, followed a second later by Chris. Three gunshot wounds to the chest had ended his life. Robert Callahan performed first aid on Cassie and called the ambulance. She stopped the video when the police arrived to inspect Chris' prone form.

His only surviving family included a sister and her two kids, but when Harris tried to find them, she'd come to yet another dead end. Christina's house had been abandoned but remained neat and tidy. With no luggage in the house and missing toiletries, Harris considered that she and the kids were on vacation. Their car was gone, but according to the financial records, no plane tickets had been purchased. She'd used none of her credit cards over the past several months.

Were Christina and the kids on the run, paying in cash to avoid detection? That was a possibility, but Apex was also powerful enough to make them disappear. They wouldn't draw the line at women and children. They'd covered up a serial killer's machinations, his victims troubled teens.

Harris ground her teeth together, as though she could break her unanswered questions into bite-sized pieces. But it was no use. She'd come at this case from every angle, pulling every string and making use of every resource at her disposal. Despair threatened to consume her.

It reminded her of Detective David Klein's murder. Her anger at his senseless death had pushed her to make reckless decisions as they'd followed the clues from Chicago to Los Angeles. She'd drunk too much, broken too many rules. She'd felt so helpless then, too. It was only because of Cassie that she'd kept her head on straight.

With Cassie gone now, Harris had no one.

Taking a deep breath, Harris pressed her palms down flat against the surface of her desk, feeling the cool wood beneath her fingertips. The AC clicked off, drowning her in silence until she felt it closing in on all sides. But then she heard a soft laugh from the hallway. The click of a door shutting. The squeal of tires from somewhere on the street.

The urge to drink herself to sleep every night was strong, and while she'd done that in the days following the news of Cassie's death, she'd poured every bottle down the drain after that first week. Cassie wouldn't have wanted Harris to drown herself in booze.

Harris had always kept a small circle, but it wasn't until Cassie's death that she realized each one of them was tied to her friend. Jason was an even bigger mess than she was. Lorraine was a steady presence, but she had her own problems to deal with in the form of Mayor Blackwood and Warden Wickham.

Then there was Cassie's sister. Tears threatened to spill down Harris' cheeks again, but she tilted her head back and blinked them away, the speckled ceiling still blurred in her vision. She could remember Laura's face from their time in California. Not a single part of Harris regretted the night she'd spent with her. They spoke regularly on the phone, and while they both remained single, they'd agreed not to put their life on hold for each other.

After the news of Cassie's death had sunk in, devastation took root in the Quinn family, and Laura had taken a sabbatical to stay with her parents in North Carolina. Harris had become the unofficial mediary, keeping the family apprised of each new piece of information.

Grabbing her phone from the corner of her desk, Harris opened the call log and scrolled until she found Laura's name. Taking a deep breath to steady her nerves, Harris tapped on the entry and held the phone to her ear. She could hardly hear it ringing over the pounding of blood in her ears.

It was only when Laura's voice sounded on the other end that Harris was able to regain focus.

"You've reached Laura Quinn. Please leave a message after the beep, and I'll get back to you as soon as I can. Have a nice day!"

Harris ended the call without leaving a message.

She enjoyed hearing the happiness in Laura's voice, but it hardly seemed worth it for the utter loneliness that followed.

It had been two months since she'd spoken with Laura. Two months since Laura had said she blamed Harris for not being there to protect her sister when it mattered most. Harris couldn't find any fault in the other woman's logic.

She'd only said what Harris had been feeling every day since the moment she heard her best friend had been murdered.

4

Cassie woke from her slumber in gentle stages. Muffled birdsong made its way to her ears through the thick walls of the facility. It was a cheerful noise, at odds with the monotonous tick of the clock on her bedroom wall.

It was the sound of time marching forward that urged her to open her eyes. Sunlight streamed through her window, warming her body with a gentle caress even as it stabbed at her eyes. She blinked against the bright illumination until her vision adjusted.

The room she had called home for the last three months looked the same as it always did. A bed, a dresser, and a nightstand filled the space, cheap but adequate for her needs. Omega had given her a few personal items, like an alarm clock she never used and a little fan to keep her cool at night. He'd also provided some clothes and basic necessities, but out of everything, it was the stack of books from Dr. Bower that she prized most.

A ripple of sadness coursed through her as she realized she'd have to leave them behind.

Tossing off the blankets and swinging her legs off the bed as she sat up, Cassie did a cursory check-in with her body, noting which parts ached and which felt strong. She'd cultivated the habit over the course of the last several months, but the thoughts were errant as she walked through her plan for the day.

She wasn't sure when she decided to escape the facility. Somewhere along the way, she'd started taking stock of security rotations, observing which employee would be the least likely to notice their keys missing. At first, it was simple curiosity. While the rehab technicians were professionals in their field, they didn't appear to have military backgrounds. Just normal people living normal lives in her abnormal world.

Omega had told her the privately owned facility sat on a plot of land in the middle of the Viriginia woods, miles away from any notable town on a map. He'd cautioned her not to press the employees for more information. They wouldn't tell her anything without his approval, he'd said, and the less she knew, the better. The location was used for keeping VIP guests off the radar, including celebrities looking to remain out of the headlines or star witnesses requiring a secure location for recovery.

Despite there only being a handful of employees, Cassie didn't know much about them. She was on a first name basis with her nurse and physical therapist, along with the chef who made her meals every day, but she had no idea where they went after they clocked out or how they had come to work with Omega in the first place.

Thoughts of Omega reminded her that while he was out on business this morning, her time was limited. She wanted to help him track down Pearl Everly, especially if that led to more answers about Apex, but she had other business to attend to first. Chris' final plea before Omega killed him had been to keep his sister and her kids safe, and the request sat heavily on Cassie's shoulders every single day.

Waking up each morning with him staring at her from across the room didn't help either.

Cassie had no trouble remembering the way Chris' gaze had locked onto Cassie's, pleading for her to follow through on the promise to take care of his family. There had been such relief in his eyes after she'd agreed. When he spoke, his voice had been tight and gruff, like it had taken every ounce of his energy to produce his next words.

Someday, I hope you can forgive me.

The pain that followed those words hadn't just been physical. The hot lead that had burned its way through her chest when he'd shot her would have been terrible enough, but the betrayal added another layer of agony to the experience. The scar on her shoulder would fade with time, but could the same be said for the invisible wounds that had been left behind?

Cassie pressed her bare feet to the cool linoleum floor, grounding herself in the present moment, even as movement from the corner of her eye threatened to drag her back into her memories. She knew who she would see when she faced the specter, but the knowledge didn't make it any easier to look into his haunted gaze.

Chris' eyes had been vibrant in life, but now they were a pale shade of green, like death had covered them in a layer of dust. His face was translucent and void of any emotion. Only the shining blood on his chest stood out like a harsh smear of paint against the backdrop of her spartan room.

"Why did you do it?" she asked, knowing he wouldn't give her the answers she wanted. He never did, no matter how many times she asked.

Shaking her head, Cassie stood and turned her back to the phantom, changing into fresh clothes and forcing herself back on track. Chris' family couldn't wait any longer. Despite the questions still running through her mind, she'd made the man a promise.

And once this was all over, maybe she'd cease to see her would-be murderer at every turn.

Cassie left her room with the quiet click of her door trailing behind her as she trudged down the hallway toward the kitchen. It was a small space with the appliances on one side and a handful of small tables on the other. It reminded her a bit of the breakroom at the museum.

The chef greeted her with a joyful hello, and a few minutes later, he placed an egg sandwich, a parfait, and a steaming cup of coffee on the table in front of her. Cassie ate her breakfast at a leisurely pace as the man chatted away at the counter, telling her nothing of importance while he chopped vegetables for a lunch she wouldn't be eating.

Next was the physical therapy room, where she spent most of her time here at the facility. It was spacious, filled with exercise equipment along a row of floor-to-ceiling windows and bright blue mats strewn across the floor. It smelled of disinfectant, but Cassie had come to associate the scent with cleanliness and her own physical progress.

Joe was all smiles and juicy gossip as he twisted her in this direction and that, checking in every so often to ensure her shoulder wasn't giving her any problems. An exclamation here or a murmur there was enough to keep him talking, which was about all she could handle with her mind focused on what came next.

Forty-five minutes later, guilt ate at her as she slipped his keys out of his bag before leaving the room with a wave.

The security guard by the front entrance acknowledged her with a nod as she passed his station on her way out of the building. She was half an hour ahead of her typical schedule, but she didn't want to wait any longer. What if Omega came back early, or Joe noticed his keys missing?

When she'd first gotten the greenlight to take outdoor walks, she'd only been able to stand by the front entrance, tip her face toward the sun, and feel it warm her skin. That had been heaven after being cooped up for so long, but it wasn't long before she'd wanted to explore the surrounding woods.

Joe had accompanied her for several weeks. He'd said it was for her own safety, in case she tripped and reinjured her arm, but Omega had most certainly instructed him to keep an eye on her.

Eventually, Cassie had gotten strong enough that she didn't need a companion. She'd extended her walks until they lasted for hours. It had been a pleasant reprieve from the monotony of her everyday life, though now they served another purpose.

With any luck, no one would realize she had left for good. For the first few hours, anyway.

Without looking back, Cassie stepped into the woods, keeping one hand fisted around the stolen keys in her pocket. She had no money, no phone, no ID. All her personal effects had remained at the hospital where she'd died. One way or another, she'd figure it out.

The woods were blanketed with morning dew, the shade at least ten degrees cooler. She shivered against the shadows that clung to her skin, but kept her shoulders square and her head held high as she put more distance between herself and the rehab facility.

The path before her was well worn. She knew the location of every raised root and dip in the dirt, and her feet automatically found the best purchase as she moved forward. But once she was out of view of the building behind her, Cassie stepped off the trail and into the wild Virginia woods.

Brambles caught on her pants and tugged at her skin. The crunch of fallen twigs underfoot sounded like gunshots to her ears even though the singing birds and chirping insects were far louder. Hell, a single chipmunk had sounded more like a bear crashing through the forest. More than once, Cassie stopped and strained her ears to locate the source of the ruckus, ensuring she wouldn't find herself at the end of her journey before it had even begun.

She circled the building at a distance to avoid showing up on security footage. As far as she could tell, they hadn't hidden any cameras within the branches of the trees. Still, Cassie couldn't stop herself from searching.

In less than ten minutes, Cassie found herself behind the large trunk of a tree at the edge of the parking lot behind the building. Joe's little hybrid vehicle was parked in the far corner, away from the other cars in the lot. A pang of guilt lanced her chest, but she pushed it down. Borrowing Joe's car felt like a small price to pay for rescuing Chris' family. Omega might be convinced they were safe where they were, but she felt like time was running out.

Pulling the keys from her pocket, she hit the unlock button and watched as the taillights flashed. She'd never driven a hybrid before, but it couldn't be that different from a regular car, right?

Cassie crouched low and darted across the forest floor, her shoes scuffing against the pavement until she got to the driver's side door. Cassie pulled it open and climbed inside, tossing the keys into the cupholder and hitting the button to start the engine. A small air freshener hung from the rearview mirror, filling the space with an overpowering citrus scent.

The vehicle purred to life—as did the radio. Booming bass erupted around her, and she let out a yelp before scrambling for the volume knob and lowering it all the way. If her heart hadn't already been racing, it sure as hell was now. How had Joe not destroyed his hearing yet?

Cassie glanced up and made sure the parking lot was still clear. Would this be the last time she ever saw this building and the people inside its walls? Maybe that thought should have caused some sort of emotion to flood her body—they had saved her life and helped her rebuild her body, after all—but only one thought came to mind.

I'm free.

Strapping her seatbelt into place, Cassie put the car into gear and eased off the brake pedal, letting the vehicle coast forward. She adjusted her seat until she felt more comfortable—and more in control. It had been a while since she'd driven, and even though it was like riding a bike, the unfamiliar vehicle set her on edge. Or maybe it was the fact she was committing a crime.

A single glance in the rearview mirror sent her mind careening. A pale green gaze met Cassie's, and her heartbeat ratcheted up another few degrees. A shiver of fear rolled down her spine and settled in her gut. Being this close to the dead was never easy, but it was made worse when the haunting specter took the shape of your friend and the person who'd nearly killed you.

Tearing her gaze away from the mirror, Cassie reoriented her focus and urged the vehicle forward. As she rounded the building, she kept her eyes on the dirt path that led to her freedom. She didn't slam her foot down on the gas despite the twitch in her foot telling her to hightail it out of there.

From the corner of her eye, she caught a figure standing outside the guard's office. The side mirror gave her a better view of Joe standing there with the guard, pointing after the car and shouting. His face was bleached of all color and his eyes were as wide as saucers. The guard spoke into the radio he'd pulled from his hip.

Cassie stomped down on the gas pedal, and the car lurched forward, slamming her back into her seat. Dirt swirled in the air and rocks kicked up under the wheel wells, popping against the acceleration. She slid her gaze from the road in front of her to the rearview mirror. The two men waved their arms and called after her through the haze of dust. The guilt of her betrayal was at war with the conviction she felt over having made the right choice.

For a moment, she was worried she'd have to barrel through a gate at the end of the driveway, but as the main road came into view, she realized they relied on the thick bushes and tall trees hiding the entrance from view. Any security at this end of the property would draw too much attention.

A smile crept across Cassie's face as the wheels of the vehicle hit asphalt. It grew wider until she grinned from ear to ear. Rolling down the window, she let the wind rake its fingers through her hair while she sucked fresh air into her lungs.

It tasted like freedom, fresh and sweet and full of promise.

5

Cassie spent the next two hours looking in her rearview mirror every five minutes, ignoring Chris' constant, silent presence and waiting to see Omega's furious features from the driver's seat of every car that passed. Once she realized she'd made it out unscathed, she turned her attention to the road ahead. Well-worn backroads, dotted with potholes and lined with trees, turned to main thoroughfares through small towns with a single stoplight. Locating the highway and heading south was easy enough, as was following the signs toward Savannah. The hybrid would have no trouble getting her where she needed to go.

Heading back to Georgia had been her only real option. She needed money for food and gas. A change of clothes wouldn't hurt either.

The thought of rescuing Christina and her kids on her own was heroic but impractical. Dangerous, even. Apex had proven time and again they weren't to be underestimated, and if this was a trap like Omega believed, she'd only get one shot at getting them out of whatever hellhole the company had thrown them into.

Both Jason and Harris would be able to help her track them

down, and each was capable of taking care of themselves during a rescue operation. Hell, they were more qualified than she was.

But she knew which would be the bigger asset. Jason was a formidable ally, but he'd been erratic in Nashville. His obsession with tracking down Omega had evolved into mania, and he'd been overbearing and overprotective. It came from a good place, but she needed someone who trusted her to take care of herself.

She'd go to Harris first. Cassie's stomach lurched at the idea of stepping out of the shadows and revealing to her friend that she was still alive. Would Harris' shock give way to relief or anger? Would she insist on telling Jason, Laura, and her parents the truth, or would she keep Cassie's secret until Apex was no longer a threat?

Hours later, Cassie turned down her street with hands that ached from gripping the steering wheel so hard. She was a bundle of raw nerves, both exhausted and on edge about what came next. As much as she'd wanted to go right to Harris and rip the Band-Aid off, she never would've made it without getting stranded somewhere. And while she wasn't against hoofing it to Harris' house, the fewer people who saw her among the living, the better.

Cassie hadn't thought this all the way through, but as she came to a stop a few houses down from her own, the truth settled in her bones like a lead weight. Leggings and a loose shirt wouldn't stop her from being recognized out on the street, even if three months had passed since her neighbors had last seen her. Being shot and killed by a federal agent meant her death had made national news, and her auburn hair rarely allowed her to blend into a crowd.

She craned her neck to survey the contents of Joe's car. A crumpled-up hoodie lay on the floor in the back. She grabbed the heap of fabric and yanked it on. It was about three sizes too big and smelled of his cologne, but it'd hide her in plain sight. Tucking her hair into the hood, she pulled it down low over her eyes.

As she turned her attention back to her house, the front door opened and a figure stepped out into the waning light. Dusk had settled, but even through the encroaching darkness, Jason's broad shoulders and powerful frame were unmistakable. A well of emotion threatened to crawl up her throat and escape in the form of a sob, but she swallowed it back down. This was no time to lose her shit.

The pain of seeing him was excruciating, like thrusting her hand over an open flame. He was in her house, taking care of her dog. It had been three months, but here he was maintaining her old life. He hadn't given up on her. He'd drive himself crazy looking for answers, and as more time passed, he'd become more reckless.

She could get out of the car right now. Tell him everything. Even if he never forgave her, he'd help her take down Apex. After that, maybe they could work toward a fresh start.

Cassie gripped the door handle, the metal cold beneath her sweat-slicked palm. Her heart pounded as she considered the consequences of her actions. But she had just enough sense left to release her grip, her heart shattering in the process. She had to keep up the ruse. The more people who knew she was alive, the more they'd be in danger.

Bear followed Jason out of the house, his head hung low as he made a half-hearted attempt to sniff the grass around him. Even from this distance, Cassie could tell he'd lost some weight. His tail hung low, not quite tucked between his legs, and he barely picked up his paws from the pavement as he walked forward.

Jason led Bear down the driveway, and Cassie blinked away her unshed tears and shook out her hands. As they walked away, she dove into the backseat. Chris' phantom presence dissipated, but Cassie hardly noticed as she peeked out from behind the headrest. Jason stood at the edge of the sidewalk, first looking one way and then the other. He eyed the hybrid before turning in the other direction. Bear paused to sniff the air, but a quick tug on his leash had him moving again. Relief and disappointment swirled inside Cassie like a tornado, poised to tear her apart.

When the two of them were out of sight, Cassie slipped from the car and landed on the sidewalk with shaky legs. After she'd received those threatening letters—which had been Chris' roundabout way of warning her away from Apex—Jason had installed a security camera to monitor her front door. Lucky for her, he'd never gotten around to putting one in the back.

Not willing to waste a single second, she took off in the opposite direction, turning left and then left again until she was parallel to her street.

Cassie counted the houses until she found the one behind hers, then slipped along a row of bushes. Joe's sweatshirt was dark enough for her to blend into the surroundings. A dog barked somewhere in the distance as she plunged into the line of trees that separated her property from her neighbor's. The chain-link fence that bordered her lot wasn't tall enough to keep Bear in if he wanted to escape, which made it that much easier for her to climb over.

Creeping up to the back door, she eyed the various pots she kept out on her back patio. They were full of dirt, but devoid of any plants. She'd meant to replant them sometime this spring, and it seemed Jason hadn't found the time to do it either. Not that she could blame him.

Lifting one of the pots, she reached underneath and felt for the spare key she'd taped there ages ago. Smiling as her fingers reached the cool metal, Cassie used a fingernail to pry it loose. Then, holding her breath, she slipped the key into the lock and turned it, letting out a shaky exhale as the door swung open. She stepped inside, closed the door, and leaned back against the frame. Her body shook from the adrenaline coursing through her veins.

Whatever Jason had made for dinner lingered in the air. Something Italian with herbs and spices. The unidentifiable meal made her feel even more like an intruder in her own home. Had he moved any of the furniture around in the last three months, or was it all in the same spot? She wondered if he kept any of his belongings here or if he returned to his apartment each night. Was her fridge stocked? Would there be a stack of mail on the counter, waiting for her?

Cassie tiptoed forward, her sneakers silent as she crept down the carpeted hallway. She stopped outside her bedroom, the dying sun barely illuminating the space with the curtains drawn over the window. Nothing had been moved from its usual spot, and yet the room felt foreign.

Jason's cologne hung in the air as she stepped over the threshold. The comforter lay rumpled atop the bed, his clothes piled in the opposite corner. Any lingering willpower to keep her emotions at bay disappeared. Cassie clapped a hand over her mouth to stifle her sob, choked and broken. Tears fell from her eyes and cascaded down her cheeks.

Movement caught her attention, and her gaze snapped to one of her old sweatshirts lying on the bed. Jason must've tossed it there after he'd worn it. Or maybe he slept with it at night. His way of keeping her close.

Before she could dwell on that thought, a multi-colored head poked out from under the garment, green eyes locking onto her before an angry meow exploded from Apollo's mouth. He wrestled his way out of her sweatshirt and launched himself into her arms.

Sobbing harder now, Cassie buried her face into his fur and let the rhythmic vibration of his purring comfort her. He kneaded her shoulder with both paws, claws sticking into the fabric like they were made of Velcro.

"I know, buddy," she whispered, lifting her head just enough to look down at him. "I missed you too. I'm so, so sorry."

Apollo butted his head against her chin, purring louder. Knowing he wouldn't let her go even if she tried prying him away, Cassie shifted him to one arm so she could use the other to grab a small travel bag from her closet and toss it onto the bed. There was a chance Jason might realize it was missing, but that was a risk she'd have to take. She gathered a few outfits, then pulled the emergency cash from her stash under the nightstand. She shoved all of it inside the open bag before hooking it into the crook of her free arm.

Stepping back out into the hallway, she took another deep breath of the spiced air. Her stomach growled and ached in response. She hadn't eaten since breakfast. If she was quick, she'd be able to grab a snack, and Jason would be none the wiser.

Taking a step toward the kitchen, Cassie froze when she heard a deep male voice outside the front door. The slide of the key in the lock set her back in motion, and she pulled Apollo free from her sweatshirt, even as he tried to dig his claws in deeper. Dropping him to the floor, she backed up into the darkness of the hallway just as the front door opened. Apollo had been rubbing his body against her shins, but as soon as he heard Jason and Bear return, he sauntered toward them with his tail held high, as though proud to tell them the good news.

Before she could second guess herself, she sprinted toward the back door and opened it only far enough to slip through with her bag. Before it shut behind her, she heard Jason's voice for the first time in months.

"What is it, buddy?" He chuckled, but the sound was rusty. "We weren't gone that long. Miss your big brother already?"

A quiet sob escaped her as she pulled the door shut behind her. This had been a mistake on so many levels, and every fiber of her being screamed to walk back inside and into Jason's arms. A series of high-pitched barks sounded from the hallway. Jason may not have known who'd been inside, but Bear had little doubt.

Through her blurred vision and heaving sobs, Cassie sprinted across the yard and threw her bag over the fence before scrambling after it. She was just past the trees when she heard her back door open. Jason shouted, loud and angry at first, and then desperate by the time she reached the row of bushes in her neighbor's yard. She didn't dare look back, despite every muscle screaming at her to do just that. She put her head down and pushed farther and faster.

When Cassie reached the corner, she heard scuffling behind her. Instinct had her looking over her shoulder, and she stumbled to a halt as a figure dashed through a pool of light shining down from a streetlamp. The shape registered just before Bear barreled into her legs and sent her sprawling to the pavement. It was firm and cool, reminding her that this was no dream. Bear whined, loud as a siren, and licked her face. His tail wagged uncontrollably.

As happy as she was to see him, Cassie couldn't stop herself from looking back the way he'd come. It would only be seconds before

Jason appeared. She didn't think he'd caught sight of much more than a dark silhouette moving on the other side of the fence, but if he saw her now, illuminated by the streetlights, he would know it was her.

"Sit, Bear. Sit." Cassie tried to sharpen her voice into a command, but her throat was still clogged with emotion. Bear squatted down on his haunches, but his butt never touched the concrete. His whole body vibrated with excitement. She stood and brushed dirt from her clothes, then grabbed her bag. "Stay. Stay there."

When Cassie walked away, Bear followed. He normally listened to her every command with no hesitation, but it'd been too long since he'd seen her. Peering down the street and through the darkness once more, she made a decision she hoped she wouldn't regret.

Cassie patted her thigh and took off toward the hybrid, Bear on her heels. Jason would look for him when he didn't return home, but by that time, she'd be long gone. Picking up dog food hadn't been a part of her original plan, but she had enough money on her now. Plus, she'd feel a little safer with Bear by her side.

As if to prove her right, Bear emitted a low growl as they approached the vehicle, eyes locked on the car parked behind hers. It hadn't been there before. Heart in her throat, Cassie slowed to a brisk walk, keeping an eye on the dark sedan.

The license plate gleamed beneath the streetlight. Its numbers and letters blurred as she focused on the state in which it had been issued.

Virginia.

The door popped open, and Bear pressed himself against her leg, his growl growing louder with every passing second. One glimpse at the dog was all the attention Bear received before the man turned his focus back to Cassie.

She wondered if her gulp was audible as she took in Omega's stern face.

With a frustrated sigh, the man tapped the roof of the car. "Get in. *Now.*"

6

Jason yanked open the front door to the precinct. He locked eyes with the security guard at the front desk. "Is she back there?"

He already knew the answer. Of course Harris was in her office tonight, just like she was every other night of the week. And most weekends, too.

The man let out an exasperated sigh. "Mr. Broussard—"

"I'm not leaving until I see her."

It was a testament to the fact that they'd done this song and dance multiple times that the guard buzzed him through the door to the back without further argument. Jason didn't offer any thanks as he charged past the man and into the half-lit hallway. Even if all the lights were out, he'd be able to find Harris' office—and not just because her desk lamp was the only one of three turned on at this time of night. He'd been here so many times in the last few months, he'd know his way around blindfolded.

If Harris didn't want to see him, that was too goddamn bad. If she was busy, he'd wait. All night if he had to.

Heart pounding out a staccato rhythm, Jason pushed through her partially open office door.

Harris' head snapped up as he stomped over to the front of her desk. Her mouth was turned down into a scowl, and her eyes narrowed as she took in his disheveled appearance. He hadn't bothered changing out of his sweatpants and stained t-shirt, both of which had needed to be washed for about a week now.

Jason's gaze locked on Harris. "Bear is missing."

She went still, her scowl turning into something more like a confused frown. Instead of answering him, she glanced over Jason's shoulder. He turned to find another officer standing in the doorway, looking between the two of them.

"It's fine," Harris said. "Close the door, will you?"

The officer gave her a cut nod, then glanced at Jason with a hard look in his eyes. Then the man leaned forward and pulled the door shut with a soft *click*. Jason turned back to Harris, who gestured to the seat opposite her. He didn't bother taking it.

"Bear is missing," he repeated, emphasizing the words like this was all the explanation she needed. And wasn't it? Didn't she understand what this meant?

Leaning back in her chair, she looked far more relaxed than she had any right to be. "What happened?"

"I took him on a walk. When we got home, he started barking at the back door. I opened it, and he ran away."

"So, you lost him."

Jason pinched the bridge of his nose. He couldn't get his head on straight, couldn't find the right words to explain this. "He was chasing after someone."

"I don't understand."

Exhaling, Jason paced the length of the room. The only illumination came from the lamp on the desk, and it seemed only fitting that the darkness of the room mirrored his thoughts. When he reached the far wall, the dusty blinds closed to block out the streetlights outside, he turned around and started over.

"I came home with Bear after our walk. Apollo ran out from the bedroom, meowing and rubbing all over the two of us. He hasn't done that since—" He choked on Cassie's name, but Harris would understand. "There was a sound from the back, and then Bear went ballistic. I saw movement in the backyard, so I opened the door and he took off. Someone was running away. They were already on the other side of the fence."

"An intruder," Harris said, placing her hand on the computer mouse and clicking around. Her fingers hovered over her keyboard, ready to take notes. "Did you see their face? Any defining features?"

"It was Cassie." Her name came out broken, like shards of glass had punctured his throat. "I know it was."

Harris typed nothing, her voice coming out as a whisper. "You saw her face?"

Jason's lip curled up on one side. "No. Just a shadow on the other side of the fence. But Bear ran after her."

"Bear ran after *someone*." Harris shook her head. "Jason, it wasn't her."

"It was," he shouted, slamming his hands down on the back of one of the chairs. "Bear wouldn't have gone after anyone else like that and not come back."

Harris was silent for a moment, considering him. "Did you look for him?"

A feral growl of frustration escaped his lips. "Of course I did. For the last hour. He's gone. They both are. And so is the spare key she kept under the potted plant out back. The back door was unlocked when I opened it. I *always* lock it."

"Still could've been an intruder. Was anything missing?"

He cursed at himself for not looking before he came here. He was too concerned about finding Bear. "I'll check when I get home."

Harris shook her head. "Sounds like a would-be burglar. You probably got home just in time."

Jason leaned forward on the chair, his hands still gripping the back like it was his only tether to sanity. "Apollo would've been freaked out if a stranger had been in the house. Bear wouldn't have left and not come back. If he was hurt, I would've found evidence of it somewhere."

"So your only conclusion is that it was Cassie? That's a stretch, even for you."

Jason rounded the chair now, standing right in front of her desk, looking down his nose at her. It was times like these when Harris felt like a stranger to him. How could she not *want* to believe it was Cassie?

"They never found her body," he said.

"I'm well aware."

"Apex has her, and no one is doing a damn thing about it."

Harris gripped the back of her neck, massaging the muscles there like they'd just gone three rounds in the ring. "We've done everything we can, Jason. I know you want to walk right up to their front door and knock it down, but it's too dangerous. You need to let this go."

"Have you?" He leaned over her desk, placing his hands on the shiny surface. Her jaw ticked. "How many times have you watched the video in the last week, Adelaide? Huh? Tell me you haven't looked at it even once and I'll drop this right here, right now."

Harris looked away. It was all the admission he needed.

"I agreed to stay out of your way so you could do your job," he continued. "I've told the Savannah Police Department everything. The Nashville Police Department. The Feds. I've answered every question a hundred times. I've done what you asked me to when we found out what happened, and they've done nothing in return. So, now it's my turn. I want everything you have on the case."

She laughed, but the humor didn't reach her eyes. "You're joking."

"I'm not."

"Even if I wanted to, I can't give you that information."

"You've slipped Cassie confidential information before."

"Yes, because she's Cassie," Harris said. "You're not her."

The words hung in the air like poison. The room was silent except for the quiet hum of the air conditioning. Beyond the walls, the muffled sounds of traffic reminded Jason there were people going about their business, living their lives like everything was normal.

"Do you even care that she's gone?" he asked.

As soon as the words were out of his mouth, he knew it was a mistake.

Harris' voice was as quiet as an arrow and just as deadly. "Get out."

"I want the information you have on—"

Harris slammed her hands down on her desk and shot to her feet.

"I don't give a damn what you want, Broussard. You're not getting anything from me or anyone else in this department." Her eyes flashed with anger. "How *dare* you think I don't care that Cassie is gone? How *dare* you believe for even a second that I haven't done everything in my power to find her? David died, and I nearly lost myself because of it. Cassie was the only person who kept me together, and now *she's* dead. Just because you're in pain doesn't mean the rest of us aren't. If you want to keep picking at your wounds, fine. But don't expect me to do the same."

Jason wished he felt guilty for pushing her like this, but all he felt was his ever-present anger. "I won't give up trying to find her."

"Neither will I," Harris said. "But I'm done dealing with you, Jason. Go home. And don't come back. If we learn anything new, I'll make sure you're informed."

Jason looked from her clenched jaw to her narrowed eyes. She meant every word. Nothing would change her mind. He'd crossed a line, but instead of feeling remorse, he just felt free. The obligation of playing by Harris' rules no longer weighed him down.

Turning on his heels, he threw open the door and stomped back the way he'd come with one thought screaming louder than all the others.

I'll do it myself.

7

Omega had waited until Cassie loaded Bear into the car and slipped into the front passenger seat before getting behind the wheel himself. He pulled away from the curb with all the urgency of a Sunday driver, as though he had no fear that Jason might waltz out the front door and spot them.

The streetlights illuminated the interior of the vehicle as they drove by them. She hadn't caught the model of the silver Honda, but it was sleek and shiny and had that new-car smell. The engine was nothing more than a quiet hum in the background. The silence pressed between them, heavy and oppressive. Her fingers twitched to turn the radio up as loud as she could stand it, just so she didn't have to endure Omega's admonishments. Even Bear was silent as he sat upright in the backseat, his mouth closed and his eyes focused on the man driving.

The specter of Chris Viotto watched her with practiced silence.

The quaint houses of her neighborhood soon gave way to the busy streets of downtown Savannah. Omega merged onto the highway, heading west. The streetlights were fewer and farther between now, casting them both in shadow. Traffic was light this time of night, with the occasional pair of headlights bearing down on them from the other side of the freeway. The urge to ask where they were going bubbled in Cassie's chest, but she shoved it back down as far as it would go. Breaking the silence would be admitting defeat.

After shifting to the outside lane and setting the cruise control, Omega spoke, jolting Cassie from her internal monologue. "What's in the bag?"

She looked down at the duffel between her feet. "Huh?"

"I want to know," Omega said, his voice coming out even but from between clenched teeth, "what the hell you needed so badly that you'd risk everything we've done up until this point?"

"Clothes," she responded. "Money."

"Did anyone see you?"

"No."

"Are you sure?"

No. "Yes."

He ran his tongue over his teeth, his jaw taut. "I never took you for an idiot."

Cassie whipped her head around. "Excuse me?"

Bear issued a warning in the form of a low growl.

"What's with the dog?"

"He's mine," she said, folding her arms. "Followed me out of the house. I couldn't leave him behind."

"Can you control him?" Omega asked, his gaze flicking up to the rearview mirror. Cassie wondered if he was looking at the traffic behind him or if he was sneaking glances at Bear.

"Yes." She glanced over her shoulder and said, "Lay down."

Bear's growls cut off as he eased himself down onto the seat until his front paws hung over the edge and his back legs were kicked out to the side. Though he looked more relaxed, Cassie didn't miss the way he watched Omega with perked ears. If he saw Chris sitting beside him, he ignored the specter's presence in favor of keeping an eye on the driver.

Omega adjusted the rearview mirror down. "I'm not risking my life or yours for a dog if he gets in the way."

"He won't." Cassie let her firm response hang in the air. "But let's circle back to you calling me an idiot."

"You are an idiot."

"I'm not—"

"Idiots do idiotic things. You did an idiotic thing." Omega's jaw ticked as he ground his teeth together. "What were you thinking? Or were you not thinking at all?"

Cassie turned her head and stared out the windshield. The trees that lined the highway were nothing more than a dark blur. A blush rose to her cheeks at Omega's tone of voice, but she refused to feel guilty for the choice she'd made.

"You left me no other option. You weren't going to help Christina and her kids, so I decided to take matters into my own hands." Curiosity replaced her anger for a moment. "How did you find me so fast?"

"Joe has a tracker on his car in case it ever gets stolen. You never had a chance."

Cassie grimaced. "I wouldn't have done it if I had any other choice." This time, she turned to Omega so she could see his reaction. "I don't want to go back to the facility."

Eyes remaining on the road, Omega said, "We're not."

Something like fear and anticipation swirled in Cassie's gut. "Then where are we going?"

"Alabama."

"Why?"

"That's where they're keeping the sister and her kids."

Cassie's jaw dropped. She didn't dare to hope. "What?"

"It's a trap, like I told you." Omega flipped his blinker as he got into the other lane, allowing a large pickup truck to pass him. After he returned to the outside lane, he said, "It's stupid to go after them, but I can't risk you doing anything else to jeopardize what we've worked for. You've left *me* no other option."

"You say that like we're not trying to save the lives of a mother and her two young children. They're going to be traumatized."

"They were going to be traumatized either way. What's done is done. Just be grateful you're getting your wish now." Omega took his eyes off the road to look at her, his gaze stormy. "But this is the first and last time you pull a stunt like this, Cassie. Neither one of us can afford the consequences of you going rogue."

The threat was crystal clear. Cassie suppressed a shiver of fear. Behind her, Bear huffed out an annoyed sigh, as though he knew she wouldn't approve of him growling again. All she wanted was to curl up back there with him and bury her face in his fur.

If she did that, Chris would disappear and she wouldn't have to feel his watchful eyes on her.

"Why are you agreeing to this now?" Cassie asked, hoping she didn't sound as suspicious as she felt.

"I can't have you running off again. I'm hoping you'll realize I'm not the bad guy here." Omega shook his head, less frustration rolling off him now. "I was hoping we could've taken care of some other business first. I told you I wouldn't leave them forever, but I have to keep my eye on the bigger picture."

Cassie didn't think the bigger picture was worth the lives of innocent children. There was no telling when Apex would decide they weren't worth keeping around. "You said they're in Alabama?"

He nodded. "In a bunker out in the middle of nowhere, on a piece of land owned by one of Apex's shell corporations. I've got a team meeting us there. A small one. Couldn't afford to take anyone else off their assignments."

Cassie had more questions now than she'd had when she got into the car, but she understood Omega well enough to know he wouldn't answer them. The rhythmic hum of the highway beneath the car's tires filled the vehicle, making her eyes droop.

"You got any strong *feelings* about what might happen next?" Omega asked, flicking his turn signal before passing a semi-truck. "We're not going in blind, but I'm not sure what the blowout from this could be. We might be knocking over the first domino that leads to a shitstorm."

Cassie closed her eyes and searched within herself, but all she found were her fraught nerves and beating heart. She shook her head, wishing she had something more to offer. "No. Sorry."

There was a beat of silence before Omega said, "Keep trying. Maybe something will shake loose."

Cassie closed her eyes again and leaned back against the headrest, working to drown out the white noise of the highway. In the past, she'd only been able to call forth a vision on rare occasions. More often, they appeared in her dreams or hit her when she touched something of significance. After a few deep breaths, her heart rate slowed. Her body relaxed against the seat. And then—

Cassie opened her eyes with a frustrated sigh. "Nothing."

"You've been through a trauma," Omega said, though his voice wasn't all that soft as he said it. "Things might not be working like normal. Have any run-ins with ghosts?"

It took all her willpower not to turn and look to the back seat. "Not anything out of the ordinary."

Omega squeezed the steering wheel beneath his hands, the leather squeaking. "Keep trying. Like your other muscles, you've got to build up to what you were capable of before. You're just out of practice."

"Yeah, you're probably right." Cassie's abilities hadn't disappeared, not like they had in the past, but they felt stiff and unused, like her shoulder. "I just need time."

Omega adjusted his seat and leaned his head back. "We've got about five hours until we arrive at the bunker. No time like the present."

8

All Cassie managed to see before they got to their destination was the back of her eyelids. She'd fallen asleep three or four times, but Omega didn't seem to mind. Every time she'd looked over at him, his eyes were locked on the road. Bear, on the other hand, had finally laid his head down on his paws and closed his eyes, though he'd probably gotten no more restful sleep than she did.

Chris remained in the same spot, silent and watchful.

They stopped once at a gas station to use the bathroom and grab something to eat. Cassie let Bear out to do his business on a patch of grass no bigger than a couple of square feet. The parking lot was empty except for Omega's car, but soon she'd need to pick up a leash for Bear. People got twitchy around dogs his size, and she had no interest in taking more risks than necessary.

The highway was a smooth river of asphalt beneath their tires. As they drove deeper into Alabama, the lights became sparse, failing to illuminate the dark expanse around them. Cassie's already frayed nerves continued to ping with awareness, though she couldn't begin to guess what her body was trying to tell her.

It was close to two in the morning by the time they turned onto a service road. Omega instructed Cassie to hop out of the car and swing the gate open. He pulled through and stopped on the other side just long enough for her to latch the metal bar back in place and return to her seat. Bear stayed alert to their surroundings, his ears forward and head oscillating between each window.

Trees towered over them on all sides while the darkness reached out to trail its fingers along the sides of the car. Cassie longed to see the night sky above them, which had been nothing more than a heavy blanket of clouds, but the canopy was too thick. The only light came from their headlights, which sliced through the thin fog that clung to the ground like a blunt knife.

Omega drove down the gravel road at a snail's pace, only pulling over once the gate behind them was out of view. The car bounced over the uneven ground before coming to a halt. When Omega cut the engine, the lights switched off and plunged them into complete darkness. They sat in silence while the outline of individual trees came into focus once their vision adjusted to the black of the night. Something swooped down in front of the car before disappearing back into the woods, but Cassie couldn't tell if it was a bird or a bat.

Omega stepped from the car, letting the door fall shut behind him with a soft *click*. Cassie followed his lead, cracking her back and stretching her limbs before reaching for the back door to let Bear out.

"Leave him," Omega said.

She scowled over the roof of the car at him, but she doubted he saw it in the dark. "He won't make a sound."

"Can't risk it." Omega circled around to the back of the vehicle and popped the trunk, a soft light emanating from inside. "Not just for our sake, but for his too. Could be a lot of bullets flying at us."

The scowl melted. She looked back at Bear through the window, his tail wagging at the sight of her. "Will we be gone long?"

"If everything goes according to plan, no." Omega pulled on a Kevlar vest before handing one to Cassie. "We know the layout of the bunker and have a pretty solid idea of how many of Apex's hired thugs are inside. My guys are good. We should be in and out in no time. But I can't make any guarantees."

Cassie nodded, watching as he strapped a utility belt to his waist. He opened a locked briefcase and pulled out a handgun, checking the magazine before slipping it into the holster on his hip. Flipping the briefcase closed, he pulled a much larger case toward him and opened it to reveal an assault rifle. The barrel was shorter than she'd seen on other ones.

Cassie didn't realize she was frowning down at the weapon until Omega said, "These are for me." He studied her. "You ever shoot before?"

Cassie swallowed down her anxiety. "I have. I don't like them."

"It doesn't matter whether you like them," Omega said, lowering the lid of the trunk before pressing down until it latched. The small click was whisked away on the breeze and they were once again surrounded by darkness, though it took only seconds to readjust this time. "It's about whether they'll keep you alive."

"Then why won't I need one tonight?"

Instead of answering, he nodded at the car. "Tell your dog to be quiet. And make sure he doesn't scratch the upholstery. This is a rental."

Cassie walked over to the door and popped it open. She held a hand through the opening to keep Bear from jumping out. "I'm sorry, buddy. You have to stay."

Bear ran his head beneath her fingers and she obliged, scratching behind his ears and under his chin, which elicited a whine. Her gaze drifted to the specter on the opposite side of the car. If everything went according to plan, this could be the last time she saw him. Would she feel a sense of loss or relief?

Turning her gaze back to Bear, she whispered, "Be quiet and stay. Be good."

When he plopped back down on the backseat with another huff, she straightened and shut the door in the same manner Omega had closed the trunk, whispering, "I'm sorry," as she did.

"Stay close," Omega said, already heading into the trees. Cassie scrambled after him, darting between thick tree trunks and over gnarled roots she could barely make out. When she caught up, he whispered, "Woods should be clear, but it's easy to get turned around. Can't afford to waste time looking for you if you get lost."

"Don't we need to wait for your team?" she asked.

"They're already in place. Now be quiet."

Cassie bit her tongue. Now was not the time to push back, no matter how much Omega aggravated her. Once again, she missed the quiet comfort of the person she'd known as Robert. But that man was long gone.

As though following an invisible thread through the trees, Omega never faltered and never slowed. He hadn't offered her night vision goggles like the pair he wore, so Cassie remained close to the man's back, trying not to think about who—or what—could be lurking in the forest around them. While Omega's footsteps were nothing more than the whisper of a leaf across the grass, Cassie found every loose stick in the entire damn woods. Each time, Omega would turn his head to glare at her. What did he expect? She was no secret agent. Harris or Jason would be much better equipped to do this kind of work.

Omega would've given *them* guns.

The older man slowed and held out an arm to stop Cassie from walking past him. He let out a low whistle she would've mistaken for some kind of bird, the sound blending in with the chirping crickets and rustling leaves that swirled around them.

A few seconds passed before Omega received a return call. It was lighter and a little higher pitched than his had been, and not too far away. Instead of moving, Omega let out his whistle again. The return call came much faster the second time.

Cassie stayed hot on Omega's heels as he strode forward, his shoulders less tense now. It wasn't until they were all but on top of the group that Cassie could make out the silhouettes of five men dressed in dark clothing, each sporting an array of weapons.

The group turned to face Omega as he knelt in front of them. One member kept his eyes and gun trained forward. Following Omega's lead, Cassie squatted beside him as he spoke with his team.

"Any movement?"

"No sir," one of the men replied. "Shift change in about a half hour. These guys will be itching to get out of here. As far as they know, it's just a regular day."

"Think they'll thank us for putting them out of their misery?" one of the other men asked.

The group chuckled, and Cassie grimaced. Omega hadn't said anything about killing, but the assault rifles made his intentions clear. She had to remind herself that the men inside were as dangerous as the group in front of her.

"Let's make this quick," Omega said. "Get in position."

The group stood and spread out in different directions. Omega turned to Cassie, gesturing toward a tree to her right. "You're staying with Spot. Get behind that trunk and don't move until I give the signal."

She didn't move. "Spot?"

Omega's voice had lost all patience. "He's the spotter. Get behind the tree."

Cassie did as she was told, if for no other reason than to hurry this up.

As the minutes ticked by, a chill crept deeper into Cassie's bones. Anxiety ratcheted in her chest with each shallow breath. The sounds of the forest blurred around her as her mind kept returning to how scared Christina and her kids must be. What sort of physical shape would they be in when Omega and his team rescued them? What if the three of them didn't make it out of this alive?

A series of louds pops signaled the start of the assault. After a moment of silence, a barrage of noise spread throughout the dark woods. Cassie's body jolted to the side when Spot squeezed off a shot without warning. She barely managed to stop the scream that had clawed its way up her throat. The crickets and cicadas went stark silent, as though also holding their breath to find out what would happen next.

Eventually, the bullets quieted. The creatures in the trees refused to continue their chirping melodies, turning the forest into a silent grave. A minute later, Spot spoke for the first time, his voice higher than she'd expected.

"All clear," he told her. "Walk straight down the hill till you get to the entrance. They'll meet you there."

Standing on shaky legs, Cassie muttered a quick thank you before doing as he'd instructed. Her footsteps seemed louder than before, even over the pounding of her heart. She placed her hand on each passing tree trunk to catch her weight as she moved forward.

It wasn't long before the bunker came into view. From the outside, it looked like a small shed a hunter would use. Just on the other side of the entrance, a series of concrete steps led underground.

She reached the top of the stairs, grateful there were no dead bodies in sight. One of Omega's men ascended, his gun hanging loosely in his hands. Behind him, a woman carried a small boy on her hip, his arms slung around her neck and his face pressed into her shoulder. She used her free arm to plaster a young girl to her side, her hand pressed firmly over the child's eyes.

Cassie backed up as the entourage exited the bunker, the men fanning out to check their perimeter. Only Omega stayed behind, a dim flashlight illuminating their surroundings enough for Cassie to get a glimpse at the family in front of her.

Christina's eyes were wild as her gaze bounced from the soldiers to the woods, finally landing on Cassie. She had some dirt smudged on her face, which made her gaunt cheeks look even more sunken. The bags under her eyes were so purple, Cassie couldn't tell if they were from a lack of sleep or if Apex's soldiers had taken their frustration out on her face.

A cool breeze wound its way past them, and the little boy, Jonah, looked up. His face was clean, his skin pale and eyes frightened. From Christina's other side, the girl, Jessi, pushed her mother's hand away from her eyes. She also looked healthy, but just as tired and scared.

It took a moment of staring into Christina's eyes—as green as Chris' had been in life—for Cassie to be able to speak, her stomach churning. When she did, her voice broke on the woman's name.

"Christina," she said, trying to swallow past the emotion in her throat. "You're safe now."

"Who are you?" Christina asked, her voice strong and clear.

"I'm a friend," Cassie began, the hardest part bubbling its way up her throat. "A friend of your brother's."

Christina's eyes widened, and her gaze roamed over Cassie's figure, landing on her auburn hair. "You're Cassie." The woman's gaze focused somewhere over Cassie's shoulder before meeting hers again. "Chris."

For a moment, Cassie thought he was hovering somewhere in the trees behind her. Could Christina see him too?

Then the woman asked, "Is he here?"

Cassie's voice wavered as she replied, "No."

"Is he—did he make it out okay?"

Cassie swallowed down the emotion rising in her throat, but she couldn't stop her chin from trembling.

After what felt like an eternity of silence, Cassie finally spoke. "I'm so sorry."

Christina's face crumpled, her eyes welling with tears. She looked beyond Cassie again, as though hoping her brother would appear to prove them all wrong. She cleared her throat, then locked down her emotions. Before either of them could say another word, Omega stepped forward.

"We'll discuss this later." The words came out with a bite. "Time to move."

9

ANASTASIA BOLTON KEPT HER HEAD HELD HIGH AS SHE FOLLOWED HER colleague down the carpeted hallway of Apex Publicity's New York City headquarters. She'd always appreciated the lush crimson material with its gold accents. It was understated but luxurious, like most everything in this building. The floral wallpaper was vintage but classic, accentuated with marble details along the edges. Each painting on the wall was an original, some even signed by artists that any common person might recognize.

But Anastasia took in none of that as she kept her gaze locked on Sienna Vogel's back, watching the woman's silky blonde hair swing back and forth like a glossy curtain as they made their way toward Daniel Haussmann's office. Anticipation crawled its way up her spine and curled atop her chest, as heavy as Sienna's cloying perfume.

Anastasia had long since honed her ability to appear unflappable. No one could ever use her reactions against her. No one could ever doubt she had everything under control. That kind of composure had taken her far in life and within the walls of this company.

Today, however, she'd been seconds away from letting herself slip.

Calling Sienna an adversary gave the woman far too much credit, but Anastasia didn't get this far by underestimating anyone. Alarm bells had gone off in Anastasia's mind as soon as her colleague had sauntered into her office. Sienna had looked down her nose and smiled, announcing that Apex Publicity's Chief Operating Officer wanted to see her in his office straight away. Then she'd turned on her heel and walked away, knowing Anastasia had no choice but to follow.

Daniel could've called Anastasia into his office from his phone or sent his secretary to fetch her, but he'd chosen Sienna as his lackey instead. Had she volunteered to do the deed, or had Daniel sent her for a reason?

As they neared the man's office, Sienna looked over her shoulder and smiled at Anastasia. The woman's porcelain skin was like ivory against her midnight dress, her blue eyes cold and piercing. Her classic beauty softened the sharpness of her tongue, but Anastasia had seen through Sienna's veneer from day one.

In another life, they could've been friends.

Sienna knocked on Daniel's door with prim satisfaction, looking like a cat come to drop a mouse at her owner's feet. Anastasia rolled her eyes at the woman's back, taking a moment to smooth a wrinkle from the front of her crimson pantsuit.

Daniel called for them to enter, and Sienna threw a knowing smirk over her shoulder before pushing open the door and stepping inside. Anastasia ignored her as she entered the room, coming to stand between the two chairs opposite the desk that sat in the center. Already familiar with the bookshelves of antique tomes and the smattering of collectibles from his travels, her gaze landed on the figure sitting hunched over his work surface.

A little over sixty, Daniel Haussmann was one of the younger men in the upper echelons of the company. He could often be heard cracking jokes in the hallway, his booming laugh contagious to even the most cold-hearted employee. But when he glanced up at the two women, his eyes held none of his usual humor. Today, he just looked tired.

He shoved a pile of papers into a folder and slid it to the side of his desk. "I apologize for the interruption, Ana. But this can't wait."

"It's not a problem."

The click of the door followed by the clack of heels was Anastasia's only warning that Sienna had not left the room. The other woman rounded Daniel's desk to stand off to the side, arms folded over her chest like a disapproving mother staring down at her child. The woman's smirk betrayed how much satisfaction she was getting from this situation.

Anastasia watched Sienna's movements from her peripheries, never taking her eyes from Daniel's worn face. "What seems to be the issue?"

"Someone has retrieved Viotto's sister and her children from their last known location. The team guarding them is dead."

Shock flared throughout Anastasia's body like she'd been hit by a bolt of lightning. "When did this happen?"

"Last night, sometime in the early hours before dawn. Hit right before a shift change."

"Why wasn't I personally made aware of this?"

"You're being made aware of it now," Sienna answered.

"That's enough, Miss Vogel," Daniel said, more exasperated than venomous.

He turned his attention back to Anastasia. "Sienna happened to be in the office when the information came through, and she reported it to me straightaway." He sighed, and his weariness doubled. "Ana, I know I don't have to explain to you, of all people, the current precipice on which we stand."

Anastasia refused to give in to the panic that threatened to crawl out of the pit that had formed in her stomach. She lifted her chin and clasped her hands in front of her, if only to keep herself from clawing out Sienna's eyes.

"Of course not," she said, lacing her tone with practiced confidence. "But I had anticipated this outcome. And, frankly, it's the one that could benefit us the most if we play our cards right."

Sienna scoffed. "This has been nothing more than a waste of resources. It would've been one thing if we could've gotten information out of the woman—"

"She didn't know anything," Anastasia interjected. "That was clear from the beginning."

"It *was* a waste of resources then. You should've disposed of them the second you knew they were useless."

Anastasia stared daggers at the other woman. "I knew someone would rescue them sooner or later. Now, we have a chance to follow the trail back to our opposition."

Sienna stood straighter, looking haughty. "We have no opposition."

"Don't be naïve."

"Do you doubt Apex's ability—"

"I doubt nothing. The fact that you don't know there's someone out there who can cause issues for us tells me all I need to know."

Turning to Daniel, Anastasia continued before Sienna could interrupt again. "Do we have any footage of the rescue? Any evidence left behind?"

Daniel shook his head. "It was a skilled team. They were in and out of the area within a half hour. Nothing left behind."

"Professionals," Anastasia mused. She tapped a finger to her chin, eyes roaming around the room, unseeing. "This has Omega's fingerprints all over it."

"Omega?" Sienna laughed, devoid of any humor. "You might as well say the Easter bunny did it."

Daniel and Anastasia both ignored her. The man's voice was resigned as he said, "My thoughts exactly."

"Why would he care about Viotto's family, though? Perhaps he doesn't know the woman has no information?"

"Wait." Sienna stepped forward. "You're saying Omega *is* a real threat?"

Anastasia plastered on a consoling smile. "You have so much left to learn, Miss Vogel. I hope you're taking notes."

While Sienna scowled, Daniel acted like he hadn't heard the exchange. "It would be nice to take him off the board. I thought we had him back in Nashville."

Anastasia had thought it was too good to be true, and she'd been right. Though she wasn't about to rub her boss' face in it now. "This will give us a second chance to find him."

Daniel nodded, his distant gaze clearing as he stood and looked between the two women. "Ana, I want you to go to the facility. Bring whichever team you need. Find us something, anything on Omega."

"Of course." Anastasia hesitated before uttering her next words, "Sir, Senator Hughes—"

Daniel held up a hand. "There's no one I would trust more to find Omega than you, Ana. Miss Vogel will take lead on the Senator Hughes situation for now."

Anastasia nearly stepped back in surprise. She'd been the one to bring Senator Hughes on board, securing his trust and his money. "Sir, I assure you I can handle both."

"I'm sure you could," he said, "but we're not taking any risks. Not when we're this close."

Anastasia nodded, knowing there would be no changing his mind. Sienna was smug as she led Anastasia out of the office and back down the hall, the walls pressing in on all sides. It was a small miracle the other woman remained silent before they parted ways.

If only she knew how well and truly fucked Anastasia was.

10

Cassie, Omega, Christina, and the kids spent the night at a safehouse about an hour from the bunker. He'd arranged it while she'd been sleeping in the car, but when she asked how he'd secured it, he refused to answer. At that point, she was too tired and too relieved to press him for more details.

There were two bedrooms, a sizeable kitchen, and a dated yet clean bathroom. Omega had ushered Christina and the kids into one room and Cassie into the other. It contained a twin-sized bed and a dresser, and there was just one window overlooking a narrow alleyway below. The walls pressed a little too close, and the mattress was a little too lumpy, but Cassie's eyes fell shut as soon as her head hit the pillow. She didn't even realize Bear had spent the night with the kids until she woke up the next morning.

The alluring scent of coffee and the murmur of voices roused Cassie from her fitful sleep. She'd gotten about four hours. She thought about closing her eyes again but decided to join the others before Omega started interrogating Christina over breakfast.

As soon as Cassie swung her legs out from under the covers and planted her feet on the floor, movement caught her attention. At first, she thought Bear had snuck into her room once he heard her stirring, but the shape was all wrong.

Chris was back, his pale eyes and bloody chest gleaming in the early morning light.

So much for her theory that all he wanted was to see his sister and her kids safe.

Under the watchful eye of her sentinel, Cassie stepped out of her room and into the living room, wincing at the stiffness in her shoulder. A woman she didn't recognize sat with the kids on the floor. Piles of LEGO bricks surrounded Jonah, and he placed one on top of another in an attempt to build the tallest tower he could. Jessi lay flat out on her stomach, filling in the lines of a coloring book with considerable precision. Bear lounged between them, muscles relaxed but gaze alert as he followed Cassie's movements with rapt attention.

Cassie returned the kids' smiles as she walked by, entering the tiny kitchen on the other side of the apartment. There was just enough room for a small, round table and four chairs to fit on the white and green checkered floor. Like the linoleum, the refrigerator seemed to be a relic from the sixties, as did the worn countertop. But Cassie only had eyes for the coffee maker.

Christina and Omega sat opposite each other, each with a steaming mug in front of them. Cassie offered up a small smile before stepping up to the machine and pouring her own. She lifted the cup to her mouth and allowed the steam to wash across her face while she breathed in the earthy aroma. The smell transported her back to her own kitchen, and for a few seconds, she could pretend she was in Savannah and the last few months had never happened.

But then the ache in her shoulder pulsed angrily, and she was slammed back into the present moment.

With her coffee still too hot to drink, Cassie slid into an empty seat next to Christina, meeting the woman's verdant eyes. They were so much clearer than they'd been yesterday. "How'd you sleep?"

Christina chuckled. "Better than I have in a while, but still not great. Woke up a few times confused about where I was. When I did sleep, I had nightmares. The kids did too. But your dog helped calm them down each time. He's incredible."

A swell of pride filled Cassie's chest until she thought she might burst.

"He knows who needs him most." She glanced into the other room. "They seem to be doing okay this morning."

"Better than I expected," Christina confirmed, holding a plain black mug to her lips. "For now, at least."

Cassie turned to Omega, taking in his neat hair and beard, still damp from his shower. "Who's the woman in the other room?"

"Child psychologist. Thought they should see one as soon as possible."

Cassie nodded and took a sip of coffee to cover her surprise. She didn't think Omega was cruel, but his attitude toward Christina and her kids had been callous in the past.

"I appreciate that," Christina said. The look in her eyes was expectant as she set her mug back down. "You said we had to wait until Cassie was awake to talk?"

Cassie looked between the two of them, her grip firm on the warm porcelain handle of her cup. "Talk about what?"

"I have a lot of questions," Christina said. "Like, what happens now? Where do my kids and I go from here?"

Omega took a sip of his own coffee before he answered.

"Your disappearance from the facility will raise alarms. Apex will want to know who rescued you and why. The quicker and farther away we get you from here, the better. Once we dismantle Apex, you can go back to a normal life."

Christina looked haunted as she stared down into her half-empty coffee cup. "I'm not sure our lives will ever be normal again."

Cassie reached over and placed her hand on Christina's forearm. "I don't know how much Chris told you about me, but I hope you believe me when I say I know how you feel. I've been through my fair share of horrors, and as cliché as it sounds, it really does get better with time."

"I want to believe you," Christina whispered, "but all I feel is terror. All the time."

"That won't go away immediately, but sooner or later, you'll feel hope again. It's important to hold onto that."

"And Chris?" Christina asked, glancing up at Cassie with pinched eyebrows. "Do you know what happened to him?"

Cassie looked to Omega, unsure if she was asking for permission or a way out of answering. All he did was nod. Despite not wanting to tell Christina the truth, Cassie knew the woman could handle it. She had to understand what Chris had sacrificed to keep them alive.

"I was there when Chris died," Cassie said, her voice wavering.

She flicked her gaze to the opposite side of the kitchen where Chris stood against the far wall, looking as he always did these days. Part of her had hoped she'd see some new emotion flicker across his face now that his sister was here, but it remained passive.

Cassie drew in a deep breath, letting the flow of oxygen steady her nerves. "Apex forced him to work for them and used you as collateral. He had a plan to bring them down from the inside."

Christina didn't bother swiping away the tears that poured down her face. "Did they find out what he was up to?"

"No." Cassie could see Chris in his sister's face, and that made it even harder to say what she needed to. "He was told to kill me. We were in a parking garage when he held me at gunpoint."

Christina's hand flew to her mouth. "No," she breathed. "He talked about you all the time. He cared about you."

"I know. But he cared about you too. And your kids. You guys meant everything to him."

"But you're here," Christina said, searching Cassie's face. "And he's not."

"He did pull the trigger." Cassie tugged at the top of her shirt until she revealed the fresh scar. "We think he was intentional with his aim. It gave us a chance to pronounce me dead at the hospital, then transport me to a private facility where I recovered. As far as Apex knows, I'm dead."

Christina stared at the scar for a long time before her gaze slid to the side. "Your other scars look older."

Cassie let go of her shirt and wrapped her hands around the handle of her mug, a distant comfort against the memories she'd live with for the rest of her life.

"Like I said. I've been through my fair share of horrors."

There was a beat of silence, as though Christina didn't know how to respond. Then she asked, "Did Chris say anything before he—he—?"

"He made us promise to keep you safe. He thanked me when I agreed."

The words came out choked, then she was back there, in that garage. The distance at which Chris stood now was about the same as it had been then.

"I would've agreed to, regardless. And then he said—" Cassie sucked in a lungful of air to steady her voice. "He said he hoped I could forgive him someday."

Christina's words were hard to decipher through her tears. "How did he—? I mean, how did it happen?"

"Someone shot him," Omega said, meeting Cassie's gaze with his own hard eyes from across the table. "To protect Cassie. He didn't suffer."

Christina nodded, like that was any consolation. Then she buried her face in her hands and sobbed. Cassie let her own tears trail down her face, allowing herself to feel all the emotions she'd been drowning in for months. Anger, guilt, and sadness were like lead weights tied to her limbs. But relief and hope buoyed her until she wasn't sure which way was up.

"I'm sorry," Christina said, when she found her words again.

"Please don't apologize," Cassie whispered. "I'm the one who's sorry. I'm—"

"No." Christina shook her head, meeting Cassie's gaze with her red-rimmed eyes. "No, you don't have anything to be sorry about. Chris was a good man, but he did a terrible thing. He had his reasons, but that doesn't make any of this easier. On either of us."

Christina blinked back fresh tears. "God, I'm so angry at him. He was always the selfless one. The one who carried the weight of the world on his shoulders. I told him that wasn't his responsibility, but he could never shake that feeling. It's why he wanted to be a Federal Agent."

"It suited him," Cassie said.

"He was a good agent." Christina's gaze was steady and sure. "As tragic as his death was, I'm alive. My kids are alive. And so are you. I wish he were here too, but I know he thought this was the right thing to do. He cared about you, Cassie. More than he probably ever let on."

Cassie's gaze slid to the specter of Christina's brother that stood at her back. His eyes, paler than they'd been in life, were steady as they watched the scene playing out before him. Cassie thought of the conversation they'd had on their trek through the forest. The way he'd pushed through his discomfort to tell her how much she meant to him.

"We talked about it," Cassie said. "He knew I didn't feel the same way, but he wanted to be upfront with me."

Christina smiled, a mix of admiration and grief. "After my husband died, Chris tried to be more open with his feelings. We grew a lot closer over the past few years. Neither one of us wanted to hide how we were feeling or mince our words. Life's too short, you know?"

Cassie's mind strayed to David's tragic death. She'd been more honest with him than anyone else in her life at the time, and yet there was so much that had been left unsaid between them. Is that how Jason, Harris, and her family felt about their relationships with her now that they believed her dead?

"Yeah," Cassie murmured. "I know."

After a beat of silence, Christina broke it. "It must've hurt him so much to pull that trigger. I hope you can forgive him someday."

"I think I'm already halfway there," Cassie said, her gaze traveling to Chris once more. The fluorescent lighting in the kitchen highlighted his lifeless skin, shining off the crimson blood on his chest. It was bright and slick, as though it were still fresh.

Omega cleared his throat. With a solemn look, he reached into his pants pocket and drew out a small item. A watch. Cassie couldn't hold back a gasp when she recognized it.

Christina took it from Omega's outstretched hand. "That was his."

Cassie met the other man's eyes as the crinkled edges softened. "You kept it."

He nodded. "Seemed like the right thing to do."

Cassie's head spun. Omega didn't do sentimental, but she saw the sincerity in his gaze. It made him a little more human.

Christina cradled the watch in the palms of her hands, fresh tears rolling down her cheek. "I wasn't completely honest with Apex."

Omega and Cassie exchanged a look.

"What do you mean?" he asked, brows knitting together.

Christina set the watch down. "Chris was careful when he talked about his job. The last thing he wanted was for us to get caught in the crossfire of whatever he was working on."

Omega leaned forward. "But?"

"But we talked about the possibility of him getting killed in the line of duty. What would happen to us. What we needed to know. He didn't want us to doubt how much he cared about us." Christina turned to Omega. "Do you have a laptop or a tablet I can use?"

Omega rose from his seat, the wooden chair scraping against the floor. He strode into the living room, then returned a moment later with a small laptop, setting it down in front of Christina without a word. His intense gaze remained trained on her face.

"The guards interrogated me for days when we first arrived." Christina shuddered, as though the chill of that place still lived in her bones. "I didn't know anything then, and after a few days, they finally started to believe me."

"What about your kids?" Omega asked.

"They left them alone, thank God. I made it clear I'd be less cooperative if they hurt them, and they're too young to know anything anyway. Or maybe those guys weren't complete monsters."

Christina pecked out a URL on the keyboard before she hit enter. "I didn't think this website was relevant when they were questioning me. But when you told me what Chris did—how he sacrificed himself—I realized maybe he left something behind."

Omega scooted his chair closer to her to see the screen. "What website?"

"I don't know how it works, but Chris made me memorize the URL of this website he created. Only he and I knew the login credentials." She paused to type them in. Cassie also moved closer, and by the time she'd angled herself to see the screen, a new page was loading. "He told me to go here if he died of anything other than natural causes."

Cassie met Omega's eyes across the table. Did he feel the same electric current running through his veins as she did?

"There's a voice note here for me," Christina whispered. Then, turning to Cassie, "There's one for you too."

11

Cassie stared at the computer screen, confusion and disbelief swirling inside her body like a mini tornado.

A simple black screen with white text stared back at her. There were three buttons down the center of the page, each consisting of an audio file only a couple minutes long. The first one was tagged with Christina's name, the second one with Cassie's, and the third one was simply labeled, *Important*.

"What should I do?" Christina asked.

"You should listen to yours first," Cassie whispered.

When had Chris uploaded these messages? Had he known he wouldn't make it out of that garage alive? She glanced over at his specter, but he remained motionless.

Looking back to his sister, Cassie said, "We can leave if you want."

"No." Christina's hair shimmied around her face as she shook her head. "No, I want you to stay."

"Okay. We will."

After a few more seconds, Christina lifted a shaking hand and hit play on the first message.

"Hey, Sis," Chris said from the computer's speakers. He sounded so tired. "Not to do that cliché thing in the movies where they say, 'If you're listening to this, then I'm probably dead,' but, well, if you're listening to this, I'm probably dead." There was a pause. His voice was slow and measured, but not like he was reading from a script. More like he was choosing every word with the kind of care his sister deserved in a time like this. "I know that's not funny, and you're probably rolling your eyes at me right now. I've made a handful of these over the years, but this is the only one that's felt like this. Like I might not have a chance to come home and delete it before it reaches you."

Christina let out a small sob, but her eyes stayed glued to the screen, watching as the playback cursor ate through the file one second at a time.

"If this plays out the way I think it will, I'm afraid you might hate me forever. I hope you don't, but I'll understand if you do." He sighed, his voice wavering for the first time, and Cassie imagined him running a hand down his tired face. "I just want you to know that I love you, and I love Jonah and Jessi. More than you guys will ever know. You're my sister and my best friend, and you and those kids of yours kept me grounded over the years. I don't think I'll ever find the kind of love you and Ben had. That used to bother me. Used to make me jealous. But some people just aren't meant for that, I guess. And it's okay. I understand now what I was meant for. Why I became an agent."

There was such a long pause after Chris' last sentence that Cassie would've thought the recording ended there if she couldn't see there was still about thirty seconds left. When he spoke again, it sounded like he was fighting back tears.

"I have to do something really hard, Chrissy. It's gonna make me look like a monster, but I need you to know that I chose the lesser of two evils. I'm probably still going to Hell"—he made a sound somewhere between a laugh and a sob—"but my conscience is as clear as it can be. Don't believe everything they say about me, okay? I did what I did because it was my only choice. I just wanted to keep you and your kids safe. And I pray to God that I did. I love you, Christina. Tell Jonah and Jessi to be good and that their Uncle Chris will always watch out for them. No matter where I end up."

There was a short buzz of silence before the track ended. Christina's soft sobs replaced the sound of Chris' voice. Cassie placed a gentle hand on the other woman's back, shaking slightly as Christina wept.

Cassie slid her gaze over to the spirit on the other side of the room. Chris' stare was intense, as though trying to communicate through his eyes alone. He was right there, just out of reach, and she had so many questions for him.

After a few moments, Christina wiped the tears from her eyes and turned the computer toward Cassie. "Do you want to be alone for this?"

Cassie shook her head, knowing Omega wouldn't leave if she asked him to. But she had nothing to hide from either of them.

Lifting her hand from the other woman's back, Cassie noted how much it shook as she leaned forward and pressed play on the second audio file. Though she couldn't be certain, she thought he'd recorded the two clips back-to-back, given that he spoke in the same tired cadence.

"Hey, Cassie. If you're listening to this, it means you found my sister and explained everything. I don't think you'll ever truly understand what it means to me that you two found each other, that you played some part in keeping her safe. I hope you and her will stay in touch, if you're not too angry at me. I think you guys would get along great. If nothing else, you can bond over embarrassing stories about me. She has quite a few, I'm afraid."

Cassie wished she could laugh at the lightness of his tone, but the bubble of emotion rising in her chest was so far from humor, it was all she could do to fight back more tears.

"Sorry, I'm nervous. I don't want to do this, Cassie. I hope you know that. If this plays out the way I think it will, there's a chance—a much bigger chance than I'd like—that you'll never get to hear this and never know why I did what I did. I've tried everything in my power to destroy Apex and get my family out from under them. Everything other than this." Chris let out a shaky breath. "I know we already talked about this, but I care about you so much. I'm afraid you'll think my feelings for you were a lie, a manipulation tactic, but they weren't. If anything, I downplayed them because I knew you'd never feel the way I felt. And that's okay. I don't blame you."

Cassie fought to hear Chris over the pounding of her heart and the rush of blood in her ears. If she owed him anything, it was this.

"Maybe we'll both get lucky and your abilities will stop this before it ever gets started. But I don't think that's going to happen. I've been afraid of dying before, but this time it feels real." Chris sighed. "I knew I should've written down my thoughts before I hit record on this. You always did have a way of making me feel like I didn't know which was way up. That's a compliment, by the way." His chuckle died off quickly. "I know I don't have any right to ask anything of you after all of this, but please take care of my sister and her kids. They deserve a good life. A normal one."

There were only a few seconds left in the recording, and Cassie couldn't decide if she never wanted it to end or if she wished she'd never clicked on it to begin with.

"Apex is a cancer. Not only to this country, but to the world. Someone has to stop them. I thought it was going to be me. But there's a reason the queen is the most powerful piece on the chessboard. If everything goes according to plan, they'll never see you coming. They've underestimated you from the beginning. If they hadn't, they never would've knocked on your door and gotten you involved.

"You're gonna be the one to take them down, Cassie. You're gonna be the one to rise from the ashes." Chris laughed, and this time, there was actual humor in the sound. "For your sake, I hope I'm not still hanging around to see that. But I do hope we meet again. Maybe in another life."

The recording ended there, and this time, it was Christina's turn to put a comforting hand on Cassie's back.

The spectral form of Chris had stepped forward, his gaze more penetrating than ever. He looked like he wanted to open his mouth and speak, but his jaw didn't move. All he did was stare through wide eyes, as though that was explanation enough for everything he'd said.

Cassie broke eye contact and swiped her finger down the trackpad on the laptop. The arrow on the screen hovered over the play button for the third recording. She didn't look at Christina as she asked, "Do you mind if we listen to this one too?"

"Go ahead."

Omega leaned forward as Cassie clicked down on the button. Immediately, she could tell this had been recorded at a different time and a different place than the first two. While there had been no background noise in the other files, distant voices and traffic underscored Chris' voice here.

Chris quickly rattled off an address. "Everything you need is in there. The passcode is the same as the one for the website. No one should know about it, but keep your eyes peeled. Apex is everywhere."

Omega already had his phone out, tapping away at the screen. "It's the location of a storage container in Michigan." He looked up at Christina. "You know anything about this?"

"I live in Michigan," she said. "Chris always told me that if anything happened to me, I'd be taken care of."

"Must be money or information to get into some secure bank accounts." Omega sounded disappointed it wasn't something more concrete for them to follow up on. "I can have someone take you there to get what you need."

"Then what?" Christina asked, looking at the website in front of her like another audio recording would pop up to provide her with the answers to all her questions. "Where do we go from here?"

Omega stood. "You can't go back to your house. Best I can do is help keep you safe somewhere far away from Apex."

Christina blinked. "But Chris just said Apex is everywhere."

"If we get our way, they won't be for long."

12

Harris didn't bother knocking before she shouldered her way through the door to Jason's office, not knowing what to expect when she walked inside. Half an hour ago, Lorraine had called and told her she needed to come talk to Jason. She'd issued the directive in hushed tones, like she didn't want to be caught on the phone, and then hung up.

With the excuse of grabbing an early lunch, Harris headed out. It wasn't a complete lie, at least. She'd see what was going on with Jason, and then when he settled down, she'd grab something on the way back to the mountain of paperwork that had taken up permanent residence on the corner of her desk these days.

Like it would be that easy.

Harris respected Jason and his military background. He was ambitious, goal-oriented, and good to her best friend. When he became a private investigator, Harris had thought it'd be a good way to put Cassie's abilities to good use when the precinct didn't need her. Jason managed to turn his rundown office into something respectable amid the sea of seedy businesses that occupied the building.

That had been the case before Cassie disappeared, at least.

Died, Harris reminded herself, despite the pang in her chest at the thought.

Now, the space looked like a tornado had hit. Papers were strewn everywhere in haphazard piles or spread out across the floor. Empty carryout containers littered the spaces in between, and both garbage cans overflowed. The air smelled sour and stale, like spoiled food and lack of air conditioning.

For a second, Harris thought she'd walked through the wrong door. Jason was nowhere in sight.

Lorraine stepped out of the bathroom off to her right, meeting Harris' gaze with a sad smile.

Told you so, she seemed to say.

"Jason?" Harris called out.

She wanted to be angry at him for going so far off the deep end, but all the frustration drained from her body when he stood up from behind his desk.

It was clear he hadn't slept much since she'd last seen him. His skin looked sallow, and the bags beneath his eyes were darker than ever. His hair was disheveled, and she swore he had on the same clothes he'd been wearing when he'd barged into her office, claiming Cassie was still alive.

Jason met her gaze and narrowed his eyes, then focused on Lorraine. "You called her?"

"Now is not the time to act rashly," Lorraine said, her voice as calm and quiet as ever. But she looked worried. And Harris couldn't blame her.

Harris shut the door behind her. "What's going on?"

"Nothing you have to worry about."

Harris shook her head. So much for all her frustration falling away in lieu of her worry.

"If I have to arrest you for obstructing justice, I will." Harris only half meant it. That would be a last resort.

"Jason," Lorraine said, her voice hardening this time. "Tell her, or I will."

Jason ground his teeth together, but then his shoulders sagged a fraction of an inch, and he looked away from both of them. "She'll just talk me out of it."

"Maybe that's not a bad idea," Lorraine said.

"Whatever it is," Harris said, "I promise to give you the benefit of the doubt, okay? Just tell me what's going on."

Jason remained silent as he straightened some piles of papers on his desk. The closed windows muffled the sound of traffic from the street down below. If she hadn't thought it would set him off, Harris would've asked if he could crack one or two of them and let in some fresh air.

"I'm collecting everything we have against Apex," Jason said. "From Cassie's time in North Carolina to all the shit with the Hughes family, plus what she worked on while she was in Nashville."

Harris walked forward until she was in the middle of the room. The sour stench of garbage grew stronger, but now that she was looking, the papers appeared a bit more organized.

When she reached the couch, she picked up a missing dog poster from the cushion beside her and glanced over it. "Have you heard anything about Bear yet?"

"No," Jason said, a hard edge back in his voice.

Harris looked back up at him. "I've got the department on the lookout. We'll find him."

"I doubt that."

She put the flier back on the seat and folded her arms. "You're gathering everything against Apex. Why?"

Jason looked her dead in the eyes and said, "I'm going to the press."

Harris dropped her arms, her entire body going rigid. "Are you crazy?"

"Hear me out." The edginess in his voice gave way to excitement. Or maybe desperation. "It could give us the advantage we're looking for. Put Apex's back against the wall."

"They've come out on top every time that's happened, Jason." Harris glanced over at Lorraine to make sure she wasn't hallucinating. Considering the other woman's pallor, she wasn't. "There's a reason no one's ever pinned them for their crimes."

"You don't have to remind me. But there's also a reason Cassie was on their radar. She's been involved with them for a while now, and we've got plenty of threads to pull on. Something will shake loose sooner or later."

Harris threw up her hands. "They could kill you without blinking an eye."

"I'll be careful."

"Cassie thought she was being careful, too."

"Don't," Jason snapped, his wild eyes hardening. "Don't go there."

"We're already there." Harris stepped forward. "What we know about Senator Hughes' family and what Apex has done to protect them is huge, but we don't have any evidence. More than that, they still have you on video *murdering someone*."

Jason let out a low growl. "I didn't murder him."

"*I* know that, but if you go to the press about Apex, they will throw you under the bus just the same. The general public won't give you the benefit of the doubt. Nor will a judge and jury." Harris softened her expression and her voice. "Then they'll see that as proof of the crime you committed, and then what help will you be to any of us?"

"Help?" Jason scoffed. "What help am I now? You won't let me work on the investigation in any capacity. You won't believe me when I tell you that Cassie is still alive and needs our help." Jason's voice cracked, tears forming in his eyes.

Harris' mouth went dry and she couldn't find the words to tell him it would all be okay.

"Nothing matters but this," he continued. "It's bigger than me. Bigger than some power-hungry company. Putting Hughes in the Oval Office is important enough that they're willing to go to whatever lengths necessary to make it happen. We need to figure out what they're planning. If I have to sacrifice myself to stop them, then I will."

Harris had to blink back her own tears before she could speak. All the air had been sucked out of the room, suffocating her.

"I hear what you're saying," she said, hoping to God that he believed her, "but I don't think it's the right move. Who could we even trust with this sort of information?"

Jason chewed on the inside of his cheek before he answered. "Annette Campbell."

It didn't take much for Harris to conjure an image of the plucky reporter. She remembered the way the light bounced off her blonde curls, and how her tall, lean frame ensured she stood out from any crowd. Annette was beautiful, sure, but she was also intelligent and ambitious. Harris had butted heads with the woman on more than one occasion, including that time the reporter had pretended to date a cop to get information from him. It had almost cost them their investigation. The memory made Harris scowl, but she smoothed it away a moment later. Annette had come a long way since then, and she'd been cooperative with the police the last few times they'd crossed paths.

Still, could they trust her with this?

"That's an interesting choice," Harris said.

"Cassie's talked about her," Jason said. "She trusts her."

More air left Harris' lungs at the mention of Cassie in the present tense, like he'd punched her in the gut.

Thankfully, Lorraine spoke up before Harris could think about it for too long. "Who is she?"

"A reporter," Harris said. "A good one. We've worked together a few times. But going public is still a huge risk. They could come after all of us."

Jason shrugged, his face impassive at the thought. "We're not going to take Apex down without making bold choices."

"We don't have enough concrete evidence of Apex's crimes," Harris said. "Even if Annette believed you, she would have to verify a lot of information. These things take time. Sometimes years."

Jason held out his hands like Harris had just offered him everything he'd been asking for. "All the more reason to start now."

Harris locked eyes with Lorraine. Lorraine was on the same page as her. It would be next to impossible to talk Jason out of going down this path.

All she could do was slow him down.

"If we're doing this," Harris said, "then we're doing it right. I want to see everything you and Cassie have gathered, and we'll compare it to what we have on file. Then we'll track down concrete evidence. The more we—and I do mean *we*—bring to Annette from the jump, the less legwork she'll have to do. Which means she'll be able to publish sooner and put all of this to rest."

Jason's nod was borderline enthusiastic. "And the sooner Cassie will be able to come out of hiding."

Harris dropped her gaze to the floor, stomach churning. Hope rose within her chest, against her will. She was trying so damn hard to accept that Cassie was gone and move on, but every time she spoke to Jason, that became harder to do.

Before Harris could say anything to mitigate expectations, her phone rang. Digging it out of her pocket, she looked down at the number with a frown. She didn't recognize it.

"I need to get this." Harris leveled Jason with a look. "Don't do anything until we've got what we need. Once that's done, I'll set up a meeting with Annette."

Without waiting for an answer, Harris lifted her hand in goodbye, then turned on her heel and slipped out the door and back into the hallway. She was hit with the same scent she'd encountered on her way in—a toxic mix of mildew and vanilla, like someone had tried and failed to cover up the odor with an air freshener. And yet it was still better than the stench of week-old takeout.

Jogging down the stairs, she finally answered the call and raised the phone to her ear.

"Harris."

"Assistant Chief of Police," a male voice replied. "Glad I caught you. My client has decided to cooperate with the authorities, but she's only willing to talk to one person."

Harris slowed her descent down the stairs. Her voice echoed in the stairwell as she spoke. "I'm sorry, who is this? Who's your client?"

"My name is Gil Sangway," he said, sounding miffed she hadn't known already. "I'm Piper McLaren's lawyer."

13

CASSIE LET THE RHYTHMIC SOUNDS OF THE CAR SPEEDING DOWN THE highway lull her into a trance. Caught in a state of limbo, she was neither awake nor asleep. Only the occasional flick of the turn signal and Bear's sporadic pants from the back seat were enough to bring her out of her reverie for minutes at a time.

Forcing Omega's hand when it came to rescuing Christina and her kids hadn't been the smartest play, but she couldn't deny the results. It was difficult to worry about future consequences from Apex when the weight of her promise to Chris had been lifted from her shoulders.

Not that he'd gotten the memo, considering his steady presence in the backseat.

It was that thought that caused her eyelids to flutter open in time to see them pass a sign for the city she called home.

"Pearl Everly lived and died in Savannah, Georgia," Omega said. Reaching into the back seat without taking his eyes off the road, he added, "She was sixteen when she disappeared."

When Omega handed her a baseball cap and pair of sunglasses, she inspected them with a snort. "Are these supposed to disguise me?"

"More or less."

By the time she'd settled her miniscule disguise in place—which paired well with the loose workout clothes she'd donned that morning—they'd pulled off the side of the road along a chain-link fence enclosing a tiny cemetery.

Cassie peered through the window at the gravestones spread across a small plot of land. There was a large weeping willow in the center, its branches drooping as if mourning the souls laid to rest amongst its roots. The sense of grief weighed her down at the same time it beckoned her closer.

"The dog will have to stay in the car."

"I know," Cassie said, not missing the way Omega refused to use Bear's name.

Without another word, Omega stepped out of the car. She did the same, shutting the door and leaning back against it as he came around to stand at her side.

The grass was neat and trim beneath their feet, like it'd been mowed recently. Small American flags flapped in the wind in front of an army of tombstones. Trees spotted the more open sections of the field. One was as dead as the cemetery's inhabitants, a tall but crooked sentinel. The warm breeze carried the sounds of songbirds and crickets. Her sunglasses and hat provided a reprieve from the sun, which beat down on them from a clear sky.

Cassie's body pulsed with a hum that grew stronger the longer she stood there. It called out to the spirits on the other side of that fence. An answering buzz told her she had snagged someone's attention.

"Tell me more about Pearl," Cassie said. "How did you first hear about her?"

"I overheard a lot in my years driving for Anastasia." Omega's voice was quiet and measured, sounding more like the man she'd met the day she landed in Nashville. "As much as Anastasia trusted me, she was always careful not to reveal too much. Even if I could follow up on the information she spoke about, I could rarely put two and two together enough to act on it. Even then, I'd have to decide if it was worth blowing my cover for. Nothing ever was. Not until you came along."

Cassie stiffened. Another gentle breeze caressed her cheek, fanning the blush that had risen there.

She risked a glance at his eyes. "How did you become her driver?"

Omega smiled but kept his gaze averted. "That's a story for another time."

Cassie let the subject go for now. "Anastasia mentioned Pearl while she was in your car?"

Omega nodded, his head on a constant swivel. There was no one else in the cemetery, and there were only trees and shrubs behind them, but even Cassie felt exposed here on the side of the road.

"As you know," he said, "Anastasia rarely shows her hand. I could tell she was scared."

"Of a sixteen-year-old girl?"

"Maybe not of Pearl." Omega's voice was contemplative. "But of what Pearl knew."

"What could a sixteen-year-old know that would threaten Anastasia or Ap—Alpha?"

"That's what I'm hoping you'll be able to tell me."

Cassie crossed her arms over her chest in an attempt to keep from balling her hands at her side. "What else can *you* tell *me*?"

Omega turned to her, his face solemn but his eyes bright with the promise of a new discovery. "Pearl Everly was Jack Hughes' illegitimate daughter and Douglas Hughes' half-sister."

Cassie's breath hitched. "He had another kid from another woman?"

Omega nodded. "Unlike Douglas, Pearl was born as the result of an extra-marital affair."

Shimmers of movement caught Cassie's attention. Interest in her presence grew the longer she stayed.

She ignored them for now.

"How did you find this out?" she asked.

"It took a while. From what Chris gathered, I was able to backtrack and find out who her mother was, when and where Pearl died, and why this case was so curious to police. That's when I discovered the truth about Pearl's father."

"Another kid." Cassie shook her head. Images of other missing kids flashed through her mind. It wasn't that long ago she'd been at Camp Fortuna, investigating the murder of Henry Holliday. "Just like Douglas."

"Pearl was nothing like Douglas." Omega held his chin between his thumb and forefinger. "According to police reports, Pearl's mother, Crystal, was not interested in having a relationship with Jack once she found out who he really was and that she'd been the other woman. She had full custody of Pearl, and Jack paid her a considerable amount of money for her silence. Later, he increased that amount to ensure his visitation rights."

Cassie furrowed her brow. "He'd wanted nothing to do with Douglas. Why was Pearl different?"

"If I had to guess, he didn't want Pearl to end up like Douglas. Not only had Douglas become a serial killer, but he had the means to destroy Jack's entire life. If Pearl knew the truth about her illegitimacy, then she'd had that same power."

"So, Jack thought he'd do right by Pearl and be a part of her life?"

Omega nodded. "He visited a few times a year. They weren't close, but Pearl never objected to seeing him because he'd give her money and presents."

"A relationship like that still could've had a negative effect on her."

"If it did, Crystal didn't mention it." Omega's expression grew solemn. "Pearl didn't get to live long enough to find out what kind of adult she'd become."

Cassie swallowed the lump in her throat. "Did Pearl fit the profile for Douglas' victims?"

"No." Omega scratched at his beard. "Crystal married a few years after Pearl was born and gave birth to a son. They were a middle-class family who had every intention of sending both their kids off to college. Neither of the children ever got in trouble with the law, and as far as I could tell, neither of them frequented any of the places Douglas scouted for his victims."

"If Douglas found out Jack had a real relationship with his illegitimate daughter, it would've been all the motivation he'd need to go after her," Cassie said. "Could Douglas have found out about Pearl?"

"The police questioned plenty of people about her disappearance. They couldn't find anyone with motivation enough to kidnap and potentially murder a sixteen-year-old girl."

"And without a recovered body, we don't even know if Pearl *is* dead."

Omega nodded toward the cemetery. "If she's been murdered, she might be hanging out at her gravestone even though her body was never found."

Cassie's gaze raked over the cemetery, wondering how many of the people buried there had died with secrets as big as Pearl's. "Jack was never a suspect in his daughter's murder?"

"No, he had a solid alibi."

"Did they interview Douglas?"

Omega shook his head. "By the time Pearl disappeared, Douglas had already been investigated regarding the other disappearances. As far as I can tell, no one knew he and Pearl were half-siblings."

The rest of Cassie's questions disappeared when Omega pushed off the side of the car and walked toward the cemetery. Cassie only hesitated for a second before crossing the threshold.

The breeze was a little cooler on this side of the fence, and the ambient sounds of the world dimmed. That hum in her veins grew louder, and the answering buzz vibrated her bones. What were once glimmers of movement coalesced into ephemeral forms.

Omega didn't notice the change as he walked toward the weeping willow and stopped in front of a grave.

Catching up, Cassie's gaze fell to the stone in front of them. It was small and plain, like the family hadn't wanted to put much money or effort into the marker in the hopes that Pearl would, one day, come home alive.

Cassie sunk to her knees and studied the name and dates in front of her. But it was the gravestone's epitaph that caught her attention. "May the truth set you free," she read aloud.

"Either someone knows more than they're letting on," Omega replied, "or the family is hoping that, someday, the truth will be uncovered. And so will she."

The wind swirled around Cassie's shoulders, rustling the leaves in the tree overhead. A loose petal from one of the bouquets resting against a nearby grave skittered along the top of Pearl's headstone before it came to a stop near the edge.

In a daze, Cassie leaned forward and brushed it away. As soon as her fingertips came into contact with the cold stone, a vice-like grip closed around her throat. She grasped at her neck, but the hands were invisible, even as the pressure increased.

"Cassie?" Omega's voice sounded so far away. "What's wrong?"

She couldn't breathe, let alone answer. Panic set in as her vision clouded. Omega's hand landed on her shoulder. The sensation was drowned out by the compression around her neck and the deafening creak of a floorboard in a home that should've been empty.

As she toppled forward into the dirt, she smelled something sweet instead of earthy. The slamming of a car door jarred her head. The roar of an engine jostled her whole body. Bright sunlight pierced her eyes despite the sunglasses still perched on her face, and then there was more pain as her body fought to suck in oxygen.

She fought against the bonds around her, fought to live, but she grew weaker with every passing minute. She knew this was the end, and yet she couldn't stop fighting. She wouldn't go without a fight.

Omega rolled her onto her back and shook her. Instead of watching him fade from view like she expected, his outline grew crisper. She dragged in one gasping breath of air and then another. She coughed, dispelling the sweet smell from her nostrils. Birdsong erupted around her as though she'd taken out a pair of headphones. Bear barked from the car on the other side of the fence.

Chris knelt at her side, closer than he'd ever come to her. He cradled her head in his hands, and the pain receded. So did the panic. All became clear.

"I'm okay," she gasped, letting Omega help her into a sitting position. "I'm okay."

"What the hell was that?" Omega asked, concern and fear and anticipation written all over his face.

"Someone sending a message," she said, reveling in the oxygen that now flooded her system, her heart still pounding. Chris sat back too, fading with each passing second until he was gone altogether. "I think it was from Pearl."

Omega helped Cassie to her feet. "She's dead?"

Cassie nodded, rubbing her throat. "Taken from her own home. I smelled chloroform, I think. Heard her being put in a car. Felt her being strangled until she no longer had the energy to fight back."

"Do you know where she was killed?" he asked. "Where she was buried?"

Cassie thought back through every sensation she'd felt, every noise she'd heard, every smell she'd inhaled. But there was nothing. "No."

Omega didn't look worried. Instead, he turned and strode toward the opening in the chain-link fence.

Cassie scrambled after him, her legs still shaky. "Where are you going?"

"To the last place we know Pearl was alive."

14

Cassie stepped out of the car and onto the sidewalk in front of Pearl Everly's childhood home. It was quaint. Small, surrounded by a neat lawn and shrubs. A charcoal gray Dodge Charger sat in the driveway, gleaming in the sunlight. A cool breeze ruffled Cassie's hair, and the hum that had dissipated since she'd gotten back into the car grew a little louder.

Cassie opened the back door and leaned in to attach the brand-new harness around Bear's chest. It had taken some persuading to convince Omega to stop for the leash and allow her to bring Bear with them inside the house. Like the good boy he was, Bear sat still, except for his wagging tail, until Cassie clipped the harness into place. Once she stepped back, he leapt from the car and inspected the grass along the sidewalk.

Omega left them behind as he walked up the front path and onto the porch steps, then knocked on the front door. He'd contacted Pearl's brother, so the visit was expected, even if the dog wasn't.

The door opened and Omega exchanged a few words with whoever had answered. When he turned and waved Cassie forward, she bent down and scratched Bear behind the ear. His tongue lolled out of his head as he looked up at her, eyes half-closed in contentment.

"You have to be on your best behavior," she told him, walking forward and watching as he fell into step beside her, the leash loose in her hand. His tongue snaked back into his mouth, and though he didn't look alarmed, he was all business now.

She was also alert. An invisible tug pulled her forward. Pearl wanted to show her something inside.

Cassie followed Omega through the door and into the living room, bracing for a torment like she'd experienced at the graveyard. But it never came. A young man in a t-shirt and jeans stood before them, his feet bare against the plush carpet under his toes. His smooth skin and toned muscles made him look younger than Cassie, but the dark circles beneath his eyes and the wariness in his gaze spoke of a rough life.

"Thank you again, Mr. Barstow." Omega had shifted his whole demeanor, appearing older and less imposing. More like Robert. "This is my colleague, Cassie. The one I told you about. And this is her search-and-rescue dog, Bear."

Cassie worked to keep the surprise off her face, but she didn't miss a beat. Reaching out a hand, she said, "It's nice to meet you."

"You too. I'm Jett." His handshake was firm. "I don't mean to be rude, but you said there was new evidence in Pearl's case?"

"So to speak," Omega hedged. "You, of course, know who Pearl's father was? Jack Hughes."

Jett nodded, looking between the pair of them. "You mean to say—?"

"We don't have any conclusive evidence," Omega said before Jett could draw any wrong conclusions. "Were you aware Pearl had another half-brother?"

"Ross?"

Omega shook his head. "Douglas Hughes. Have you heard the name?"

"Can't say that I have." Then Jett's eyes widened. "Jack had another kid? Another affair?"

"Douglas was born quite a few years before Pearl. Jack wasn't married at that point, but he left them in much the same way he left Pearl and your mother."

Jett crossed his arms and clenched his jaw. "Sounds about right."

"Douglas Hughes was the Ash Wednesday Killer."

Jett's eyes grew wide again. "I didn't even know they'd solved those cases."

"The story got buried thanks to Mayor Blackwood's scandal."

Jett seemed at a loss for words. He looked from Omega to Cassie and back again. "You think he took Pearl?"

"That's what we're trying to find out. I know it's been a long time—"

Jett held up a hand. "Whatever you need, just let me know." His gaze drifted to the wall where a group of family photos hung. "My mom died about a year ago. She never knew what happened to Pearl. I don't want to go the same way."

Cassie cast her gaze around the living room. The floral couch, dozens of kitschy decorations, and framed family photos didn't match Jett's outward appearance. Cassie guessed he'd changed nothing about the house since his mother died.

"Were you and Pearl close?" she asked, looking back to Pearl's brother.

A soft smile formed around his lips. "Yeah. Close as a brother and sister can be, of course. We fought a lot, got on each other's nerves, but I looked up to her, you know? She was smart. Kind, too. But if you got on her bad side—" He whistled, his grin growing wider. "She didn't bend over backwards for nobody. Not even her father."

Movement beyond Jett caught Cassie's attention, leading her gaze into the kitchen. The doorway on the other side of the room shimmered. The details were muddied from the light streaming through the window, casting a glow over the room's surfaces. Was Chris manifesting again so soon?

No. He'd expended too much energy earlier when he'd saved Cassie from Pearl's vision. This had to be the young girl beckoning her closer.

Cassie's body trembled, and Bear pressed his warm body against her legs.

Hoping she wasn't about to relive what had happened at the graveyard, she asked, "Could we see her bedroom?"

Jett hesitated. "You really think you'll be able to find something after all this time? It's been years." He glanced down at Bear. "Will your dog be able to get her scent or whatever?"

"He's very good at what he does," Cassie said, patting Bear's head. "We can't guarantee anything, but I have a feeling it's a good place to start."

"Okay then." Jett motioned for them to follow him. "Back this way."

Omega gestured for her to go first, and Cassie fell in line behind Jett. The house had a stale scent underneath potpourri or incense. A stack of mail sat on the kitchen table. Cassie cast a glance over her shoulder as Omega paused to flip through envelopes. He abandoned the pile a few seconds later.

At the end of the hall, Jett stopped outside a closed door. "I'll warn you, Ma turned this into her sewing room and I haven't had a chance to go through it yet. Bit of a mess."

He swung the door open, and Cassie sucked in a breath. A musky smell hit her square in the face. Dust motes floated in the beams of sunlight filtering through the singular window on the far side of the room. Five full-sized storage cabinets, and at least that many smaller ones, burst with fabric and yarn and accessories. Scraps, needles, and pins covered the work table.

Bear sniffed the air, then sneezed.

"Right," Cassie said, turning to the two men. "We'll start in here." She looked pointedly at Omega. "This could take a little while."

Omega nodded, then turned to Jett. "I've got a few more questions about Pearl, if you don't mind?"

Jett frowned, but Cassie donned her best smile and nodded in reassurance. Jett smiled back and retreated down the hall with Omega.

Turning back to the room, Cassie resisted sucking in a deep

breath of air, lest she start sneezing too. She unhooked the leash from Bear's harness and ordered him to search the room, mostly for show.

Meanwhile, she turned in a circle, searching for any sign of Pearl. That hum in Cassie's veins grew louder, flooding her system with adrenaline.

A floorboard had creaked in the vision earlier. Pearl had thought she'd been alone in the house. The sweet smell that had soon followed was chloroform. The intruder's car had been just outside the house, and they'd driven her to the place where she'd been murdered. Then her attacker strangled her in the fashion of Douglas Hughes' victims.

Pearl wanted Cassie here, in her home, rather than where she'd been killed. But why?

Something bumped against her knee, jostling her from her thoughts. She looked down to see Bear staring up at her, his brown eyes large and wanting. With a sad smile, she said, "Good boy," and scratched him behind the ear, clipping his leash back to his harness before backing out into the hallway.

The men's voices drifted toward her from the kitchen. She walked toward them but stopped in front of the next door down the hall. Twisting the knob and pushing it open, Cassie flicked her gaze over the contents of the room. It was more masculine than the rest of the house, with a dark bedspread and a pile of weights in one corner. This had to be Jett's room.

A single window let in a little bit of light, but it was blocked out by the face pressed up against the glass.

Cassie gasped, taking a step backwards. Goosebumps erupted along her arms as she took in the round face of a young girl, her hair drawn back into a slick ponytail. She cupped her hands around her eyes as though trying to see inside. Her translucent form was corporeal enough to bend sunlight, as if she were really standing there.

"Pearl," Cassie whispered.

The girl met her eyes for a split second before taking a step back.

Cassie kept Bear close as she hurried back into the hallway and neared the entrance to the kitchen. Just as she wondered how she'd get out back, she spotted the door to a small outdoor patio. She grabbed the knob and pulled it open.

Jett called out from the other room. "Hey—"

Cassie stepped through and closed the door behind her. Shifting to the right, Cassie searched for Jett's window from the outside, but it was no use. Pearl was gone from the side of the house.

Bear tugged on his leash. She turned to see him staring at the old oak that stood at the other end of the fenced-in yard. And the girl hiding behind it.

As if in a daze, Cassie crossed the lawn in what felt like three strides, ignoring the sound of the back door opening and Jett calling after her, Omega offering reassurances that the other man didn't heed.

On the other side of the oak, Cassie stopped short.

In the shade of the large tree, she could make out Pearl's form as if she were still made of flesh and blood. Cassie was used to the pale complexion and milk-white eyes that most spirits had, but she never got used to seeing evidence of their gruesome deaths. A purple bruise encircled Pearl's neck like a macabre necklace.

"Please," Cassie said, ignoring the scuffle behind her. "Talk to me. Tell me where you're buried. Or who took you. Anything."

Pearl opened her mouth, but no sound came out. She furrowed her brows and tried again. Frustrated, she looked down and stamped her foot.

"It's okay," Cassie reassured her, despite the urgency singing through her blood. "Sometimes you can't talk. What about images? Feelings? Anything that can help me."

Pearl stamped her foot again. And again. All the while, she faded from view, stamping and pouting.

When she'd appeared in the hallway, she hadn't meant to lead Cassie to her old bedroom, but out through the back door.

"Bear," Cassie said, kneeling and pointing to the spot Pearl had once occupied. It was between two large roots that stuck out of the ground. "Dig."

Bear darted to the spot, tail wagging as he engaged in one of his favorite hobbies.

Cassie looked over her shoulder just in time to see Jett shove Omega off him and dash across the yard, one finger pointed in her direction as though preparing himself to lecture her. She had no idea what she'd say in response, especially after they walked into his house and dug up the past.

But just as Jett reached her and opened his mouth, Bear's nails screeched across metal. Omega joined them, and all three stared down at the army-green tin her dog had unearthed.

"What's that?" Jett asked, all anger gone from his voice.

Cassie stood. Her gaze locked onto the container. "Something that once belonged to Pearl."

15

Jason stepped out of the elevator and into the bustling newsroom with his head held high. Phones rang, papers rustled, and voices murmured as workers talked to their contacts, bounced ideas off their colleagues, and read their pieces out loud to themselves in hushed tones. Laughter punctuated the noise, as did a blaring horn from the street below. Reporters paid as much mind to those noises as they did to Jason.

Lying to Adelaide and Lorraine made his stomach twist into knots, but they were being too cautious about the whole situation. Ross Hughes would be named one of the two major presidential nominees any day now. They only had so much time to put an end to this situation and avenge Cassie.

Not that she was dead.

Somebody brushed by him, huffing out an annoyed sigh that he'd stopped in front of the elevator. Stepping to the side, Jason watched as a dozen people forged ahead with their work. None of them realized a freight train headed straight for them.

Sticking to the outer wall, Jason hiked his small backpack up his shoulder and made his way to the far side of the room, toward a few separate offices closed off by a wall of windows and an array of doors.

All the blinds were drawn, but it wasn't difficult to find the one he was looking for. The first placard he came across listed her name.

Annette Campbell.

He'd read some of her articles. They were well-researched and well-written. Jason had no idea what she'd be like in person, but when they'd spoken on the phone, she was polite and interested in what he had to say.

Knocking on the door, he waited until he heard her muffled "Come in," before entering. It was bare of any decoration. Piles of papers covered every surface in neat stacks, like she'd placed each one just so.

The woman behind the desk looked up, her blonde curls bouncing. She was conventionally pretty, even wearing a bulky cardigan and minimal makeup. The sharpness in her gaze drew him closer.

"Jason Broussard," he said. "We spoke on the phone earlier?"

"You're early." Annette hadn't stopped typing at her computer since he walked in, not making a single mistake despite her eyes never leaving his face. "Take a seat. I'll be done in a minute."

Jason did as he was told, heaving his bag from his shoulder before plopping down in the chair across from her. Annette followed his movements before returning to the computer screen, her fingers flying over the keyboard at a rate that would make Lorraine jealous.

After a minute, Annette moved one hand to her mouse and clicked around a few times. Then, leaning back in her chair, she gave Jason her full, undivided attention. "It's nice to finally meet you, Jason." She paused and tilted her head to the side. "Can I call you Jason?"

"Of course." He knitted his eyebrows together. "You make it sound as though you've heard of me."

She smiled, revealing straight, white teeth. Annette had appeared on the news when she'd first started out, but it had been a while. She could've been an anchor, but her talent lay in investigative work. Uncovering stories other people wanted to keep buried came with its own notoriety.

"Because I have heard of you," she said, looking him up and

down. "Assistant Chief of Police Adelaide Harris speaks highly of you."

"Does she?"

"Sometimes."

"That sounds more accurate."

"Your phone call was intriguing." She checked her watch and frowned. "But I don't have much time to spare. Shall we get to it?"

"Like I said on the phone, I have a story that could shock not only the city of Savannah, Georgia, but the entire nation."

"I've heard that before," Annette said. Her eyes flicked back to her computer like she'd rather get back to work than talk with him. "I'll be honest with you, the only reason you're here is because of your connection to Harris." A frown pulled her lips down. "And Cassie. I'm sorry, by the way. I didn't know her well, but she was a good person."

Jason stiffened in his seat. "Cassie's not dead."

Annette raised her sculpted eyebrows. "What makes you think that?"

"We don't have her body."

Annette searched his face, as though waiting for him to continue. "You'll need more than that to convince me or the public."

"I don't care about the public. And while you were my first choice for this story, you're not the only reporter in this building who would be willing to talk to me."

Those sculpted eyebrows pulled together, and Jason didn't miss the flash of annoyance in Annette's gaze. "You should know that I don't intimidate easily, Mr. Broussard."

He ran a hand over his face. "I'm sorry. I'm not in the best state of mind right now, and Cassie's disappearance has been rough on me. I'm not here to intimidate you. If you decide not to run with the story, I'll understand. But I'd rather not take this to someone else. There aren't many people I can trust."

"How do you know you can trust me?"

"I don't. But some of your stories have garnered national attention. You stick to the facts, even when they're not flattering. You don't seem afraid to ruffle a few feathers."

"You certainly know how to tease a girl," Annette said, her sharp gaze sparkling. Then she looked down at her watch again. "But like I said, I don't have much time. Can we skip the ambiguity and get to the good stuff?"

"I have one condition before I tell you what I know."

"Which is what, exactly?"

"This has to remain confidential for as long as possible. Until you write the story. You can't tell your boss or your colleagues. You can't talk to Harris about it. Preferably, I'd like it if you didn't talk to anyone at all, but I know you'll need to corroborate some information."

Annette leaned forward on her desk. "That's a tall order."

"I know."

"I don't think I can make that promise, Jason. At the very least, my boss—"

"No. We have to be discreet. This isn't just so we don't get steamrolled." He hoped she saw the pleading look in his eyes. "This is for our safety."

Annette picked up a pencil from her desk and tapped it against the surface while she assessed him with narrow eyes. "I'll do what I can to keep this quiet." When Jason opened his mouth to argue further, she held up a hand. "It's the best I can do. If there's enough here to write a story, my editor will find out at some point, whether we publish it in the *Morning News* or not. I'm not willing to lose my job over this—or piss off any of my contacts at the SPD. But if this story is as big as you're making it out to be, then I'll find a way to keep it off anyone else's radar for as long as possible."

Jason sank back into his seat with relief. "Thank you."

Checking her watch for a third time, Annette met his eyes with a stare that left no room for argument. "You've got two minutes. Give me the cliff notes."

"Have you ever heard of Apex Publicity?"

"The big PR company? Sure."

Jason leaned forward, a smile playing over his lips. "What if I told you they covered up the Ash Wednesday Murders for years, then had

Douglas Hughes killed when keeping him alive was no longer in their best interest?"

Before Annette could answer, Jason went on. "What if I told you Douglas Hughes was Senator Jack Hughes' biological son, and that Apex wants to put his adopted son, Ross, in the Oval Office to become their puppet? That their intention is to destabilize our country to benefit foreign adversaries like China and help them supersede us as a global superpower? And that all this will earn them more money, power, and influence than any single entity should ever have?"

A beat of stunned silence passed before Annette spoke. "How much evidence do you have?"

Jason sat back in his chair. "Enough to make Apex nervous, but not enough to nail anyone to the wall. That's where you come in."

"In that case," Annette said, "I'd better reschedule my next meeting."

16

Cassie pulled the metal tin from the earth between the oak tree's massive roots at the edge of the yard. Her hands shook as she walked it back to the house, wiping the dirt off the corroded metal surface. Inside, she set it on the kitchen table.

Before she could ask Jett if he wanted to do the honors of opening it, Omega released the clasp on the tin, pushing the lid back until it hung from rusted hinges. Dirt and mildew assaulted her senses, but it would've been worse if the contents hadn't been sealed in plastic bags.

The three of them stared at the journals. The ticking of a clock and Bear's quiet pants punctuated the silence. The hum that had coursed through Cassie's veins was quieter now, but she couldn't drag her gaze from the metal box in front of her. Was this everything they'd been searching for?

"These are Pearl's journals," Jett said, breathless. "We couldn't find them. The police figured the kidnapper had taken them. Someone who didn't want their secrets uncovered."

"Her father?" Cassie suggested, meeting Omega's eyes.

"Only one way to find out," Omega said, reaching into the tin. He grabbed three plastic bags and handed them out.

Jett stared down at the journal in front of him. "Shouldn't we go to the police with this?" He looked up at the other man. "The local cops, I mean. They'll want to know."

"I'll be sure to inform them as soon as possible," Omega reassured him. "But I want to know what sort of evidence we've got first. No point in bothering them if this is just a bunch of love notes to her high school crush."

Cassie bit her tongue. He knew as well as she did that these buried journals were more than that. But Jett, still dazed, nodded and peeled open the bag that had protected one of his sister's journals for all these years. Cassie and Omega did the same, each sinking down into a chair to read. Bear stayed at her side, head resting on his paws.

The journal in Cassie's hands was from several years before Pearl disappeared. It was full of the kind of entries she'd expect from a preteen—annoying things her brother did, the fights she got into with her best friend, and yes, even the kids she had crushes on. Cassie skimmed the pages, guilt twisting like a dagger in her stomach as she turned each page, reading about the minutia of the girl whose life had been stolen from her.

Cassie shut the diary and stood to lean over the metal tin in the center of the table. A few more journals sat inside, similar in size and shape to the others, each a different color and pattern. Another baggie contained a small pink jewelry box. Below that sat a smaller notebook, plain in comparison to all the others.

Cassie reached in and drew it out. Bear lifted his head in curiosity but put it back down when she sat in her seat. Unsealing the bag, Cassie pulled the item from its tomb and flipped it open. The first sentence made her heart stop.

I met my dad today.

The other two didn't notice the way she sucked in a sharp breath, too absorbed in their own research.

He was nice, I guess. Kind of boring. Mom says I shouldn't think those things about people, especially my own father, but I can't help how I feel! I can tell he's rich, and he acts like some of the kids in school. Like he's better than me. He didn't say that, but I felt like he was thinking it. Well, if he thinks he's so much better than me, then why is he even here? Roger has always been my real dad, even though he's weird and likes to put pineapple on his pizza. I asked Jack what he likes on his pizza, and he looked at me like I had two heads. WHO DOESN'T EAT PIZZA!?!?

Cassie couldn't hold back her smile. Even from that first meeting, Pearl had been able to see right through Jack.

The next entry was about him, too.

Jack showed up today. Mom said it was out of the blue, but I don't know what the color blue has anything to do with it. She was angry that he hadn't called first, and so was I. She said she'd take me skating in the park! When Mom suggested Jack take me instead, he said he couldn't, so we just sat in the living room and watched TV together for an hour. Worse than that, he made me watch the news. I mean, what's the point??

Cassie kept reading. Some of the entries were neat and intentional, like Pearl had spent half her time making sure all the words were legible, and some were nothing more than angry slashes across the page. But all of them were about Jack.

Not every visit was a bad one. Pearl wrote about getting ice cream and flying in a helicopter. Jack's presents became more elaborate, and Pearl became less incensed by his impromptu social calls. She talked about how Jett was jealous, but less so when she let him play with some of her toys. Her mom, on the other hand, always became moody and closed off after Jack showed up. Roger was stalwart in his love of Pearl—as well as his disapproval of Jack.

A longer entry detailed the day she found out her father was a well-known politician. She'd done some research and taken notes, but none of it was scandalous—other than the fact that Jack was married and had adopted a son. Pearl was surprised and hurt that Jack hadn't told her that bit of information, and when she confronted him about it, asking if she could meet her brother, she said Jack looked like he'd seen a ghost.

Had he been afraid of her meeting Douglas?

Only the flipping of an occasional page from Omega and a sporadic sniffle from Jett reminded Cassie she wasn't alone. Bear kept his eyes closed, but his ears twitched at every sound. Neither Pearl nor Chris reappeared, the house calm and quiet around her.

Jack was angry about something today, but I couldn't tell what. His life is perfect, so what does he have to be angry about? He's rich and handsome, with a beautiful wife and a perfect son. I wouldn't be surprised if Ross became a politician like him. But Jack was tense and kept telling me to be careful when I walked to and from school, or anywhere else in the city. He even suggested hiring me a bodyguard! Can you imagine how embarrassing that would be? Mom must've thought the same thing because she said, "What would everyone say if they found out?" That shut him up real fast. They stared at each other like they were having a whole conversation in their heads, but when I asked Mom about it later, she wouldn't tell me. She doesn't know that I figured out she had me while Jack was still married to his wife.

A few months before Pearl disappeared, she wrote about how Jack was always on his phone, which annoyed her because she wasn't allowed to be on hers when he visited. This entry was written in the messiest handwriting Cassie had seen yet.

Jack is always on his damn phone! Mom would be so mad if she knew I was swearing, even if it's not out loud, but I don't know how else to get my anger out. He shows up a few times a year, hands Mom a wad of cash, then watches as she leaves me alone with the guy who abandoned us when I was a baby. And I'm supposed to be grateful? Sure, I like when he gives me money to go shopping, but I also know he's not the one picking out my Christmas presents. Mom probably gives him a list and he hands it off to his secretary or something. Why does he even bother?

Today, I did something bad. Or something amazing. I'm not sure yet. For all the money Jack has, you'd think he'd hire someone to teach him how to use his own phone. He was getting so frustrated, and it was so annoying, so I asked him if I could help. I didn't think he'd say yes, just take the hint and keep his grumblings to himself, but he handed over his phone and said he couldn't open an attachment in his email. I told him I knew how to fix it so he wouldn't have trouble anymore, but I would need my computer. He must trust me a lot because he just said okay and then went back to watching the news while I went into my bedroom. From there, it only took a few minutes to copy everything from his phone over to my computer. I don't even know why I did it, other than I could. He's probably got a lot of important stuff on there, and I don't want to mess with any of that, but he's been keeping secrets from me for years and I'm tired of waiting for him to open up.

Cassie's breath hitched. Her back twinged from hunching over the table. Straightening, her spine cracked with the movement, but it offered little relief. Anticipation built inside her until her hands shook, and she had to force herself to slow down as she read so she didn't miss a single word.

I've been going through the contents of Jack's phone. I started with the pictures because I figured those would be easiest. Most of them are professional shots of him and his family or him on the road campaigning. Surprise, surprise, there are none of me or Mom. I'd say that doesn't hurt my feelings, but I'd be lying. There was a folder I couldn't open. Maybe it's government information, or maybe something worse. I'm not sure I want to know.

Then I started going through his emails. Most of them were boring, and it's taken me weeks to find something I even understand. There are hundreds from this woman named Anastasia Bolton. At first, I thought maybe Jack was having another affair, but then I thought maybe she was his secretary. Turns out she's neither. She works for this publicity company called Apex, and it seems like Jack did something wrong that they need to fix.

Cassie's heart pounded at the mention of Apex Publicity. Pearl couldn't have had any idea who they were or what they were capable of at the time, but did she look them up later? Information would've been sparse, but maybe she'd connected some dots. A few entries later, another scribbled passage told Cassie all she needed to know.

It makes SO MUCH MORE SENSE why Jack got all scared when I said I wanted to meet my brother. Turns out, I've got another one. That's three now! This brother is named Douglas, and he's much older than the rest of us. He also lives right here in Savannah. But the way Anastasia and Jack have been talking, it doesn't seem like I'd want to meet him. Sounds like he's a bad guy who's gotten into some trouble, and that's what she's been trying to fix.

The handwriting in the following entry was neater, but the blotches of ink indicated Pearl had been pressing down hard as she wrote the entry with fury.

I figured it out. Jack was scared for me to go out on my own because of Douglas! He knows his own son is the Ash Wednesday Killer, but he refuses to tell anyone about it. He's known for months. I hate watching the news, but even I know there have been a bunch of kids who've gone missing. Jack needs to say something before someone else gets hurt. If he won't, then I will.

Cassie swallowed past the lump in her throat. With a shaking hand, she turned the page. The entry was short, but it wasn't rushed.

Jett, I hope your obsession with that metal detector means you find these journals someday. I know we didn't always get along, but I hope you know you were the best little brother anyone could've asked for. If you read all of this, then you know the truth, just like I do. But that also means they got to me before I could do anything about it. It feels scary to write that. But I know what kind of person Jack is now. Mom always told us to do the right thing, no matter how tough it is, right? Well, that's what I'm going to do. Jack was so angry when I confronted him. I thought he was going to kill me. But he just made me delete everything off my computer. Good thing I kept copies of everything. Please be careful. I don't think Apex is just covering stuff up for Jack. They're more dangerous than you can imagine.

I love you, Jett. Tell Mom I said I'm sorry.

Cassie took a breath as she flipped the page, only to find it blank. Pearl hadn't written more about her confrontation with Jack. He was undoubtedly responsible for what had happened to her, but had he done it himself?

With a spark of realization, Cassie drew the metal container closer and stared at the small jewelry box. Lifting it out, she unwrapped it and stared down at the pale pink exterior.

"We couldn't find that either," Jett said, eyeing the pink box in Cassie's palm. "Jack gave her a bunch of jewelry, and we figured the kidnapper took it to pawn."

Cassie lifted the lid on the box. Inside were several pairs of earrings, a few bracelets, and a handful of necklaces, all adorned with diamonds or pearls.

Jett laughed, but it was watery. "Jack was always buying her pearls, and she hated it. She never wore them. Drove him crazy."

Cassie tugged on the tiny drawer inside the box. Instead of more jewelry, she found several USB drives tucked safely into the slots.

Jett leaned closer. "What's that?"

Cassie locked eyes with Omega. "Exactly what we've been searching for."

17

A BEAT OF SILENCE PASSED THROUGH THE KITCHEN WHILE THE THREE OF them stared down at the cute jewelry box in Cassie's hand. They were each leaning forward over the wooden table, enraptured by the discovery.

Omega was the first to speak. "What makes you say that?"

Cassie tapped the notebook in front of her. "This whole journal is dedicated to Pearl's relationship with Jack Hughes. From the day she met him until their final confrontation."

"Confrontation?" Omega asked.

"Pearl thought her father was hiding something from her, so she tricked him into giving her his phone and copied the contents onto her computer. She found out that Apex was covering up for Douglas, so she forced his hand by trying to make him do the right thing."

Omega ran a palm across his beard. "That obviously didn't go according to plan."

Jett stared between the two of them. "I'm missing something here."

Cassie looked to Omega, who hesitated for only a second before giving her a nod of approval.

"Jack knew his son Douglas was the Ash Wednesday Killer." Her voice came out with breathless excitement. "His publicity company was helping him cover it up to avoid a scandal."

"So was it—" Jett's sentence cut off with a choked sob. "Was it Jack who took her?"

"I'm not sure." Cassie looked down at the last page in the notebook. Then she slid it over to him. "She wrote you a letter."

Jett closed his eyes as tears tracked down his face. He placed his hand on the notebook and tugged it closer. After a moment, he wiped his eyes, looked down, and started reading. Cassie turned to Omega to give Pearl's brother some semblance of privacy.

Omega pointed to the USB drives and asked quietly, "These contain what was on Jack's phone?"

Cassie nodded. "She mentioned pictures and emails, but I'm sure there was more. She said there was a folder she couldn't get into."

"I know someone who'll be able to open it for us."

"She also mentioned emails between Jack and Anastasia. That's how she found out she had another brother, Douglas. That's also how she found out he was the Ash Wednesday Killer. We'll be able to prove Jack knew, and that Apex covered it up."

Omega quirked the corner of his mouth down. "We'll be able to prove Anastasia covered it up, but we'll need something bigger than that to implicate Apex as a whole." Now he had a glimmer of excitement in his eyes. "Luckily, this is just one of many options at our fingertips."

Cassie wondered if it would be enough to get Anastasia to abandon ship. If Apex was going down, would she be willing to turn on them to save herself? Time and again she'd proven her loyalty to the company, but everyone had their limit.

She opened her mouth to let Omega in on her thoughts, but Bear pushed to his feet, his head swiveling in the direction of the door. Cassie stilled, watching as a figure coalesced in the center of the living room. Taller and broader than Pearl had been, it only took her a few seconds to realize that Chris was back.

Only this time, he didn't just stand there and watch her from his usual spot against the opposite wall. Pale eyes wide and bulging, his mouth opened and closed in rhythm. He repeated the same phrase or sentence over and over, his eyes somehow growing wider. Cassie stared at him without blinking, as though that would help her figure out what message he wanted to give her.

Just as she was about to stand and see if she could get close enough to hear him, a polite knock sounded on the door.

Jett and Omega turned toward the sound. Cassie froze, her mind whirring. Savannah was a big city, and while her face wasn't currently plastered across the news, there had been some articles and segments on television about her death. They were so close to what they'd been searching for. Now was not the time to take risks.

Another knock emanated from the door, and Cassie stood, ready to bolt into the hallway.

Jett rose from his chair, wiping tears from his eyes and shaking his head as if to clear the daze that clung to him. He walked around the table and went into the living room, passing right through Chris and making the specter dissipate as though he'd been made out of nothing more than a collection of dust motes.

Omega stood from his seat. "Don't answer that."

"It's probably just my neighbor," Jett replied, turning back to face Omega. "She's been checking on me since Mom died." He cleared his throat as if trying to dislodge the emotion stuck there. "She knows I don't have anyone left."

Before Omega could stop him, Jett opened the door to a group of people. Three men stood back on the doorstep, all suits and sunglasses. A woman stood in front of them. Black hair. Bright red lips.

Think of the Devil, and she shall appear.

A small gasp left Cassie's mouth, and the woman's gaze shifted. Her face morphed from one of bored politeness to ravenous hunger the second she laid eyes on Cassie. There was a slight movement, like she'd waved her hand at one of the men. Then a muffled *pop, pop.*

Omega reacted first, whipping out a gun that Cassie hadn't even known he was carrying.

Jett staggered backwards, then crumpled to the floor, bright red blooming against his torso.

A scream tore up Cassie's throat. A wide smile disfigured Anastasia's face. The gleam in her eyes wasn't one of surprise, but vindication.

Like she never truly believed Cassie was dead to begin with.

Next to Anastasia, the man with the silenced gun gestured toward the inside of the house, as if asking for permission to kill the rest of them. The other men stood still behind Anastasia, eyes hidden beneath darkened sunglasses. Jett bled out on the floor in front of them, unbreathing. Another scream clawed its way up Cassie's throat and died. She couldn't breathe.

"I want them alive," Anastasia said, eyeing her manicured hand and allowing the men to step in front of her.

A deafening bang filled Cassie's ears. Omega had his back turned to Anastasia and his gun pointed behind Cassie. She whipped around in time to see a man fall, his body halfway through the back door.

They'd surrounded the house and come in through the rear entrance.

Omega turned back toward Anastasia, shouting at Cassie to run.

Cassie slammed the lid shut on the jewelry box, scooping it inside the crook of her elbow. She snatched the small, open notebook off the table, her heart cracking open despite the adrenaline pumping through it. Jett would never get to learn what had happened to his sister.

She darted for the back door, Bear and Omega on her heels. Gunshots sounded, Omega's louder than the others. No bullets hit her as she burst out into the backyard. One of the suited men grunted. Omega's bullet had found its target.

"Where are we going?" Cassie shouted over her shoulder.

"Run until you can't run anymore," he shouted back.

Cassie made for the back gate behind the oak tree. She screamed as Pearl manifested in the opening, charging at her with wild eyes. Invisible hands wrapped around her neck again, yanking her back a step. Real hands closed on empty air as one of Anastasia's men grabbed the back of her shirt. Cassie clutched the jewelry box and notebook tighter as Bear launched himself at the man and sank his sharp teeth into his arm. The man screamed, cut off by the sound of another gunshot. Bear let go as the man crumpled to the ground, blood pouring from his mouth in fading gasps.

The pressure around Cassie's neck faded, her ears still ringing. Without stopping to look behind her, she took off down the sidewalk. The pounding of her feet against the concrete jarred her arm. A deep ache pounded in her shoulder. She gritted her teeth against the discomfort.

"Somebody will call in the gunshots," she panted.

"Good." Omega didn't even sound winded. "It'll slow them down."

"Not for long."

"Long enough."

"You got a plan?"

Omega's reply came out like a growl. "I'm working on it."

18

ANASTASIA STOOD IN THE LIVING ROOM OF PEARL EVERLY'S CHILDHOOD home, her heart pounding even as her stomach sank.

Cassie Quinn was still alive.

Despite their incredible resources, Apex hadn't found Cassie's body. Anastasia figured Robert—*Omega*—had whisked her off somewhere to recover. They'd surveilled Cassie's friends and family, and all of them had been devastated by the news. Anastasia was sure no one from Cassie's life knew the truth.

Now, Anastasia had proof.

Anastasia had gone against Daniel Haussmann's orders to visit the bunker where Christina and her children had been held. The operation had been done by professionals, and Omega had proven capable of slipping through their fingers without a trail for them to follow.

It had taken a long time for Anastasia to realize she was the reason Omega knew the name Pearl Everly, but only seconds after Christina's rescue to realize it was the next logical step for Cassie and her benefactor.

Pearl was the last connection between Jack Hughes and his biological son, Douglas. Jack had sworn he'd watched his daughter wipe all the downloaded correspondence off her computer, but if she'd been smart enough to get it in the first place, then she'd been smart enough to make a copy.

"Clean up this mess before the cops get here," she ordered her men through gritted teeth, gazing down at the dead body of Pearl's brother before her eyes found the unmoving form of one of her soldiers. If Cassie were here, would she be able to see their spirits?

Anastasia stepped around the dead body at her feet. "Be sure to check the backyard, too."

"Yes, Ma'am," Stolus replied, bending down to lift Jett Barstow off the ground.

"DiMarco," she said, turning to the man kneeling on the floor. "How bad is it?"

DiMarco undid his vest to show two bullets had hit him center mass. Omega had been aiming to kill. "Hurts like a son of a bitch, but I'll live."

"Cage is dead," someone called from the back.

Anastasia swore. Two down, one injured. Not the worst way this could've gone, but far from ideal. She had one more man waiting out front near Omega's vehicle. Her order not to kill their targets had cost two people their lives. She didn't mourn them as anything more than soldiers, but it irked her that Cassie and Omega had slipped through her fingers again.

Anastasia folded her arms tight and crossed the living room to the kitchen. She stopped in front of the dining room table. A green metal box sat in the center. Several plastic bags and notebooks lay strewn across the surface.

Cassie would've taken the most damning evidence with her.

Eyes locking on a small pile of dirt next to the box, she called out, "Check the backyard. See if they dug something up."

"Yes, ma'am."

With a single finger, Anastasia flipped open one of the notebooks and turned a few pages. Journal entries. She peered into the box and noted a few more that had been untouched.

She spoke to the man closest to her. "Bag this up. Bring it with us."

"Yes, ma'am."

Anastasia crossed the kitchen and entered the hallway, taking her time as she peered into each room, searching for anything of interest. The thrill of finding proof of Pearl's hidden evidence never hit her. Apex would be disappointed they had yet another fire to douse when it felt like the whole building was already engulfed in flames.

Stopping in the doorway of what appeared to be Jett's room, Anastasia peered through the window and watched one of her men inspect the other side of a large oak tree out back. He knelt down, reaching his hand inside a dirt hole. The green box's former resting place.

Anastasia shook her head and once again cursed the man who had kidnapped Pearl from her childhood home. He'd strangled her to death before remembering he was supposed to interrogate her about any possible hidden evidence. The girl had only been sixteen and an easy mark. It would've taken all of five minutes to break her and reveal the contents' location.

But Gary Slate had been unhinged. He'd been too excited to kill with the promise of no repercussions.

He had not lived to see the next morning. Apex had made sure of that.

Anastasia shivered at the memory of pulling the trigger and ending the man's life. It was her punishment for choosing the wrong operative to carry out a vital mission. She'd taken the penalty like a champ, not showing an ounce of fear or revulsion until she was alone in her own home. Her tears had blended into the water coming from the showerhead.

It had been her first time taking a life.

Sirens sounded in the distance, edging closer to the house. Anastasia turned on her heels. A headache pulsed in her temples. She dug her fingers into the side of her head to relieve some of the pain.

Anastasia swore under her breath again. If Apex had been able to see the future—if had they known how many skeletons the man had hidden in his closet—they would've cut ties with Jack Hughes a long time ago. Douglas and Pearl had been the biggest, but far from the only secrets he'd wanted hidden in plain sight.

Jack Hughes had been Anastasia's first big client. He was a bit of an asshole who got a little too handsy at times, but it was par for the course. As a politician, he wasn't afraid to ruffle a few feathers to get what he wanted. She'd respected that much about him, at least.

The sirens grew nearer. Anastasia smoothed her hair back and dropped her hands by her sides, clenching them into fists. She'd built her reputation on making Jack Hughes' problems go away, and now they were rising from the dead, one by one.

Anastasia couldn't tell Apex that Cassie had made off with evidence they'd long thought dead and buried. She still had a day, maybe two, before the company found out what was really going on. They'd send someone after her—but was she still valuable enough that they'd give her the benefit of the doubt before turning the barrel on her?

The doorbell rang, and one of her men answered. The officers on the doorstep inquired about the shots fired. Her men would take care of it, one way or another, leaving her to deal with the most pressing issue at hand.

Anastasia needed to get her hands on the evidence Cassie Quinn had stolen. She'd do it by appealing to the woman's bleeding heart. A small smile formed on Anastasia's blood-red lips. She pondered who Cassie would come running for the fastest.

19

Cassie didn't stop running until Omega pointed at a rusty pickup truck parked along the side of the road in front of an empty lot. The windows were rolled down halfway, so all he had to do was reach inside and pop the door open, then peel a panel away from under the steering wheel to reveal a mess of wires. A moment later, it roared to life under his touch. She loaded Bear into the back and hopped up front, clutching Pearl's journal and jewelry box to her chest, ignoring the stench of stale cigarettes and mildew that emanated from the fabric of her seat.

Only after Omega pulled away from the curb and her heartrate slowed did she find the words to ask, "What do we do now?"

Omega heaved deep breaths but his voice came out steady. "Right now, we have to make sure no one is following us."

"Your car," Cassie said. "It has all our stuff in it."

"Unfortunate." Omega slowed for a stop sign and turned right. "Nothing we can do about it now."

"My clothes," Cassie said, tilting her head back onto the headrest. "My money."

"My weapons. My computer." There was a slight pinch to Omega's voice. "At least they won't find anything they can use against us, but we just lost considerable resources."

"Are we staying in Savannah?" Cassie asked, risking a glance at the man.

Omega was silent for a moment. "Staying. For now, at least." He glanced over at the jewelry box she still clutched to her chest. "I'd like to see what Pearl found out about Apex."

With a silent nod, Cassie returned her gaze to the road. They drove around the city for a half hour, then stopped at a pet store to get some food and water for Bear. Afterwards, Omega bought a cheap laptop and a couple burner phones at an electronics shop.

He handed over his cell and told Cassie to find a café. She searched for one that had internet and allowed dogs on the outside patio, then read out the directions for him.

They parked the truck several blocks over. There was no telling how long it would take for the vehicle's owner to figure out it had been stolen. They'd likely have to find alternative transportation later.

Omega left Cassie and Bear outside with the computer while he went in and grabbed them a pair of coffees and a couple sandwiches. Her stomach growled in response to imminent food. Bear sat at attention by her feet, alert yet relaxed, his head swiveling and tongue lolling as he surveyed the bustle of the people around them.

Cassie had missed this about Savannah—the light traffic, the chattering tourists, the birdsong. The temperature had risen since the morning. Her hat and sunglasses kept her from feeling any adverse effects from it. She didn't feel comfortable enough to close her eyes and tilt her face to the sun, but she did relish in soaking up the warmth it provided. Now that her heart was steady again, she'd take advantage of their momentary respite.

There was no telling what the next few days would bring.

Omega returned to their table in the corner of the patio, setting their purchases off to the side while he pulled the laptop closer. They both sat with their backs against the brick wall of the shop to keep watch on the street in front of them and to avoid the sun's glare against the dim computer screen. Bear sank down to his stomach, but he never relaxed enough to lay his head down on his paws.

Cassie set the jewelry box on the table and pulled open the bottom drawer, retrieving three small, black USB drives.

Omega gestured for her to pick one and insert it into the computer. "Dealer's choice."

Cassie waited for some mystical feeling to wash over her, driving her to pick one over the other. After a few seconds, nothing came. She picked up the first one she laid eyes on and handed it to Omega, watching as he plugged it into the side of the laptop. A second later, a window popped up containing several folders. Cassie leaned forward to read their titles.

"Pearl organized all the photos," she said. "Campaign photos, family photos, random."

Omega clicked on the folder titled *Random*. Inside was another folder along with several hundred photos. He clicked on the untitled folder. It prompted him to input a passcode.

"This must be the locked file," he said. "My guy will be able to get into this before long."

Ejecting the drive, Omega grabbed another and pushed it into the appropriate port. "I'm more interested in those emails. We'll go through the photos eventually, but I don't want to waste what little time we have."

Cassie looked toward the street, as though waiting for someone to walk around the corner and point a gun at her. The universe had a dark sense of humor, but it seemed that—at least for now—it was content on letting the pair of them work. Even Chris had remained absent.

Another window popped up and Omega leaned in. "Bingo."

Cassie grabbed her coffee, peeling off the lid and blowing across the hot liquid while she watched him move the computer mouse around the screen. There were more folders, all organized into different categories.

"She was a smart kid," Cassie said, sadness creeping into her chest.

“Too smart,” Omega agreed. “That’s what got her killed.”

“But was it Jack or Apex? Does he know what happened to her? Is he that much of a monster that he’d let them sweep her murder under the rug like that?”

Omega shrugged, scrolling through the dozens of folders to read their labels. “He was enough of a monster to let his firstborn kill indiscriminately for over a decade, so you tell me.”

Cassie took a sip of her coffee. Pearl had paid for Douglas’ crimes far sooner than the man himself. And poor Jett never got to know the truth before he died. Cassie hoped Pearl and Jett had already reunited somewhere on the other side of the veil.

“Here we go.” Omega clicked on a folder labeled *Douglas Hughes* and then clicked on the first file in the list. It was written in plain text, and Cassie had trouble reading the blocky lettering of the code. “These are in date order, so we’ll be able to go through a complete timeline of information shared between Jack and Alpha.”

Cassie peered around the empty patio of the café, checking for any sign of customers near them. There was none.

“How much do you think they discussed over email?” she asked. “Seems like a rookie mistake.”

“Enough that Pearl figured out what Jack was hiding. And he *was* a rookie, at least compared to Anastasia. He let his own kid take his phone in another room long enough for her to download everything she could.” He clicked his tongue. “There’s more here than I thought. We’ll need somewhere more secure to go through all of this properly.”

Omega backed out of the folder and read through some of the other files.

“Building projects,” he read aloud. “Receipts, that could be a good one.”

He clicked on it and scanned some of the files, but Cassie looked away, sipping her coffee and hoping the caffeine would replace some of the adrenaline that had been rushing through her system an hour ago. What could they do with all of this information? Would it even be enough?

And there was still that nagging notion in the back of her mind that they had no idea where Pearl was buried. She might not have any relatives left alive to place her body in the grave her parents had set aside for her, but after all Pearl had done, both while she was alive and after she was gone, Cassie felt obligated to lay her to rest. She deserved so much more than that.

Omega popped out the second USB and replaced it with the third. Cassie glanced over when the window popped up, furrowing her brows. There was only one folder in this one.

Five Winds.

The two of them shared a glance before Omega clicked on it, immediately requesting a password. He cursed under his breath.

Picking up his phone, Omega said, "I'm going to send this off to my contact." He tossed a rare smile in her direction. "We're close now, Cassie. I can feel it."

Cassie nodded, but all she felt was a sinking sensation. She trusted Omega with her life, but what happened when she was no longer useful? They were on the same side, but would he ride off into the sunset with this information and leave her waiting for the other shoe to drop? How long would that take, and would she have to stay hidden—stay *dead*—until it did?

"I'd like to send it to one of my contacts, too."

Omega stilled, the smile sliding from his face. "Why?"

"Two heads are better than one, right? This is important enough that we should be attacking it from all angles. I'd like to make sure we have all our bases covered."

"We have to make sure this doesn't fall into the wrong hands."

Cassie blew out an angry breath, and Bear looked up at her, assessing whether he needed to intervene. She placed a hand on his head and stroked his fur. "I trust my contact with my life. She's proven to be discreet and smart. Half of what we know is because of her."

"Lorraine Krasinski."

Cassie kept her expression neutral. Omega knew who she was? Should that worry her? "She's the reason we found you."

Omega sighed through his nose. "All right. I'll send it to her as well. It'll have to be anonymous. She can't know you're alive. Not yet."

Cassie had expected that, but she didn't argue. It was safer if Lorraine remained in the dark, no matter how much she was itching to console her friends.

It took him a few minutes to encrypt the email. Then he typed in Lorraine's email address, followed by a message instructing what to do once she got it.

After pressing send, Omega closed the laptop and grabbed his sandwich out of the bag. Cassie picked hers up and scarfed it down. Omega took three bites in total and was down to one left. Cassie hardly tasted hers as she swallowed, the texture like ash against her dry throat.

Omega paused, still holding onto his last bite, and scrolled through his phone. "Blackwood is holding a press conference." He looked back up at Cassie. "Apparently, he's got some news to share."

20

Blackwood slid behind the podium as Cassie and Omega tuned in to the broadcast. His wife, publicist, secretary, or any other person of support were absent from his side. A police officer stood at the edge of the screen, pushing his hands out in a gesture to get the crowd to step back.

Clutching her coffee to her chest, Cassie watched with rapt attention. From the camera angle, all she could see was the man himself set against the backdrop of City Hall. She was sure there were plenty of reporters in attendance, but whoever was working the camera had zoomed in enough that the figure in the center took up most of the screen.

Along the bottom, text read *Former Mayor Makes First Public Appearance Since Scandal.*

It'd been three months since Cassie had last laid eyes on Richard Blackwood. He was still handsome, with his strong jaw and sharp nose, but his usually tailored suit hung loose around his chest and arms. His hair was slicked back in its usual manner, but she swore his temples were grayer than she remembered.

"Thank you all for coming here today," Blackwood said into the microphone. “It means a lot to me, not just as your former mayor, but also as a citizen of the great city of Savannah.”

Cassie found herself leaning forward, coffee forgotten, as Blackwood spoke. The sounds of traffic and pedestrians faded into the background.

The cameraman panned out a little bit, showing the reporters huddled in front of him. Some held microphones aloft, while others carried heavy cameras on their shoulders. A riot of familiar blonde curls appeared in the middle of the crowd before someone blocked them.

“I want to start off by saying that it has been three long months since news broke of my affair. I want to once again relay my sincerest apology to my wife, my family, and the people of this city. I acted in a manner unbecoming of a husband and a mayor, and I feel a deep shame for what transpired.

“In the past three months, I have looked inward and wrestled with the decisions I have made over the course of my career. I am proud of many of them, as I have seen our city grow in surprising and satisfying ways. I know my legacy will forever include this scandal, but I hope that, one day, people will also be reminded of the accomplishments we attained together.”

Blackwood scanned the crowd, somehow looking more solemn than when he’d begun. If he’d meant this speech to relieve him of the burden he’d been under for the last three months, it didn’t look like he was quite accomplishing that.

“As you can see, my wife is not here with me today. My friends are also absent. Turns out, I don’t have many of those left, if I ever had them to begin with.”

Blackwood took a moment to inhale, looking down at the empty podium before him, as though the surface held the answers to his unasked questions. When he looked up again, a determined glint in his gaze had Cassie leaning forward even more. Soon, her nose would be pressed against the screen of Omega’s phone.

“Because of this, I realize I have nothing left to lose by speaking the truth. This is not meant as an excuse or to make you forget what I've done. As I said, that will forever be a part of my legacy. As much as I've taken from the people that I love, from the city that I care about so much, I hope to give something back that will make a difference on a broader scale. My aspiration is to put more good into the world than I've taken out of it."

The crowd was so silent, you could hear a pin drop.

"Soon, we will know which two candidates will be facing off during the presidential debates. It will come as no surprise, I think, that Senator Ross Hughes will be a frontrunner in that race."

Cassie sucked in a breath at the same time Omega swore under his. The crowd's murmurs were loud enough now that the microphone could pick them up. Was he about to announce his intention to run?

"In fact, by the time the debates are over, I imagine Hughes will win by a landslide. From what I can tell, as a fellow politician, he has a good head on his shoulders and very few skeletons in his closet." A wry smile transformed his face. "The same cannot be said about his father."

Blackwood's eyes glinted with something too close to mania. He ran a hand through his slicked-back hair, forcing several strands to fall out of line. But his shoulders were squared. He looked out to the crowd with a set jaw.

Cassie held her breath for what Blackwood would say next.

"Not so much time has passed that we do not all remember the tragic story of Henry Holliday, the little boy who disappeared without a trace, only to be discovered a few days later thanks to some savvy Savannahians. Joy Abbott was arrested for his murder before we came to know the true identity of the Ash Wednesday Killer. His name might be hard to dredge up now because it wasn't long after that when my story was splashed across the headlines."

Cassie held a hand to her mouth. The murmurs in the crowd had grown quieter.

"The timing of that scandal was interesting, don't you think?" Blackwood leaned forward, curling his fingers around the edge of the podium.

As Blackwood's voice grew more spiteful, it also grew louder. One of the cops looked over his shoulder at the man, his brows furrowed.

"The Ash Wednesday Killer was Douglas Hughes. If you're wondering whether there's any relation, rest assured there is." A few gasps went up from the crowd, and for the first time, Blackwood smiled. But there was nothing kind about it. "Douglas Hughes was Jack Hughes' biological son. And the senator's known about the sick bastard's proclivities for years."

"Do you have any proof?" someone shouted.

The smile faded from Blackwood's face. "Nothing tangible. I'm sure my word isn't as good around here as it used to be, but I've witnessed plenty of shadowy deals in my time as this city's mayor. One company kept coming up again and again." He leaned closer to the mic, his voice loud and clear. "Apex Publicity."

The crowd shifted, reporters exchanging glances. Some people scribbled notes or hastily typed into their phones. How many of these reporters had heard of the company before? How many had brokered their own deals with them?

"If you do your due-diligence, and I'm sure you will, you'll find that Jack Hughes employs Apex Publicity, as does his son. If you've ever felt like a politician or a celebrity has come out of the woodwork and risen to fame overnight, you can probably thank Apex. If you've ever seen that same person fade into obscurity as though they'd never existed to begin with, you can also thank Apex. They're the best at what they do."

"Are you saying that presidential candidate Ross Hughes covered up his brother's past as a serial killer?" someone else shouted.

"I don't know if Ross knew about it, but Jack Hughes sure as hell did."

"How do you know that?"

"Because Apex got *me* to where I am today. And I mean that in every sense—they are the reason I became your beloved mayor, as well as the reason I fell from your good graces. The actions were mine, both good and bad, but I never would've achieved all that I did without them. I sold my soul to the Devil, and if I had the chance to go back and do it all over again, knowing what I do now, I never would've taken that call. They're as willing to place a crown on your head as they are to stab you in the back, and it's all dependent on what *they* want."

"What *do* they want?" someone different asked.

Blackwood paused, his eyes growing distant. The camera had panned closer to him again, emotion flickering across his face.

"I don't know," he said quietly. "But whatever it is, we're not ready for it."

"Why are you coming forward now?" another reporter asked. The camera zoomed out to focus on the woman, those blonde curls front and center. There was no mistaking her.

Annette Campbell.

This time, Blackwood looked directly into the camera. "Like I said, I've got nothing left to lose."

With that, he stepped back from the podium and allowed the cops to escort him away from City Hall, despite the volley of questions being thrown his way.

Omega placed his phone down on the table, turning off the screen. "That was unexpected."

"He's either very brave," Cassie said, "or very stupid."

Omega looked her straight in the eyes when he responded. "Either way, he's a dead man."

21

Harris followed the guard down the sterile prison hallway, the fluorescent lights glaring at her from above. The woman stopped outside a heavy metal door that led to one of the private meeting rooms and then faced Harris, her expression blank. Harris offered the guard a strained smile. The woman gave her a solemn nod in return, then pulled open the door. This was another typical day for the guard.

For Harris, it was anything but.

When she'd gotten that call from Piper's lawyer, she'd almost dropped her phone, then nearly crushed it in a fit of anger. The last thing she wanted was a face-to-face with Piper. But the woman had provided them with information in the past. Harris would be stupid to pass up the opportunity to get more from her now.

Piper had been uncooperative throughout her sentencing, but the prosecutors had built a solid case. The death of Cassie and Chris had complicated the trial since they weren't around to testify, but the sentencing was quick. Piper had been transferred to the Federal Correctional Institution in Tallahassee. Out of everything, being sent away to *Florida* had offended Piper the most.

Harris stepped into the sparse room, furnished only with a table and a pair of chairs on opposite sides. Piper stared up at her with a wry smile, her skin pale and washed out against her drab gray uniform. Harris waited until the officer closed the door behind her before she spoke.

"Where's your lawyer?"

Piper shrugged. "Told him I wanted to speak with you alone. He doesn't really care what I do, as long as I pay him." She paused, the smile turning contemplative. "You look good, Adelaide. Healthy."

Harris remained standing and silent.

"I was sorry to hear about Cassie."

"You don't get to talk about Cassie."

The smile fell from Piper's face. "Why not?"

Harris scoffed. "You know why."

"I don't, actually. Care to enlighten me?"

It was on the tip of Harris' tongue to say no, but she'd driven four hours for this. There was no point in wasting more time. "You sent that woman after her in Nashville."

Cassie's death at the hands of a federal agent, and Chris Viotto's subsequent murder, had stolen headlines, but there had been a third body in the parking garage that day. Security footage showed a woman leading Cassie deeper into the building. Chris had emerged from the shadows and killed her in Cassie's defense. Then he'd turned his gun on her, too.

"Emma?" One of Piper's eyebrows quirked up, almost to her hairline. "She had specific instructions not to hurt Cassie. And she didn't. Chris Viotto did. He's the one who shot her."

"And yet, I don't think even Chris would have shot her without your meddling."

It was Piper's turn to scoff. "Please. Apex has wanted Cassie for years. I might've been the catalyst, but I was hardly the one who pulled the trigger." Piper's shoulders sagged, and she looked away. "I was just as much of a pawn as she was."

Harris eyed Piper, noting the way the other woman jiggled her leg and tapped her fingers against the table. "Again, somehow I doubt that."

Piper shrugged. "Believe what you want. I sent Emma after Cassie to warn her about Chris. It's not my fault she didn't listen."

The question came out of Harris' mouth before she could think twice about the ramifications of asking it. "Why *did* you warn her?"

"Sit down, Adelaide. My neck is starting to hurt."

"And if I refuse?"

Piper rolled her eyes. "That's your choice, but we'll both be more comfortable if you do. I'll tell you whatever you want to know if you just sit down and treat me with a shred of human decency."

It was more than Piper deserved, but Harris had already made her choice when she hopped in her car with the intention of speaking to the woman. With a huff, Harris pulled out the metal chair in front of her and sat down, leaving plenty of space between her and the table.

"Thank you," Piper said, and to Harris' surprise, she looked more relieved than smug.

Harris folded her arms against her chest. "Why did you warn Cassie about Chris?"

"I found out about Apex holding Chris' family captive. I knew enough about him to figure that he'd do whatever it took to save them, even if it meant hurting Cassie. Of course, I didn't think he'd kill her, but I guess I'm not that surprised."

Harris had been, but she kept those thoughts to herself. "How did you find out about it? They still letting you do your little podcast from jail?"

"Unfortunately, no. But I still have contacts. I've been a good girl these last few months, so the guards don't bother me much."

Harris was curious about how some of the guards might be bothering Piper, but she didn't care enough to ask. "Maybe they should be keeping a better eye on you."

"Probably, but I'm far from their biggest problem in this place. What shocks me more is that Apex hasn't stepped in and made my life a living hell. All things considered, I guess I'm not their biggest problem. No one would believe me if I told them what I know." Piper locked eyes with Harris. "No one except maybe you."

Harris didn't back down from the challenge in Piper's eyes. "Is that why you asked me here? To divulge your secrets?"

"More or less."

Harris' muscles tightened, her arms clenching against her torso. "Let's hear it then."

"For free? I'm not that stupid, Adelaide."

"You're not in a position to negotiate."

"Are you sure about that? You drove all this way just to visit little old me. My lawyer said you didn't even hesitate to come. That means you're interested in what I have to say, that it has some inherent value. At most, I'm spending years behind these walls, and at minimum, Apex will find a way to take me out of the game without raising suspicions. Can you blame me for wanting to enjoy life's little pleasures while I can?"

Harris thought that through. Apex certainly had bigger fish to fry, but they'd dropped Piper like a bag of rocks once she became less than useful to them. If they found out Piper knew something valuable, they probably would make her disappear.

Harris adjusted herself in her chair, forcing her arms back down to her sides. "I'll listen to what you have to say, and if I feel like it's worth my time, I'll agree to hear out your request."

Piper snorted. "That requires me to put a lot of faith in you holding up your end of the bargain."

Harris leaned forward, her gaze hard on the other woman. "Only one of us is doing serious time in a federal prison. If your request is reasonable, I'll do what I can to fulfill it."

Piper scrutinized Harris, perhaps looking to see if she was bluffing.

"Deal."

"All right." Harris leaned back and crossed her right leg over her left. "Spill."

Piper sat back in her chair, silent, assessing. She finally spoke, her voice serious and measured. "Apex is more of a threat to this country than anyone realizes."

"You mean Ross Hughes and the presidency."

Piper nodded, her eyes wide. "The ramifications of their actions will be felt for years to come. You can't stop them all, so you have to pick and choose the right ones."

"Okay, I'll bite." Harris tried to match the evenness of Piper's tone. "Which are the right ones?"

A laugh burst from Piper's mouth. "I have no idea. If I did, I wouldn't be here right now, would I?"

Harris narrowed her eyes and clenched her teeth. "Then why am *I* here, Piper? This song-and-dance routine is getting old."

Piper's expression turned solemn once again. "What if Ross Hughes sitting in the Oval Office isn't the checkmate you think it is? What if the real headline wasn't the skeletons in Jack Hughes' closet?"

"His son murdered dozens of children—"

"And it's a tragedy," Piper said, leaning forward, her eyes imploring. "But what if that's just the distraction? Your time as a detective wasn't that long ago, Adelaide. What's one of the first rules they tell you when chasing leads?"

"Follow the money."

"Bingo." Piper's eyes sparkled like she was staring at a pile of presents on Christmas morning. "Have you ever wondered why Apex stuck with Jack Hughes after all these years, considering what he's hiding? They took a huge risk in keeping him as a client, but he's got connections and wealth. That's what the people behind Apex are most interested in. They need those two things for a reason." She raised her hands, palms face up. "What are they doing with all of it?"

"You sound like you don't know."

"I don't." Piper shrugged, like she didn't just hit Harris upside the head with a sack full of disappointment. "Apex has been making moves for a long time, and it's only now that they're starting to show their hand. That means they're closing in on the endgame. Ross Hughes will be a nice little pawn to do their bidding, but that might not be why they chose him. Perhaps it's not because he doesn't have skeletons in his closet, but *despite* his father having secrets that need to stay buried."

"Makes sense," Harris said, "but that still doesn't tell me anything concrete."

"Like I said, if I had anything concrete, I wouldn't be here right now. But I often find what's missing to be more interesting than what's right in front of my nose. Apex once wanted Senator Lawrence Gray as their little pawn, and that fell through. The presidential election is fast approaching, but that's just a single notch in Apex's belt. There must be more that Jack Hughes can offer them."

Harris searched Piper's face, but she didn't find the answers she was looking for. "Why are you helping us? You used to work for Apex."

"So did Cassie."

Harris' shoulders stiffened, and she stared the other woman down. Piper didn't relent under the steely gaze. Her hands remained still. Her legs had stopped jiggling. All she did was peer back at Harris, her expression open.

Finally, Piper shook her head and looked away. "It was a means to an end for me. They screwed me over. Now it's time for me to repay the favor."

Harris tilted her head to the side. "And what do you want in return?"

Piper leaned forward, a shark-like smile spreading over her face. "Credit."

Harris blinked, switching her legs to cross the left over the right. "You want credit?"

"Yes," Piper said, as if that explained everything. "I want everyone to know that I helped take down the big bad Apex."

As simple as that sounded, this sort of credibility could go a long way in painting Piper in a better light. She would be a hero to her fans. She'd also garner plenty of attention for her podcast and whatever ventures she decided to invest in along the way.

And all of that would take almost no effort on Harris' part.

The ramifications would be minimal. Detectives worked with criminals all the time to take down bigger fish. None of this was illegal.

"I'll see what I can do."

The smile still on her face, Piper leaned back and said, "That's all I ask."

Harris stood and left the room without another word. She followed an officer to the exit. Piper had told her next to nothing, yet there was a truth to her words. Helping Ross Hughes win the presidential election was Apex's top priority, but they were too smart to put all their eggs in one basket. There was something else brewing. Piper was right about one thing—following the money was always the first step.

Harris made her way to her car in a daze, not noticing the slender woman behind her until she felt a pinch in the side of her neck. She spun around and swung out at the person, hitting air. The tingling in her hands started almost immediately, and she dropped her keys to the ground.

As Harris stumbled, the stranger stepped forward as though to hug her, and any attempt to push the other woman away failed.

As her vision faded, the woman dragged Harris across the ground and placed her in the back seat of her own vehicle. The door slammed shut, the sound muffled as she slipped into unconsciousness.

22

Cassie didn't argue with Omega when he found another car to hotwire and followed Richard Blackwood's vehicle downtown, leaving a few cars between them to avoid detection. There was no part of her that liked the former mayor, especially after everything he put Lorraine through a few months ago, but she was willing to talk to him in order to find out what he knew.

At one point, Blackwood had been one of Apex's darlings. Now, he was in the dog house. It must've been worse than Cassie thought if he was willing to speak out about them to the press. Cassie had no idea what he'd done to get on Apex's bad side, but he'd been left alive, which was a kinder punishment than a lot of other people endured after crossing Apex.

Either Blackwood was a genius for putting everything out in the open, believing that'd be enough to deter Apex from doing anything directly, or he was stupid enough to think they couldn't find a clever way to get rid of him without drawing more suspicion.

When Blackwood pulled into a crappy motel parking lot on the outskirts of Savannah, Cassie wondered if it was because no one would think to look for him there or if he'd truly lost so much that he couldn't afford a better place to stay for the night.

Omega and Cassie waited for him to step out of his vehicle before they did the same. Bear jumped out of the back when she opened the door for him. Together, they crossed the parking lot and surrounded Blackwood as soon as he fit the key into the lock on his room. He stiffened as their shadows encroached on the wall in front of him. He turned to face them, his eyes wild, holding up both fists as though to defend himself.

Omega put up his hands. "We just want to talk."

Blackwood studied him, as though trying to discern if he had ever met the man before. Then his gaze flickered to Cassie. His eyes widened.

"You're supposed to be dead," he said

"It's a long story," she answered, keeping her voice neutral despite the way her stomach churned. "I'll tell you all about it if you let us come in."

"Why the hell would I do that?"

"Because we want the same thing you do." Omega stared right back at Blackwood. "We want to take down Apex as badly as you do."

"I doubt that."

"You'd be surprised."

Looking at Cassie again, Blackwood turned to face the door and twisted the key in the lock. He pressed the door open and stomped through. "The motel doesn't allow dogs."

"We won't tell if you don't," Cassie said, following Omega inside and letting the door shut behind her.

The motel room smelled like stale cigarettes and cleaning supplies. It was at least twenty years out of date, with peeling wallpaper and a stained carpet, but the bed was made and there was a flat screen TV sitting on a small desk.

Blackwood sat down on the edge of the bed and kicked off his shoes. "Welcome to the deluxe king suite. You're standing in the lap of luxury, can't you tell?"

Neither Omega nor Cassie said a word.

Blackwood sighed. "No senses of humor, got it."

"Surprised you're laughing about it." Omega walked over to the bathroom and peeked his head inside. Bear tracked his movements but didn't leave Cassie's side. "You don't strike me as the self-deprecating type."

"A lot has changed in the last few months." Blackwood slid his gaze over to Cassie. "I can thank you for that, actually."

Cassie's brows knit together. "What did I do?"

"You died." Blackwood shrugged. "You were kind of pivotal to my plan."

Cassie crossed her arms and leaned back against the door. She cocked her head to the side. "What plan?"

"Guess there's no harm in telling you now." The man stood and walked over to the desk against the wall. He grabbed the crumpled paper bag next to the coffee maker and pulled out a bottle of whiskey, then held it up. "Anyone want a drink?"

"I'm good," Omega said.

Cassie shook her head.

"More for me then." Blackwood grabbed a disposable cup next to the coffee maker and poured himself a healthy portion. He took a large gulp and closed his eyes in satisfaction, then took another, smaller sip before returning to the side of his bed, placing the bottle on the nightstand next to him. "What were we talking about?"

"You had a plan," Omega said, his tone dry. He now leaned against the wall on the opposite side of the room. "It involved Cassie."

Blackwood snapped his fingers and pointed at her. "Right, that."

Cassie glanced over at Omega, startled to see Chris materialize by his side. His mouth moved as though he were trying to tell her something. Cassie straightened, letting her arms hang loose at her side. Chris had tried speaking to her right before Anatasia's men shot Jett.

She braced for a knock on the door behind her. Omega noticed her movements and furrowed his brows in her direction. Blackwood didn't notice anything other than the drink in his hand.

She'd never seen the former mayor like this. He'd been unhinged during the press conference, but this was something else.

"You're aware that I was working with your little friend, right?" Blackwood asked.

Cassie jumped at the sound of his voice. When still no knock came, she tore her gaze from Chris and focused on Blackwood. "You mean Lorraine?"

"That's the one."

"Lorraine would never work with you."

"That's where you'd be wrong." He took another sip. "We made a deal. A pretty good one, I might add. She'd ruin your boyfriend's reputation, admit those photos of me were altered, and have you put in a good word for me with Apex. In exchange, I'd break off my ties with Warden Wickham, leave her mother alone, and tell her everything I knew about Apex."

Cassie's mind spun. This could've been Harris and Lorraine's plan —pretend to join Blackwood and gather dirt at the same time. It would be dangerous for Lorraine, who'd be walking into the lion's den every day, but she'd do anything to protect her mother. Perhaps even make Blackwood think she would betray Cassie and Jason.

"But then I died," Cassie said after a moment. Bear remained stoic as he pressed against the side of her leg, but he kept a watchful eye on the former mayor, who took several more sips of whiskey. "You knew you'd never get back in bed with Apex without me vouching for you."

"And that was kind of the crux of my whole plan. Ruining Broussard's reputation would've been the cherry on top, but I could've done that with or without Lorraine, especially once I got back on Apex's good side."

"What made them drop you to begin with?" Omega asked.

Blackwood swirled his whiskey around his glass like it was a crystal tumbler. His face turned sour. "I got a little too cocky. Something felt off with the whole Hughes family, so I did some digging. Found out about Jack's firstborn." He looked up then, a smile playing around his mouth. "If you're here, I'm guessing you saw my press conference?"

"We did," Cassie replied.

"Thought I was bringing Apex something they didn't already know. Turns out, they were behind the coverup all along." His smile faded. "I should've known."

"Yes, you should've," Omega said, sounding like a father chastising his son.

Blackwood glared at the man. "I wanted to prove to them Ross wasn't the choirboy they made him out to be. Then his father turned out to be the biggest sinner of all. Well, after Apex, of course."

"So, they dropped you, just like that?" Cassie asked.

"Just like that." He stared down into his cup, as though the answer to all his problems was at the bottom. "They don't take kindly to being threatened."

"Feels like there's more to the story," Omega said, pushing off the wall and moving over to stand by Cassie. At least now it would be easier to ignore Chris' spirit, but even out of the corner of her eye she could tell he was still trying to speak with her. "Either this wasn't your first time threatening them, or you're leaving out a crucial detail."

Blackwood looked up and raised an eyebrow. "Sounds like you know as much about them as I do. Former client or employee?"

"I was just a driver," Omega said. "But I heard enough over the years. Answer the question."

"I had a friend in the NSA. Dalton. Good guy, family man. He gave me intel he shouldn't have. Did me a favor. And he paid the price."

"What kind of intel?"

Blackwood drained his cup, then plucked the bottle of whiskey off the nightstand and poured himself some more. "Putting Hughes in the Oval office will damage this country for decades to come if he's willing to be their puppet. But you have to wonder who helped pave the way, and who might profit from seeing the United States crumble."

"Several options come to mind," Cassie said.

The conversation outside the Pantheon in Nashville sprang to mind. She and Jason had tracked down who'd they thought had been Omega. That discussion had been enlightening. It was the first time Cassie had realized the scope of Apex's plans. This wasn't about one politician or one election. What they had in mind would affect the entire country. Maybe the entire world.

Omega gave Cassie an expectant look. She cleared her throat before she spoke. "China seems to be the frontrunner."

"Bingo." He winked at her. "A man named Zhang Wei is a billionaire over in China. Made his money in tech. He's got his hands in a lot of industries over here."

"Does he own Five Winds?" Cassie asked.

Blackwood's head snapped up, sobering in a matter of seconds. Bear shifted on his haunches. "How did you know that?"

"Apex encouraged Ross to invest in them. Seemed like something worth looking into. Didn't get a chance because—"

"You died," Omega finished, impatient. He looked down at Blackwood. "You got proof of this?"

"Dalton hid it somewhere before he died. I didn't want Apex to realize he'd talked to me about it. It's the only reason I'm still alive."

"How did he die?" Cassie asked, her voice soft.

She might not have liked Blackwood, but she still felt sorry he'd lost his friend. Especially if that friend was just trying to do what was right. Out of instinct, she glanced to the opposite side of the room at Chris, whose mouth was still moving. Then she tore her gaze away from him.

"He killed himself." Blackwood met her eyes with a hard, angry stare. "Or so the police report says."

"What did Dalton tell you about Five Winds?" she asked. "Or Zhang Wei?"

Blackwood took a gulp of his whiskey and stood. "I think I've been forthcoming thus far. I want to know what I'm getting out of this."

"Protection," Omega said. "You just threw down the gauntlet, and Apex will respond, one way or another. If you're lucky, they'll downplay the story with some fabrications and paint you as a disgruntled former client. Make you out to be crazy. Won't be hard after that speech you gave."

Blackwood snorted but said nothing.

"You get us proof of what your friend uncovered about Apex

working with China to destabilize the United States, and I'll keep you off Apex's radar."

"Nobody can stay off Apex's radar for long," Blackwood said.

"I can." Omega leveled the man with a glare. "I've done it for years. Even when I was right under their noses."

Blackwood looked at Cassie. "It's true," she said. "He kept me safe for three months. Convinced anyone who cared that I was dead."

"Even your boyfriend?" Blackwood asked, his eyes glinting.

"Even him." Cassie folded her arms, as though that could protect her from the guilt clawing its way up her body. "But you don't just want protection, do you? You feel like you've got nothing left to lose, even your life."

Blackwood held his arms out to the side, the whiskey splashing over the side of his cup and dripping down his hand. "This is no life."

Bear stuck his nose in the air and sniffed, but didn't move from his spot at Cassie's side.

"I used to have high aspirations. I wanted to become president someday. Maybe if this all works out, I still can." Blackwood glared when Omega scoffed. "But I'll settle for my old life back. I want my money, my reputation, and my office."

"What about your family?" Cassie asked.

"My wife is gone. I'm sure Apex helped with that, too. I have nothing to my name except for the meager funds I had in an account no one knew about. But that's almost gone, too. I don't have much time left."

Cassie resisted rolling her eyes. He talked like he had a terminal illness. "How do we know we can trust you not to go crawling back to Apex? You've tried to use me before. And you threatened my friends."

Blackwood grinned, a politician's million-watt smile. "They were a means to an end. I've got a bigger fish to fry, and a larger worm to put on my hook now."

"Comparing me to bait isn't helping your case."

"Look," Blackwood said, "I'm still pissed at your boyfriend for taking those pictures, but he was just doing his job. It's been Apex digging my grave all along, and I'll be damned if I don't go down swinging. They'll never let me back in the door, and I'll never be able to trust someone won't stab me in the back. Might as well help you clear them from the board and pave my own way to the White House."

Cassie looked to Omega. "Seems like he's self-serving enough to help us."

"I'm standing right here," Blackwood protested. "Besides, this is a two-way street. How do I know you can deliver on what I want?"

"I have connections," Omega said.

"Oh, connections? Well, why didn't you say so? I'm sold!" Blackwood scowled. "This isn't the time for cloak and dagger shit. We both need to reveal our hand."

"I'm not about to do that when we don't even know if you're spouting bullshit or not. You bring us what proof you can get your hands on, and I'll bring proof that I can ensure you get your old life back."

Blackwood studied Omega for a moment before turning to Cassie. "I don't know him from Adam, but I do know you, Miss Quinn. You're a good person. Always trying to do the right thing."

"It doesn't sound like a compliment when you say it."

"It's not. But it does make you a trustworthy person. Is this guy blowing smoke up my ass, or can I trust that he'll deliver his end of the bargain?"

Cassie didn't know much about Omega either. She had no idea where his myriad of connections came from or what promises he'd been making to them in return. She had no idea who Omega really was or what he was capable of, but she'd seen enough to know that if he promised Blackwood something, he'd do his best to deliver.

"He gave you his word," Cassie said. "And he'll keep it."

Blackwood threw back the rest of his whiskey and slammed the paper cup down on the table. Then he crossed the room and held out his hand, ignoring the low growl emanating from Bear's chest.

"Then you've got yourself a deal."

23

Cassie and Omega backed out of Blackwood's room after they shook on their deal and exchanged numbers, more than a little happy to leave their tentative new ally behind to work on his end of the deal. She trusted the former mayor to hold a grudge. Instinct told her he was done playing by Apex's rules, which could either work in her favor or get the man killed. Cassie's stomach twisted at the thought of Apex burying another skeleton where no one could find it. She didn't want to be part of the reason he got killed.

Bear stayed at her side, but Chris remained behind in Blackwood's room as they filed out the door. At some point, he'd fade and reappear somewhere else. Maybe in the backseat of the next car they stole or the hotel room where they'd spend the night. She was grateful his presence hadn't been a prelude to someone else getting shot, but what was he trying to tell her?

Omega was silent as they walked past the motel, abandoning their second stolen car in the parking lot. As fate would have it, there was a place to rent a vehicle next door, and that's where they headed next.

After paying with a fake ID and credit card, the guy behind the desk brought their vehicle around to the front and handed off the keys. It was a beat-up Kia Forte that had seen better days.

As Omega pulled out of the parking lot, Cassie breathed a sigh of relief at finally being in a car they hadn't stolen.

Omega broke the silence first. "We need to go to Nashville."

Cassie looked over at him and the way he held his mouth in a grim line of determination. She'd seen that look on his face many times and knew there'd be no arguing with him. Not that she had much reason to. She'd been thinking along the same lines.

"You have a plan?" she asked.

"We need to talk to Ross."

"Not Jack?"

Omega shot her a look. "You think he'll be *more* forthcoming?"

"No." Cassie chewed on the inside of her cheek, casting a glance over her shoulder. Bear took up the entire back seat. "But what can Ross do about any of this?"

"I want to talk to him and find out." Omega drummed his fingers on the steering wheel. After merging onto the highway, heading toward Tennessee, he spoke again. "We need to know how much he's aware of. If he's in on it, we can't trust him. But if he's been in the dark, he might be willing to give us the last few pieces of the puzzle."

"He might just be a good actor," Cassie replied, "but I got the impression he didn't know about Apex covering up everything Douglas did to those kids. If that's the case, how much do you think he'll be able to tell us?"

"A lot more than he thinks, I'd reckon. He might not know specifics, but maybe he'd tell us more about what Apex has been working on and how his father's involved." He glanced over at her, his face grave. "I think it's worth a face-to-face."

"I agree," Cassie said, "but he's a presidential nominee. Getting a face-to-face with him won't be easy."

"I know." Omega drummed his fingers on the steering wheel again. "I'll work on a few ideas. Get some rest while you can. We'll stop in a couple hours for dinner."

At the mention of a nap, fatigue gripped her body, down to her bones. The dying sun warmed her through the car window as trees whizzed by.

"What about you?" she asked. He had to be even more exhausted, considering how much he'd driven over the last few days.

"I'll be fine for a bit longer. If I need to stop, we can grab a hotel for a couple hours."

Cassie nodded and leaned her seat back. Bear licked her cheek in what she was sure he thought was a reassuring gesture. The lights along the highway passed in a blur, and the darkening sky gave her little to look at as she peered out the window. She was sad to leave Savannah behind and shuddered at the thought of returning to Tennessee. With any luck, they wouldn't have to stay for long.

"Do you think Blackwood will be able to get that evidence on Zhang Wei and Apex?"

"No idea," Omega said. "But he'll try, I'm sure of it."

"Wonder how he'll manage it," she murmured, a yawn overtaking the last of her sentence.

"That's his problem. Not ours." Omega's voice was gruff but not unkind. "Now get some sleep."

Cassie wanted to argue, but she closed her eyes instead. Her body sank into the worn seat, even as her mind still spun. Her life looked like something out of a movie. How had she ended up in this mess? The web they were trying to unweave was too big and too far-reaching for her to figure out alone. They had no choice but to rely on people like Richard Blackwood and Ross Hughes.

They needed a big break. And soon.

Somewhere in the middle of her search for answers, she fell into a restless sleep. It felt like minutes had passed instead of hours when Omega stopped for food halfway through their trip. Eating gave her a modicum of energy, and she stayed awake to see the exit for Nashville.

They pulled into a parking spot at a gas station just outside the city, the sun hovering on the horizon and casting its amber glow over everything. She dug out a wet wipe from the bottom of their dinner bag and ran it over her face. It was cool against her skin as it removed the fine layer of dirt that had accumulated over the last twenty-four hours.

Cassie tossed the used wet wipe back into the bag. One last hash-brown remained at the bottom, cool after sitting for a few hours. She tossed it to a waiting Bear, who snapped it up in a single bite and swallowed it whole. His tail thumped against the seat as though to thank her in Morse code.

She smiled and then dug her fingers into her injured shoulder in an attempt to loosen the tight muscle. Omega looked over at her as she stretched out her arms but said nothing. Her whole body felt tense, but there was nothing she could do about it now. At least they were both in one piece, and Omega had a plan. Albeit, a simple one.

"You want me to just call up Ross and ask him to meet in private?" Cassie asked.

"He thinks you're dead," Omega replied, keeping his eyes peeled to any movement around them. Despite the early hour, quite a few people came and went from the station. "If you call Ross and tell him Apex tried to kill you, he'll want to know why. The man invited you to dinner at his house with his wife and kids. He trusts you, and we can use that to our advantage."

Cassie moved her hand to the nape of her neck and began massaging the muscles there, too. "You want me to manipulate him."

"I want him on our side. If we have to manipulate him, then yes." At the glare Cassie gave him, he continued, placing his palms out in front of him. "I don't think that'll be necessary. If you tell him the truth, he's going to start questioning Apex's endgame."

"How do we even get his phone number?" she asked, rolling out her neck and relishing in her improved range of motion.

"I've already got it." Omega reached into his pocket and held his burner phone out for her. "You just need to dial."

Cassie took the device and glanced at the screen. It didn't escape her notice that he hadn't answered her question.

"What should I say?" she asked.

"Whatever you need to. Put it on speaker."

Cassie took a deep breath and sighed, then tapped the number and hit the button so Omega could be privy to the entire conversation. She would've felt less pressure if she could do this on her own, but that wasn't an option.

After three rings, Ross picked up. "This is Hughes."

Cassie sucked in a breath, but when she tried to speak, nothing came out.

"Hello?"

Omega's piercing glare was enough to spark her into action. "Ross? Hi."

"Hello." Ross paused. "I'm sorry, who is this?"

"It's, um, Cassie. Cassie Quinn."

The pause on the other end of the line felt like it lasted eons. When he spoke, it was nothing more than a quiet breath. "That's not possible."

"It is, actually. Surprise, I'm not dead!" She winced. "Sorry, I know that's not very funny."

He paused yet again. Blood roared through her ears in tandem with her pounding heart. Finally, Ross said, "Prove it."

"I'm sorry?"

There was rustling in the background, and the click of a door shutting.

"Prove it," he repeated. "How do I know it's really you?"

Cassie thought back to their last conversation, which felt like it had happened in another lifetime.

"I came over to your house for dinner. I met your wife and children. You were surprised Patrick was well-behaved at dinner. Then we went into your study and talked about your father. You hadn't confronted him about Douglas or Apex's involvement after the murders. You said Douglas was sick, but that you still had sympathy for him. That maybe if he'd gotten the help he'd needed, he might not have hurt all those kids."

More silence permeated the line. Omega's gaze burned through her as though trying to will the other man to speak. Cassie looked away from the older man and checked to make sure Ross was still on the line.

"How?" Ross finally croaked. "What happened?"

"It's a long story. I'd really like to tell you, but it needs to be in person."

"Why?"

"We have some new information about your father. It's sensitive, and I'd rather tell it to you face-to-face."

His breathing was heavy on the other end of the line. "Okay. Do you want to come by the house?"

Cassie looked up at Omega, who shook his head. "The fewer people who know I'm alive, the better. Is there somewhere more private we can meet? Somewhere no one will see me."

"My bodyguards won't like that much. Especially on short notice."

"I know, and I'm sorry about that. But I'm bringing someone with me, someone I trust. It's only fair you bring someone with you too. Preferably someone who can keep a secret."

Omega's scowl deepened, etching stark lines into his forehead, but he said nothing. They both knew Ross wouldn't come if he thought there was anything suspicious about this meeting.

"All right," he said. "I'll bring my head of security. He's been with me a long time. I'll send you the address once I find something that works for both of us."

Cassie nodded even though he couldn't see her. "Thank you, Ross. I mean it. I wouldn't be asking you to do this if it wasn't important."

"Not sure I'm looking forward to hearing this new info about my father."

"I get that. But I think you'd rather know the truth than turn a blind eye to it."

"You're right," he said. "I'll see you soon."

As the line went dead, Cassie waited for the relief to hit her, but it never came.

This was only a small step, and the finish line was still out of sight.

24

JASON TAPPED HIS HANDS AGAINST THE STEERING WHEEL IN RHYTHM with the furious beating of his heart. Lorraine glanced at him from the passenger seat but said nothing. They were on their way to Warden Wickham's house. His recent retirement hadn't come as a surprise, no matter how sudden it had been.

Jason had wanted to go alone, but Lorraine knew Wickham better than most. He'd asked her along, and she'd been all too happy to agree. Wickham and Blackwood had tried to blackmail her, after all. She'd been working with Harris on a plan to turn the tables on each of the men, but Jason didn't know the details. He'd been too lost in his grief and anger to care.

At one point, he and Lorraine had become friends, rather than just employer and employee. In the last few months, however, she'd been hovering. The constant concern in her eyes made him feel guilty for the way he'd been acting. And that only made him angrier.

That's all he was these days—a concentrated ball of anger that burned in his gut with such ferocity that he was sure it would consume him from the inside out.

After meeting with Annette Campbell yesterday, he should've felt some modicum of relief. But after Blackwood's speech, the pent-up fury surged like he'd plugged it into a new power source.

It took all his mental strength to find the silver lining. At the very least, Blackwood's public announcement only backed up the evidence Jason had brought to Annette. But she'd still have to go through all the documentation he'd provided. All Jason could do was sit around and wait.

But that had never been his style.

He needed to speak with Blackwood directly to find out what he knew and what he was willing to share, but neither he nor Annette knew where the former mayor was staying these days. The logical next step was to reach out to one of the man's closest contacts.

"There's something I want to tell you," Lorraine said, breaking the silence. The only other sound was the rumbling of tires on asphalt. "But I don't want you to get mad."

By the tone of her voice, Jason could tell she'd been gearing herself up for this.

"You can tell me anything. I'm sorry if that hasn't felt true in the last few months." He glanced over at her before returning his gaze to the road. Lorraine was one of the few people he had left. She needed to hear this as much as he needed to say it. "I haven't been dealing with any of this very well."

"None of us have," Lorraine said, twisting a piece of her hair around her finger and tugging on it. "Cassie held all of us together and with her gone..."

"What did you want to tell me?"

"Right." Lorraine blew out a steady breath as though she needed to steady herself enough to speak. "Last night, I received an email."

When she didn't continue, he prompted, "An email?"

She nodded. "I tried calling Adelaide about it, but she didn't answer her phone."

It bothered Jason that she'd waited until this morning to talk to him about it, but he pushed his annoyance to the side. The email must've been important if she was this worried, and he wanted to know why.

"What was the email about?"

"It was a compressed file full of information." Lorraine took a deep breath, her words coming out in a rush. "As far as I can tell, it's a collection of documents about Jack Hughes. Photos. Emails. Banking information. There's a lot to go through, and some of the folders are encrypted. I haven't been able to get into those yet, but I should be able to crack them soon. I spent half the night going through the most accessible files, but there's still loads left."

Every muscle in Jason's body screamed at him to pull the car over so he could give her his full attention. He ignored the thought and kept the vehicle steady, resigning himself to choking the life from the steering wheel until his knuckles paled.

Through clenched teeth, he asked, "Who sent the email?"

"I have no idea. I didn't recognize the sender and I couldn't trace the IP address back to anything credible. The photos seem to be copies of the originals, and the emails were all from Jack Hughes to dozens of people. They must've come from his phone or computer."

"Something tells me Jack didn't offer up this information on his own."

Lorraine remained sober. The wheels continued to churn beneath them in a steady rhythm. The sun poured through the windshield, adding to the heat coursing through Jason's body.

"I think it might've been Omega," she said.

"Omega's dead."

"I can't think of anyone else who would send this to me. The only message in the email was how to open up the main file. There were no other directions, no demands, nothing."

"It could've been Cassie," he said, before he could stop himself. "How she got her hands on that sort of information, I have no idea."

"Jason—"

"You think Omega is still alive despite the fact that I saw his *dead body* sprawled out on his hotel bed, but it's too much to think that Cassie isn't dead even though we don't have her body?" Jason followed his GPS, whipping the car into a hard right turn onto Wickham's driveway.

He threw the car into park, slamming the gearshift forward. "Make it make sense, Lorraine."

"Maybe the dead body you saw wasn't the real Omega," she suggested, her voice soft but her eyes hard. "Maybe the email came from one of his contacts."

Jason turned to face the house in front of him. A cherry-red Camaro gleamed in the sunlight, so pristine that it looked like it had never left the driveway. Wickham was doing retirement in style, it seemed.

Lorraine followed his gaze. "He must be home."

"Let's get this over with."

When they were done here, he'd look through the new evidence and come to his own conclusion. Then he'd pass it on to Annette to add to her collection.

Stepping out of the car, they walked across the gravel drive to the stone path in front of the stately brick house. It was large, but not opulent, and the flowers out front were blooming in a riot of colors.

Jason worked to keep his tone neutral as he asked, "Have you ever been here before?"

"A couple times for staff functions. He liked to host parties." She rolled her eyes. "Show off his house."

"Sounds about right."

Jason was just about to make a smartass comment when a prickle of awareness crawled up the back of his skull.

The front door was open.

Jason held out his arm to stop Lorraine from walking any closer. She inhaled sharply. Jason peered around to ensure they were alone. He strained to discern any noises from inside.

"I'm getting my gun." Jason backtracked to the car in long strides, Lorraine on his heels.

He pulled the weapon from his glove compartment, double-checked it was loaded, then switched the safety off. He met Lorraine's eyes across the hood of his vehicle. "You should stay here."

"Not a chance."

Jason gritted his teeth, releasing a breath through flared nostrils.

"Stay behind me. Anyone attacks us, you run back to the car and get the hell out of here."

"Let's go."

The tension didn't leave his shoulders at her answer.

Jason reapproached the house and used the toe of his boot to swing the door open, keeping his gun at the ready but pointed at the ground.

It was quiet, like no one was home. He stepped inside the foyer, alert to even the tiniest of noises or movements. Lorraine was all but silent behind him.

The entrance was clean and absent of any odors like blood or bleach. The morning sunlight streaming through the front door glanced off the black-and-white checkered floor. A riot of shapes and colors were splattered across the wall, a reflection of the chandelier above.

Jason kept to the wall as he looked into the first room to the right. The sitting room contained substantial, ornate furniture, meant to impress more than to comfort. Swinging his head to the left, he peered across the entrance at the dining room, the edge of a table barely visible in the darkness created by the drawn curtains.

"Do you hear that?" Lorraine whispered.

Jason's muscles tensed at the sound of her voice in the quiet. She had moved past him, closer to the back of the house, despite his warnings to stay behind him.

He slid past her and stopped when he heard it, too. It was a lilting sound, almost like—

"Music," Lorraine said, locking eyes with him.

He nodded in the direction of the noise. "You know what's back there?"

"His office."

A new scent caught his attention. Still no blood or bleach. "Smell that?"

She sniffed the air. "A cigar?"

He nodded and relaxed a fraction. Maybe Wickham was in his office, enjoying his retirement like all was right in the world.

Jason pressed a finger to his lips then returned it to his gun as he stepped forward, creeping closer to the man's office. This door was also slightly ajar, revealing a sliver of the darkened room.

Pausing just outside, Jason listened. The music was low, but clear, and the cigar smoke was stronger. Jason placed one hand on the door and gave it a gentle shove. It swung open on silent hinges.

The blinds were drawn. A single bookcase held more awards and trinkets than tomes, and a couch and pair of chairs sat to one side. Next to them sat a small, round table and a dry bar. The single lamp on Wickham's desk illuminated the figure in the chair.

Warden Wickham slumped over the surface. Red pooled beneath him, glinting in the lamp light.

Lorraine's gasp came a second later.

"Shit," he said, crossing the room.

"What are you doing?"

"Making sure he's really dead." Jason put a finger to his neck. He was still warm but had no pulse. "Shit."

Lorraine remained outside the door. "What happened to him?"

Jason looked at where the blood fell from the man's head. "Bullet to the brain." He looked over at the still-smoking cigar in the ashtray. "Must've just happened."

Lorraine kept her eyes on the dead man's body. "Did he kill himself?"

"No gun in his hand. Bullet came from behind," Jason said. "Someone murdered him."

Lorraine opened her mouth to speak. Tires on the gravel driveway interrupted her. She and Jason locked eyes and bolted for the front door.

Blue and red lights filled the front of the house. Three cop cars pulled up behind his vehicle, their sirens silent but their lights flashing like strobe lights. Jason placed a hand in front of his face to shield his eyes. The officers stepped out at the same time, their guns raised and pointed at them.

"Drop the weapon and put your hands in the air! Do it, now!"

25

Within an hour of their call, Ross sent directions to Cassie for Harpeth River State Park. It was only a half hour from downtown Nashville. The windy, overcast day spoke to the promise of fewer onlookers enjoying the park.

By the time they pulled into the parking lot, Cassie was a mess of nerves and anxiety. Omega looked as calm as ever, his gaze roaming over every detail of their surroundings. Hikers taking the trails. Trees billowing in the breeze.

What had he deduced? Did it make him feel more at ease? She tried to draw strength from his stoicism, but her body shook with anticipation. Meeting Ross was a big step. If this went sideways, it could be disastrous for them.

"You ready for this?" Omega asked.

"Not at all. Are you?"

He shrugged. "It's gonna happen either way."

Not exactly the reassurance she was looking for. "You still think this is a good idea?"

"I think it's our best idea," he said. "If we can get him on our side, then we can find out what he's privy to. Apex'll bury us as deep as they can if we don't have allies lined up."

Cassie shuddered. Who would they send to wipe her and Omega off the board? Anastasia wasn't a soldier, but she *had* shown up at Pearl's house. This was personal, which meant she wouldn't trust just anybody to do her dirty work.

Cassie's heart pounded harder at the memory of Jett's death. It had been quick but callous. The only reason he'd died was because she was there, investigating his sister's death. Jett had survived all this time because he hadn't known anything about Pearl's disappearance. Everything Cassie touched turned to blood and ash.

Hopefully Ross didn't succumb to the same fate.

Before they could change their minds, Omega opened his door. "Let's go."

Cassie stepped out and rounded the car to open the back door. Bear stood on the backseat and wagged his tail hard enough for his body to wiggle. Cassie gave him pets and a kiss he eagerly returned. He hopped out of the cramped space and stretched into a puppy posture, then scratched behind his ear with his back foot. Whatever came of this meeting, she wanted her dog by her side.

Hooking the leash to his harness, Cassie tugged him toward Omega as they started down the path to Newsom's Mill. She'd read about the structure on the drive. The original mill had been located upstream, built by a man named Colonel Joseph M. Newsom. After having been destroyed in a flood in 1808, they'd built a new mill in 1862 with limestone from Newsom's quarry.

The trail was a short stretch of asphalt, grass and wildflowers bordering its edges. At its end, the structure loomed over them, crumbling against the forces of nature. Its walls had been witness to countless stories over the years. People had relied on the building for their livelihood. They'd toiled away to provide for their families. They were long buried, but proof of their existence remained within every stone of the structure.

Instead of following the path right up to the building, Omega hooked his way around and to the right, stepping into the tree shade. The river lay just on the other side, the sound of water a quiet but steady murmur amidst the singing of the birds.

Once they could no longer see the path, Cassie unhooked Bear from his leash and let him wander. With a wag of his tail, he stuck his nose to the ground and investigated all the interesting smells, occasionally digging a little hole in the dirt to get a better sniff.

"This is far enough," Omega said. "Feel anything?"

It was such a vague question, but Cassie knew what he was getting at. She could always feel something, whether spirits disturbing the air around her or a pull in a specific direction. Like ambient noise, those sensations faded into the background unless she focused on them. That was when they rushed to the foreground like an oncoming train and the weight of her ability sat on her shoulders like a concrete mantle.

"I saw a few millworkers down by the building," Cassie said, "and a woman standing on the bank of the river, looking across the water. She's faded, almost gone."

The figure beside Omega was crystal clear in the shade of the trees. She still hadn't shared that tidbit with Omega. Chris' pale gaze locked on hers, his mouth opening and closing like yesterday. She still couldn't hear him.

Cassie returned her focus to what she could decipher, her heart cracking at having to ignore her old friend. "No other feelings."

"All right," Omega replied. "Then we wait for Ross."

Cassie did her best to calm her racing heart while they waited for Ross' arrival. The shade from the trees caused goosebumps to crawl up and down her arms. Bear had long since disappeared into the trees, his footsteps audible amidst the fallen leaves and twigs. Omega stood with his back to the river, his head ever-swiveling.

Five minutes later, Cassie's ears perked up at the sound of boots crunching over the forest terrain. Omega stood a little taller. Two figures emerged from behind the trunks of a dozen of trees.

Ross didn't look much different than the last time she'd seen him, though instead of wearing a button-up and slacks, he wore a pair of jeans and a sweater. Was this what incognito looked like for him?

He raised a hand to wave at Cassie. His gaze flicked to Omega as he approached, and perhaps the other man's less than welcoming demeanor was enough to remind Ross why they were here. He lowered his arm and stopped close enough to speak.

Ross' eyes traveled back to Cassie. "It's really you."

Cassie nodded and held her hands out. "It's really me."

Another man stopped beside Ross, hands on his hips. One of them rested on a gun. Ross gestured to him. "This is my head of security, Vaughn."

The man nodded in acknowledgment but said nothing. He was tall, broad, and forgettable. That's probably what made him good at his job.

Cassie gestured to her own guest. "This is my friend—Robert."

Omega eased at the use of his old name.

Ross studied him, folding his arms. "You look familiar."

"I have one of those faces."

Before Ross could recognize him as Anastasia's former driver, Cassie cut in. "Thanks for coming. I know this is unconventional."

Ross chuckled. "To say the least. I'm just glad you're okay." He sobered quickly. "What happened?"

"Long story short, Agent Chris Viotto shot me but didn't kill me. Robert over here saved my life." She flicked her gaze toward him, but it landed on Chris instead.

She turned back to Omega. "He's been helping me recover for the last three months."

"Why were you recovering in secret?" Ross held up his hands. "You don't owe me an explanation, but people back in Savannah mourned you. Assistant Chief of Police Adelaide Harris spoke to me about it several times."

Cassie's chest squeezed at the mention of her friend. The ache traveled through her body until she could feel it from the crown of her head to the tips of her toes. More than anything, she wanted to talk to her loved ones. See them. Hug them. But there was no time to dwell on that right now.

"I know. It's complicated, but that's part of what I wanted to talk to you about."

"I'm happy to listen, though I'm not sure what I can do to help. My life is under a microscope these days."

Cassie bobbed her head, flicking her gaze back to Vaughn. "Are you sure you want to talk about this? Your father and Apex?"

"Like I said on the phone, Vaughn's been with me for a long time. He knows everything."

Cassie chewed the inside of her cheek. "I don't even know where to begin."

"Start with what happened in the parking garage," Omega said.

"Agent Viotto was my colleague, and also a friend. When I met him again here in Nashville, he was working with Apex Publicity against his will. Anastasia had his sister and her kids abducted and used them as collateral to get Chris to do her bidding."

Ross jolted like he'd been hit with an electric shock. "Anastasia Bolton?"

"The very one." It was hard to believe anyone who'd ever met the woman would deny what she was capable of. Did Ross wear rose-tinted glasses when she was around? "It was on Anastasia's orders that Chris shot me."

Ross remained silent. Vaughn studied her, his gaze moving from her face down to where her hands were clenched at her sides. She loosened them beneath his calculating look. A moment later, he returned his focus to their surroundings.

Finally, Ross asked, "You're sure?"

"Yes. We also have concrete proof that Anastasia knew about Douglas' wrongdoings and helped cover it up to save your father's reputation."

Ross' whole body stiffened. "You have physical evidence?"

Cassie nodded. "Yes."

"Can I see it?"

Omega spoke before Cassie could. "No."

Both of the other men looked at him, but it was Ross who spoke. "Why not?"

"Because we need something from you first."

"Like what?" Ross looked back at Cassie, eyes wide. "I didn't know about any of this."

"I believe you." Her mind worked to figure out how to make him listen before he got defensive. "Have you ever heard the name Pearl Everly?"

Ross thought for a moment, then shook his head. "Who is she?"

Cassie exchanged a look with Omega, who gave her a small nod.

"She was Jack's second biological child," she told Ross. "He had an affair while he was still married to your mother."

"Jesus Christ," Ross spat, running a hand through his hair. "I assume there's proof of this, too?"

Cassie nodded. "We have dated journal entries from Pearl detailing each one of Jack's visits. I'm sure we could get financial records if we needed to."

Ross swore, his skin paling beneath the shade. "When did this happen? How old is she?"

Cassie's heart ached for Ross. He had two siblings, both of whom he'd never met. Ross had grown up in the system, never knowing where he'd be next or if he'd see any of his friends again. Having siblings would've given him the stability he'd probably craved. And maybe he would've been a good influence on both Douglas and Pearl.

"Pearl disappeared around the time Douglas' other victims went missing, when she was sixteen. But we have yet to locate her body."

"Douglas killed her too?"

"We're not sure. But I don't think so."

Ross narrowed his eyes. "You think Anastasia did it? Or, at least, someone at Apex?"

"That's the most likely scenario."

"I know I already asked this, but—*are you sure*?" He ran a hand through his hair, dislodging a few strands. A soft breeze tousled them further. "There's no room for mistakes here, not with information like this."

Cassie rubbed at her arms where goosebumps had erupted from the wind winding its way through the trees. "We went to Pearl's childhood home, where her half-brother Jett still lived. Anastasia showed up with a few men, had them kill Jett in cold blood. We barely escaped."

Ross swore. "God, Cassie, I'm so sorry."

Cassie swallowed, battling to keep tears from gathering.

"This is turning into a shitshow." He took a deep, steadying breath. "You realize my hands are tied, right? We can't even control the narrative about Douglas after Blackwood's speech, let alone another scandal. I've got press conferences and town hall visits lined up for the next several weeks."

This was it. The moment they found out if Ross was willing to stick his neck out for the right reason.

"It all comes back to Apex," Cassie said, her breath tight in her throat. "They've been doing this for decades, all in service of something bigger. You remember when you told me about Five Winds?"

"Yeah, of course." Ross knit his brows. "What's that got to do with anything?"

"Have you ever heard of Zhang Wei?"

"He owns Five Winds, plus some other companies. We've met a few times. Seems like he wants to make the world a better place."

Omega stepped forward, narrowing his gaze and tilting his head. "Are you sure about that?"

Ross looked at him, hardening his stare. "I had my people do their research, yes."

"*Your* people?" Omega asked. "Or Apex's?"

Ross' jaw ticked, and he turned back to Cassie, a question in his eyes.

"This goes way deeper than what your father's gotten himself into," she said, keeping her voice firm but not unkind. "Has anything raised red flags for you recently?"

Ross huffed out a dry laugh. "I'm in politics. Everything raises red flags."

Before Cassie could open her mouth to speak, a branch snapped to her left. Vaughn withdrew his gun and stepped in front of Ross. Cassie backed up. Omega drew his own weapon.

"I think you've said more than enough already, Senator Hughes."

A sliver of ice ran down Cassie's spine at the familiar voice.

From between the trees, two figures emerged. Anastasia Bolton looked like she always did—tough, put-together, and always in control. The second woman materialized, a gun to her head. Zip ties cuffed her wrists together. A gag around her mouth kept her from speaking.

A strangled cry of surprise left the woman's throat as she locked eyes with Cassie.

Anastasia had brought Adelaide Harris as her bargaining chip.

26

CASSIE COULDN'T TEAR HER GAZE AWAY FROM HARRIS, HER EYES WIDE and full of terror. Maybe horrified that she was going crazy, seeing her dead best friend in the flesh, only to wake up later to find out it was all a dream.

Cassie wanted to tell Harris everything, to reassure her this was real. But with three guns drawn, she was limited on time and options. As though she could stop a bullet by sheer force of will, Cassie stepped forward and held up her hands, one in Anastasia's direction and one in Vaughn's.

"Please," she said, her voice welling with emotion. "Everyone, calm down."

"Anastasia," Ross croaked, hurt evident in his eyes. "What the hell is going on?"

Anastasia's arm remained steady as she held the gun to Harris' head. "There's been a few developments."

"Is what she said true?" Ross asked, flicking his eyes over to Cassie.

"I didn't hear it all, but—yes. Miss Quinn isn't known for being deceitful, although she's had her moments." Anastasia shot Cassie a rueful look. "We didn't get a chance to talk much the last time I saw you. You're looking good. Very *alive*."

Cassie sputtered, every word she'd been dying to spit at the woman fading before it could leave her mouth.

Omega spoke up in her place. "What are you hoping to accomplish here?"

"Simple. You leave Ross out of this, and I return Cassie's friend intact."

"You're outnumbered."

"How foolish of me."

Anastasia stepped behind Harris for cover. She swung the gun out, pointing it at them. Then she pulled the trigger. The silenced gun went off, the sound no louder than a click. Vaughn crumpled to the ground.

Ross let out a strangled cry as he stared at the dead man lying prone at his feet. Cassie stumbled backwards. A twig snapped underfoot, and she jumped, afraid Anastasia had fired the gun again. Omega's arm remained steady and pointed at the newcomers, but he didn't return fire.

Instead, he darted behind Ross and held his gun to the back of the man's head. Ross froze, his eyes going wide. Cassie let out a strangled cry but didn't move from her spot.

"Not sure that was your best move," Omega said.

"Maybe not," Anastasia said, her voice calm despite the fire in her eyes. "But it did level the playing field. And now you know how serious I am."

"You mean how desperate?" Omega asked.

Cassie's head swam. No one pointed a gun in her direction, but she was defenseless. Caught between two immoveable objects. Harris and Ross were pawns to be moved across the board while she sat on the sidelines. Ross shook as he waited to see what would happen next, and Cassie's mouth went dry at the palpable fear emanating from him. Omega had wanted to convince Ross to become their ally, and here he was holding a gun to the man's head as though no one would look for him if he went missing.

Harris' eyes were as round as Ross'. Anastasia stared down Omega, her gaze steady and calculating. Cassie didn't know which pair of figures to keep her eye on. Anastasia had tried to kill her in the past, but right now it seemed as though she'd forgotten Cassie existed.

A branch snapped in the distance. Cassie didn't jump. It most likely belonged to a squirrel or chipmunk. She didn't dare look away from the scene playing out in front of her. She needed her brain firing on all cylinders.

"I mean determined," Anastasia said, cocking her head to the side. Her steady gaze remained hard. "I want the evidence you uncovered from Pearl's house. I want everything you have on me, on Apex, Hughes—all of it."

"Did you think this would work?" Omega laughed, but his arm didn't move an inch as he kept his gun trained on the two women across from him. "I've got your presidential hopeful at gunpoint, and you have a woman I've never even met. We're not exactly at an impasse here."

Cassie whipped her head around to stare at him. The ground was unsteady beneath her shaking legs. "What?"

Omega didn't take his eyes off Anastasia. "I'm sorry, Cassie. I know she's your friend, but I'll do whatever it takes to end Apex."

Harris let out a strangled cry beneath the gag in her mouth.

Anastasia laughed, drawing Cassie's attention again. "Haven't you figured it out yet, Cassie? This man is as callous as I am. It's too bad you were stuck driving cars, Robert. You would've been more useful out in the field."

"Please," Cassie begged, turning back to Omega. "Harris is innocent in all this. You can't shoot her."

"This is bigger than her. Bigger than you, or me. Sacrifices have already been made. The only way to stop that from continuing to happen is to ensure we've dismantled their entire operation."

"Good luck with that," Anastasia cooed. "It took them decades to become what they are today. You can't bring that down overnight."

"I can certainly try."

The breeze cooled Cassie's damp cheeks. At some point, she'd started crying. There had to be something she could do, something that would satisfy both of them and get everyone else out of this alive.

Cassie chanced a look at her specter. Chris moved his mouth, wider and faster, but whatever message he tried to convey was still lost without his voice.

With no other recourse, she turned back to Anastasia. "If we give you what we have, you'll let Harris go?"

"Cassie," Omega warned.

"Scout's honor," Anastasia said, risking a glance in Cassie's direction. Her gaze was hungry. "Killing her would be messy, and I'm not interested in having more to clean up."

"We have other ways to get what we need." Cassie turned to Omega but kept Anastasia in her peripheral. "This isn't the end of the road for us."

Anastasia laughed. "You mean Blackwood? He won't deliver on whatever he's promised you. Big talk with few results. That's how he operates. The idiot thought he could bring us down by revealing a couple of the skeletons in our closet? Like we don't have contingencies for our contingencies? He should know better by now. Besides, how do you think I knew you were here? We've had someone watching him for weeks."

"Is he dead?" Cassie croaked.

"Not yet. He's not worth the resources." Anastasia's smile was vicious. "We'll let him dig his own grave."

Cassie's knees wobbled beneath her as she watched Omega. He adjusted his grip on Ross' shoulder as he risked a glance in Cassie's direction. His trigger finger never wavered. They were all a hair's breadth away from disaster.

Killing Ross would put a big wrinkle in Apex's plan, but that was only one piece of the puzzle. The chance that he might know something useful was enough to keep him close. And now Ross had a first-hand account of how dangerous Anastasia and Apex truly were. If he'd had any reservations before, they had to be gone now.

A blur of tan and black bolted from the shaded forest and

launched itself at Anastasia. Bear clamped his mouth down around her forearm—the same one pointing the gun at Omega and Ross. A scream ripped from Anastasia's throat as she dropped the weapon, blood pouring from the wound.

Harris stumbled to her knees at the same time Ross tried to turn and fight off Omega. Two shots rang out, but Cassie launched herself toward Harris. She pulled the woman up to her feet and dragged her behind a large tree. Cassie didn't bother pulling the gag out of Harris' mouth before yelling, "Run!"

Harris stood frozen, and Cassie shoved her. "Go! I'm right behind you!"

Harris nodded, then took off through the trees. Cassie poked her head around the wide tree trunk. Omega had wrestled Ross to the ground, face down. Bear stood over Anastasia, teeth bared, as she held her bleeding mess of an arm and spewed profanities.

With a knee in the middle of his back, Omega had secured Ross within seconds. Cassie looked on in horror as he then raised his gun to fire at Anastasia. But Bear was standing in the way—

"Come!" Cassie called.

Bear jolted forward a millisecond before the gun went off. He tore across the leaf-strewn ground, tongue lolling out of the side of his mouth as though he hadn't just saved her and Harris' lives, or evaded his own demise. Cassie ran her hand along the top of his head when he came to a stop by her side.

Another gunshot sounded. Anastasia screamed in agony again.

Cassie didn't stick around to find out what happened next. She took off after Harris, calling for Bear to remain close. If they were going to get out of this alive, they had to stay ahead of everyone else.

By the time Cassie caught up with her, Harris had pulled the gag from her mouth. The woman ground to a sudden halt. Cassie collided with her, gripping Harris' arms to catch her fall.

"How?" Harris sputtered, tears streaking down her face.

"Later," Cassie gasped, gearing up to sprint again. "I'll tell you everything. Later."

She sure as hell hoped they got through this long enough for there to be a later.

27

Searing pain shot down Anastasia's arm, but she refused to stop running, to slow down. Now that she was up on her feet, she had to put as much distance between her and Omega as possible. After that beast of a dog attacked her, she'd lost her gun in the detritus of the forest floor. Yet her *former driver* still held his.

The trees whipped by as she sprinted away. Branches snagged at her clothes, tugging and ripping the fabric. Brambles cut into her skin. The wind was loud in her ears as she ran, drowning out everything else around her.

Anastasia had made a name for herself by being calm, cool, and collected at all times. Right now, she felt anything but. Her legs shook as she ran. Her breaths came in haggard pants. The pain radiating throughout her body felt like she was getting stabbed with a white-hot poker over and over again. But her cheeks felt cold thanks to the wind and her tears.

Omega had managed to graze her biceps with one of his bullets. It hurt like a son of a bitch, but it was nothing compared to the bite wound. She clutched her bloody and mangled forearm to her chest, hoping that would stop some of the blood loss. That damn dog had bitten her hard, tearing her skin open in multiple places. Anastasia bristled at the thought of the grisly scar it'd leave behind.

Anastasia's looks had always gotten her foot in the door. Her mind had pushed it open the rest of the way. People listened to her, trusted her—feared her. The scar on her arm and in her shoulder shouldn't change any of that, but people would notice. It would raise eyebrows. And not in a good way.

She tripped over a branch and landed on her knees, catching herself with her hands. The impact shot through her wounds and sent a wave of nausea crashing over her. Leaning to the side, she emptied the contents of her stomach. She sat up and wiped her mouth with the back of her hand, chest heaving. What was happening to her?

The sound of snapping branches erupted behind her. She didn't look over her shoulder for the source of the noise. She pushed back up onto her feet and kept running. She had no time to lose.

She'd been too cocky, thinking Harris would be enough of an incentive to get Cassie on her side, and too naïve, believing Ross would stand against the man who called himself Omega. It'd been a long time since she had made a mistake as big as this one. If Apex didn't already know what had happened here, they would find out soon.

Using her good arm, Anastasia patted her pockets. They were all flat against her skin. She cursed. Had her keys fallen out of her pocket when she'd hit the ground? Had Harris stolen them from her during the shootout?

Anastasia kept going, doing her best to orient herself despite the trees looming all around her. She'd circled wide when she sprinted away from Omega, and now she had to curve back toward the parking lot. Omega might guess where she was going and wait for her, but she'd be on the other side. She'd have plenty of time and distance to make a second escape.

The burning in her legs had grown unbearable by the time the parking lot materialized on the other side of the trees. She stopped before she revealed herself and scanned the area.

Omega wasn't there.

And neither was the car.

Leaning against the trunk of a steady tree, Anastasia gathered all of her rage and pushed it deep inside her body, saving it for later. Harris must've grabbed the keys after all. That was fine. She'd start walking along the road. Most people would see her injuries, surmise she'd been attacked, and help her. She just hoped they'd find her before she passed out amongst the trees.

As the breeze cooled the sweat gathering on her skin, Anastasia pushed down her pain until it resided next to her anger. She imagined them as neat little packages, a pretty bow attached to each one. Pulling on the ribbon would unleash them both until anger and pain were all that fueled her.

When that time came, there would be hell to pay.

A vibration against her hip made Anastasia freeze. The vibration came again. Straining to keep her one arm immobile, she pulled her phone out of her pocket. The device was completely intact.

Guess Harris didn't think of everything.

All thought of revenge on the woman disappeared when Anastasia read the caller ID.

Hitting the answer button and bringing the phone to her ear, Anastasia made sure her voice gave away none of her desperation. "Sienna. To what do I owe this pleasure?"

The woman snickered. "The pleasure is all mine, Anastasia."

"I've got important work to do, Sienna. If you're having trouble with the fax machine, ask one of the interns."

Sienna's responding laugh was light. "Daniel wanted you to hear the news in person, but I couldn't wait a second longer."

Grinding her teeth together, Anastasia said, "What news?"

"It's so rare for you to be out of the loop, Anastasia. Are you sure you're doing okay? Maybe you're slipping."

"Or maybe your news isn't as important as you think it is. I've got bigger issues to deal with than the minutiae you concern yourself with."

"But this is about you, Ana." The woman's mock-airy tone called the anger right back up into Anastasia's chest. "You're getting transferred, isn't that exciting?"

Anastasia froze. "What?"

"He didn't say *demotion*, exactly, but we all know you aren't what you once were." Her mocking tone shifted to pity. Then amusement. "Do you think you'll have to work in a cubicle? I'll visit, just so I can see the sight for myself."

Anastasia jammed the "end call" button and slipped the phone back into her pocket.

Sienna had made a rookie mistake—big surprise there. Anastasia had witnessed plenty of transfers over the years, and few of them came with a cubicle job. The majority ended in an early grave.

So, it was official then. She was a loose end.

Pushing off the tree, Anastasia stumbled out of the forest with her jaw set in grim determination.

It wouldn't end this way.

No one tossed her away like she was nothing.

Not even Apex.

28

CASSIE COULDN'T STOP STARING AT HER FRIEND, TOO AFRAID TO HOPE that all of this was real.

After they dashed through the forest and out into the small parking lot, Harris produced a set of keys from her pocket and unlocked the car. Then she turned the keys inward, using the rigid edges to free herself from the zip ties.

Cassie told Bear to wait with Harris and then sprinted for Omega's car. They only had seconds to spare, but Omega was always one step ahead of her. Now was her chance to even the odds.

She didn't hesitate as she grabbed a large rock from along the border of the parking lot and hefted it into her arms. Lifting it above her head, Cassie threw it at the rear passenger window of the rental. The alarm blared, but she ignored it as she reached inside the car and grabbed Pearl's journal and the jewelry box full of USB drives.

She wouldn't risk taking the laptop in case Omega had put tracking software on it.

Dashing back to Harris' vehicle, Cassie let Bear into the back and then jumped into the passenger seat, slamming the door just before Adelaide hit the gas. The jolt in acceleration threw Cassie back into the seat. Pearl's belongings fell from her hands into her lap. After a sharp right turn, they fell onto the floor. She rushed to strap the seat belt over her body and click it into place. By the time they raced out of the park exit, Omega was nowhere to be seen.

Harris took the lead, donning her Assistant Chief of Police persona and sticking to business, the ride punctuated by necessary dialogue. Were either of them hurt? No. Was Bear okay? Yes. Where were they going? A motel outside the city. Did Harris have cash on her? Yes. Would they talk more once they got somewhere safer? Damn right they would.

It took a half hour to get back to Nashville, then another twenty to find a hotel seedy enough that they could pay in cash. It was a risk to travel anywhere nearby, but one they silently agreed was worth it.

As soon as they walked into the hotel room, Cassie filled an ice bucket with water from the bathroom sink and let Bear drink. He drained about half of it before jumping up on the bed, curling his tail around his body and over his nose, and letting his eyes fall shut.

Harris secured the door, closed the blinds, and scrubbed water over her face. When she returned from the bathroom, her shining face was at odds with the disheveled state of her clothes, stained with grass and dirt. She stared at Cassie like she was seeing a ghost. Did Cassie look like this too, when ghosts decided to pop up at random? Chris had yet to reappear for her to test the theory.

Harris stood in the middle of the room, arms limp at her side. Her chest heaved, her eyes wide and searching. "Cassie?"

"It's me," Cassie said. "I'm alive. I'm okay. I'm so sorry—"

"I don't know whether to strangle you or hug you."

Cassie opened her arms, tears already forming. "I vote hug."

Harris crossed the room in two strides and grabbed Cassie into a bone-crushing embrace that pushed all the air from her lungs. Even as her body screamed for oxygen, all of her muscles relaxed.

Harris' body shook with sobs. Cassie drew in deep, wheezing breaths and clung to her friend even tighter, her own tears spilling over the edges of her eyes. At some point, both of their legs gave out, and they dropped to the floor in a heap of tangled limbs, crying until their throats were raw.

Eventually, Harris pulled back and gazed at Cassie like she was afraid this would be the last time they'd ever see each other.

"How?" was the only word Harris could expel from her throat.

Cassie disentangled herself from her friend and leaned back against the bed, stretching her legs out in front of her on the rough and stained carpet.

The phrase *bone-tired* made more sense now than ever before.

She started from the beginning, telling Harris about her surgery and how she was transferred from the hospital. How Omega had them record her death and make up a story about where her body went.

Harris shook her head. "Who is this guy? How was he able to do that?"

"I'm not sure. He's well-connected. He's got a whole support network—soldiers, doctors, you name it." Cassie leaned her head back against the bed and stared up at the ceiling. It was no less stained than the carpet. "And he's got money. Knowledge and experience. He wants to take down Apex as badly as I do. More, probably."

"Enough to not care if Anastasia killed me."

Cassie looked back to Harris. "I never would've let that happen to you."

"I'm not sure any of us could've stopped it." Harris looked over at Bear. "Thank God he was there. Jason's been going out of his mind—"

"What about you?" Cassie sucked in a breath. She couldn't bear the thought of Jason right now. "How did Anastasia get to you?"

"I got a call from Piper's lawyer saying she wanted to talk." Harris shook her head. "Against my better judgement, I went to visit her. She didn't say much. Seems to think there's more to Jack Hughes' involvement with Apex than the fact they want Ross to be president." Harris lifted a hand and rubbed the side of her neck. "I wasn't paying attention when I left the prison. Didn't notice someone come up behind me. They jabbed me with a needle." Harris dropped her hand into her lap. "Next thing I knew, I woke up in fucking Tennessee."

Cassie shook her head. "I'm so sorry."

"I literally don't care about any of that right now. All I care about is the fact that you're safe. You're *alive*."

Even though she thought she'd cried out all the tears in her body, Cassie's eyes welled up again. "You should be angry at me."

"Oh, I am." Harris' face was like stone, but the worry in her eyes softened it. "I'm furious, but I understand why you did it. I just wish you could've given me some sort of sign. I've been driving myself crazy trying to figure out what happened to you. We all have."

"I wanted to," Cassie said, grabbing her friend's hands. "Trust me, I did. Omega wouldn't let me leave the facility for months, not until I was fully recovered. He hardly told me anything about what was happening. All he wanted me to focus on was getting better."

"I want to be happy he did that for you, but I don't think I can bring myself to think happy thoughts about him right now."

Cassie nodded. "I escaped. Stole a truck and drove from Virginia all the way to Savannah."

"Virginia? No wonder we couldn't find you." Then Harris froze and stared at Cassie. "You were in Savannah?"

"I went home. Packed a bag. Grabbed some cash. Jason came back from walking Bear as I was ready to slip out the door."

Harris ran a hand down her face. "Jesus, he's never going to let me live this down. He knew you were in the house. He was convinced you took Bear."

"It wasn't my intention. Bear ran out of the house after me and wouldn't go back."

"Smart dog."

"Tell me about it." Cassie paused, wanting to say something to comfort Harris, to show her that she'd never wanted any of this to happen. "I was going to show up on your doorstep, ask you for help. Chris' sister and her kids were being held hostage, and Omega refused to go get them. I decided I'd do it on my own, and I wanted you there with me. You were the only one I trusted to stay by my side and trust that I knew what I was doing."

"Why didn't you?" Harris asked. "I would've dropped everything to help you."

"I know. But Omega showed up. He was pissed, but he helped me. Christina and her kids are safe. Then we went to Pearl Everly's childhood home. Found some damning information about Jack Hughes. That's when Anastasia tracked us down for the first time." Cassie blinked away the blood-stained memories. "We barely got away."

Cassie reached over and dragged the notebook and jewelry box from the bed and into her lap. "This is Pearl's. It proves he knew about Douglas' killing spree. It also proves Apex helped cover it up. Omega sent copies to one of his contacts and Lorraine."

Harris stared down at the items in Cassie's hands, then back up at her. "Is it enough to take them down?"

"It's a good start, but no. We need to prove the company is up to something big. That's why we met with Ross." Cassie shook her head. "God, I hope he's okay."

"You think he was going to work with you and Omega before Anastasia showed up?"

"We were getting close. I have no idea if he knows anything that could help us, but it was worth a try. Now we're gonna have to find another way. We hoped Blackwood might work with us."

"Boy, do I have some news for you."

"His press conference?" When Harris nodded, Cassie sighed. "We saw it. We spoke to him right after. He's trying to get his hands on some information, but I'm not convinced he'll be able to." Cassie groaned. "This is all going to shit."

"And it's not over yet."

Silence descended over them. All Cassie could hear was distant traffic and Bear's quiet snores. The room smelled stale, and her butt was starting to hurt from sitting on the floor, but she hadn't felt this safe in days.

"Cassie," Harris began, her tone warning Cassie that she wouldn't like what came next. "Jason's been going out of his mind. He's been convinced you weren't dead this whole time. Lorraine's been keeping an eye on him best she can, but I'm worried that the longer it looks like you're really dead, the more of a chance there'll be that he does something stupid."

Cassie choked back a sob. She hated hearing the way this was affecting him, knowing that it had been her decision to do this to the people she loved.

"I know," she finally said. "But the more people who know I'm alive, the more they'll be in danger. The more distracted I'll be."

"Anastasia already knows you're alive. She kidnapped me. What's to say she won't hurt Jason or Lorraine anyway? Or your sister and your parents?"

"Last time I saw Anastasia, she showed up with a handful of soldiers at Pearl Everly's door. This time, she was alone. I think she's desperate. And the only reason she'd be desperate is if Apex is up her ass about taking care of this situation. If I had to guess, she doesn't want the company to know she keeps letting me slip through her fingers."

"Now's not really a time for guessing."

"I'm telling you, this time was different."

Harris nodded, unconvinced. "Hey, it's your call. All I'm saying is that a lot of people are going to be angry with you when you show back up. Are you ready for that?"

"Right now? No. I'll have a lot of work ahead of me. And I'll learn to live with the consequences, no matter what they are. But we have to get to that point. And that only happens once we stop Apex from achieving their goals."

"And how do we do that?"

Cassie groaned, hoping Harris wouldn't ask that question. "No idea. But I think a warm shower and a good meal are in order." She stood, holding out her hand to help Harris up. "Are you with me?"

"Are you kidding me?" Harris clasped her hand and used Cassie to haul herself up to her feet. "I'm never letting you out of my sight again."

29

Cassie squeezed herself into the tiny motel shower, not looking too closely at the stains along the edges of the tub. The hot water relaxed her sore muscles, though she didn't stand under the spray nearly long enough to ease all the strain out of her body. She wanted to save some hot water for Harris.

Not everything was back to normal between her and Adelaide, but she had her best friend by her side. For the moment, that was good enough. Over the last three months, tension had dug its way into every muscle of her body. She'd trusted Omega, but she'd also been wary of his agenda.

Now that Harris was here, Cassie didn't have to worry about who she had at her back.

After Harris took a quick shower, they set an alarm and slept for a few hours. Cassie was sore again when she woke up, but the growling of her stomach took precedence. Harris suggested they pile back into the car and grab some food, then think about their next move. Bear had been reluctant to leave his napping spot in the middle of the bed, but after some coaxing, he jumped down, stretched, and followed Cassie back out to Harris' car.

After Cassie got some food into her system, a plan formed, but

Harris didn't love the idea. Since she didn't have any suggestions of her own, however, she agreed to Cassie's scheme.

Which was how they ended up sitting around the corner from Jack Hughes' house, debating whether to kick this particular hornet's nest. The senator had flown home from Washington D.C. to be with his family after Blackwood's press conference. It was a long-shot he'd be willing to talk to anybody, but they had to try.

"It's his reputation that's on the line right now," Cassie said for what felt like the tenth time. "We can leverage that in our favor."

"I already said I agreed this needed to happen," Harris argued. "But I don't like that we've had zero time to prepare. Do you even know what you're going to say to him?"

"More or less." Cassie shrugged, but Harris still looked dubious. "The more time we sit here, the more of a chance Omega figures out our next move and corners us when we're least expecting it."

"You really think he's going to do something to hurt you?" Harris asked. "After everything he's done to make sure you were okay?"

"He was willing to let *you* die. He must've known I wouldn't have worked with him anymore after that. Not willingly, at least."

"Maybe he was bluffing," Harris said, like it wasn't her life that had been hanging in the balance. "Besides, don't we need him to pull all this off? Seems like he's a lot more connected than we are."

"Which is why I'd like to get some information he *doesn't* already have. Make sure we're both invaluable to him. That way, he won't think about pulling anything else." Cassie thought of Pearl's journal and jewelry box. "He needed me to get into contact with Pearl's spirit. Now that we have, my part in this might be over. That could've been all Omega ever wanted from me. I'm just a glorified bloodhound."

Bear whined from the backseat.

Harris turned to him and scratched behind his ear. "She didn't mean it, buddy."

Cassie allowed herself a small smile, scratching Bear's other ear. Chris sat in the seat beside him, his form rippling when she reached across to Bear. Her smile faded, and she turned back to Harris. "It's now or never. Are we doing this?"

Harris blew out a breath and jumped out of the car, striding down the sidewalk like she owned it. Bear whined again, his nose pressed up against the window, watching her every move. She disappeared around the corner and out of view.

"It's okay," Cassie assured him, twisting to run a hand down his side. Chris remained stoic. "She's just talking to the guard at the front gate. She'll be back any minute."

Silence descended upon the inside of the vehicle. Harris had taken the keys when she'd left, and it soon became warm without any open windows. Cassie didn't dare crack her door in case it drew unwanted attention. Bear panted from the back seat, watching as people walked past the car.

Harris returned a few minutes later, furrowing her brow as she walked back to the car. Cassie tensed, expecting the worst. The guard was onto them. Hughes wouldn't let them in. They'd have to go all the way back to Savannah, deal with Omega—and Jason.

But as soon as Harris slipped inside the vehicle, she broke out into a grin. "Our buddy Martin at the front gate will let us in. I may have name-dropped Anastasia to do it."

Cassie laughed, tension falling away from her shoulders. That was only step one, but it was vital they do this the right way.

"Go on, get in the back. I'll let you know when we're through."

Cassie climbed over the center console, watching as Chris' form faded from view. She settled into the middle backseat next to Bear, tipping her hat low over her giant sunglasses. The once-silly disguise had now become her lifeline. The horde of reporters standing outside Jack's gate wouldn't catch sight of her through the tinted windows, but she wasn't taking any chances. They'd already be asking why the Assistant Chief of Police from Savannah, Georgia, was being let inside the man's home.

Once Cassie was settled, Harris pulled away from the curb, went around the block, then turned into Jack's driveway. She laid on the car horn to send people out of her way. Flash bulbs went off outside the car, no doubt trying to photograph both Harris and her license plate. Harris merely grumbled under her breath, creeping the car forward at the slowest pace possible.

Cassie was ducked down far enough that she couldn't see what was happening outside the car. Shouts indicated some of the reporters had tried sneaking in after them. The clang of the gate shutting rang out a few seconds later.

Finally, Harris said, "We made it through the gate. Another minute and we'll be at the house."

A minute later, they pulled to a stop, and Harris hopped out of the car. Then she rounded the vehicle and opened the door for Cassie, who attached Bear's leash to his harness before stepping out onto the brick driveway, leaving her hat and sunglasses behind. There was no point in hiding now.

The senator's house was exactly what Cassie had expected. It was at least three stories aboveground and stretched back farther than she could see from her vantage point. The bricks were a light salmon color, recalling a French Provincial Style that fit his Old Money persona. The façade was not greatly adorned, but an ornate wrought iron parapet enclosed a small balcony.

"Think he's compensating for something?" Harris quipped.

Cassie tried not to laugh. "Wonder if this was built from all the money Apex helped him make."

"You know what's an even worse thought? This is what was left over after they took what they needed from him."

"You're right," Cassie said. "That is worse."

Harris patted her sides. "I don't have a weapon on me. Anastasia relieved me of my service gun. Not looking forward to that paperwork."

"Do you think you'll need one?" Cassie asked.

Harris eyed her. "You tell me. You're the psychic."

Cassie leveled her with a look. Before she could say anything, the front door opened, and a man dressed in all black walked toward them. He eyed Bear with a raised eyebrow. "Martin didn't say anything about a dog."

"He's a police dog," Harris said, folding her arms. "He goes with us."

The man made a noncommittal sound but didn't argue. He waved for them to follow him inside.

Harris stepped in line behind the man while Cassie and Bear brought up the rear. There was little fanfare as they made their way inside. In fact, Cassie didn't see another person while they were led down the front hall and into a parlor just off the main entrance.

"The senator will be with you momentarily. Please wait here." The man retreated from the room.

When he shut the doors behind him, both Cassie and Harris waited a moment before either spoke.

"Were you also waiting for him to lock us in here?" Harris asked. "Or am I just getting too paranoid in my old age?"

"I don't think there's such a thing as too paranoid at this point. Not after everything we've been through."

"Good point. The shrink at the station is going to have a field day with all this."

Cassie shuddered. The idea of seeing her regular therapist again made her want to run screaming in the opposite direction. Integrating back into her old life would be no easy feat, but that was trivial after everything she'd been through. She'd done all this before. Replaying events and dissecting her feelings about them was about as much fun as getting a lobotomy.

Cassie turned her attention back to the room, pushing aside her relentless anxiety about the future.

It was simple, decorated in pale turquoise and copper. A small sofa and loveseat were situated on one side of the room, and matching high-backed chairs sat on the other, each adorned with a round pillow. A low coffee table held some books on world photography and travel. They sat next to a lit caramel-scented candle.

Cassie sank down onto the loveseat with Bear at her feet. She instructed him to lie down, and he did so without hesitating, though he kept his feet under him and his head held high. He stuck his nose in the air and sniffed, as though searching for something out of the ordinary.

He didn't pay any attention when Chris appeared on the opposite side of the room, washed out from the light filtering through the window.

Harris circled the room once, inspecting the dry bar, the two floor-to-ceiling windows, and the small piano in the far corner. Cassie wondered if anyone played it, or if it was just for show. The same could be asked of the chess board on a small table nearby.

As Harris came to stand by Cassie's side, the doors to the room opened and Senator Jack Hughes walked in. He stood tall and straight in a button-up shirt, slacks, and dress shoes. The ensemble looked casual on him, like this was an everyday outfit and not what most people would wear out to a nice dinner. As he shut the door behind him, his watch glinted in the sunlight, the same color as his wedding band.

When he turned around, Cassie forgot all about the man's wealth and power. His dark eyes bore into Harris, then Cassie, and finally dropped down to Bear. A look of mild annoyance crossed his expression, but he schooled his features into a mask of professionalism.

"Assistant Chief of Police Harris," Jack said, holding out his hand. Harris shook it once. "You were vague over the phone, but I assume you want to talk about Richard Blackwood's claims. You didn't need to come all the way to Tennessee for that."

"We were in the neighborhood." Harris swept her arm out and told him, "This is my colleague, Cassie Quinn."

"I've heard that name before." Jack didn't reach out to shake Cassie's hand, and she wondered how much he'd heard of her and whether he knew what she was capable of. Jack checked his watch. "I did this as a courtesy to the Savannah Police Department, but I don't have much time. As you can imagine, I've got a lot of fires to put out."

"Right. Why don't you sit down?" Harris asked, gesturing to one of the chairs opposite Cassie.

Jack raised an eyebrow and smirked but didn't say anything about Harris asking him to sit in his own home. He did so, crossing one leg over the other. His expression was calm, but Cassie could tell they'd already gotten under his skin.

If only he knew what was coming.

Harris sat, then looked to Cassie and nodded. Harris got her in the door, but Cassie held the power here. She had knowledge that would make Jack's life much more difficult if he didn't cooperate. Hopefully, it wouldn't come to that.

"I spoke with Richard Blackwood after his speech," Cassie said. "I doubt he has any regrets about his public statements about you, but the real target of his ire is Apex Publicity."

"Yes, I heard they dropped him as a client," he said, feigning pity. "Such a shame. He had potential."

"You should consider getting out from under their thumb as well."

Jack tilted his head back and laughed. "I'm sorry, but why in the world would I do that? They've built my brand. Made me millions. Helped me forge a legacy."

"What legacy is that, exactly?" Cassie asked. "The one you'll have as a senator, or as a father?"

Jack stared at Cassie for a moment, then turned his attention to an invisible piece of lint on his pants. "I hardly knew Douglas. I can't be blamed for the actions of another man, even if he was my own flesh and blood."

"You can if you knowingly covered up his crimes."

"You have no proof of that."

"Actually, I do."

Jack got to his feet and took a step in Cassie's direction. Bear let out a low growl and the man stopped in his tracks.

"I have proof that you knew what Douglas was doing," Cassie continued. "What's worse, I have proof that Apex helped cover it all up. Swept it under the rug until they were forced to do something about it. Your legacy has already been tainted, Senator. Do you really want to see it destroyed?"

Jack stared at Cassie as though he could set her aflame from his gaze alone. "How dare you lob empty threats at me in my own home?"

"It's not a threat," Cassie said, her tone filled with practiced ease. "And it's not empty. Does the name Pearl Everly ring a bell?"

A look of panic crossed Jack's face for the first time.

But before he could answer, the doors to the room swung open, and a silver-haired woman strode inside.

"I've never heard that name before," she said, staring daggers at the man, "but I would love to know what she has to do with my husband and whether he's kept yet another secret hidden from me for all these years."

"Dear—"

"Don't *dear* me," she snapped. "I deserve to know."

Harris stood. Her arms hung loose at her sides, but her shoulders were stiff. "Ma'am?"

The woman rounded on her with a face full of fury, though Cassie didn't think it was aimed at them. "Call me Jillian. I'm not really interested in hearing *Mrs. Hughes* at the moment. I apologize for being late. It seems my husband forgot to invite me to the meeting."

Cassie exchanged a look with Harris. Trepidation crawled up her spine and settled in her gut.

Jillian crossed the room and sat in the other chair. Her face was regal, even as she attempted to contain her ire. Once she was settled, she turned back to Cassie.

"Now, where were we?"

30

Harris didn't know what to make of Jillian Hughes.

She sat in her chair like a queen holding court, her chin held high as she surveyed her subjects. The expression on her face was stoic, but she gripped the armrests like they were the only thing keeping her in place. The woman's body trembled in anger, though she refused to look at her husband.

Senator Hughes had paled when his wife entered the room, and his skin remained drained of color. There was only a foot of space between their chairs, but they couldn't be farther apart. How much had Jillian known before Blackwood's press conference?

Cassie sat with one hand attached to Bear's leash, and the other placed on her lap. She leaned back into the loveseat with one leg crossed over the other, as though sitting in a friend's living room, listening as they told a story. Bear occasionally flicked his ear in a new direction when he heard a noise from outside or somewhere deeper in the house.

Harris remained standing. It was where she felt most comfortable and most prepared for whatever was next. Now that Jillian had entered the fray, there really was no telling what would happen.

Adelaide could relate to Jillian's anger. Harris had never stopped caring about Cassie, but the truth of her friend's deception still stung.

"Well?" Jillian asked, looking at Cassie. "If you've got another bomb to drop on us, I'd do it before someone else does."

"Jillian," Jack said, "you're being dramatic."

Jillian's whole body tensed, but she didn't tear her gaze away from Cassie's.

When Cassie looked up at Harris, she shrugged. They had to have this discussion one way or another.

Clearing her throat, Cassie said, "Pearl Everly was Jack's daughter."

Jillian's jaw clenched. "I shouldn't be surprised you had yet another child without my knowledge. Was it with the same woman?"

Jack kept his gaze on the floor, a hand covering his mouth. Cassie answered for him.

"No."

"Interesting." The woman's gaze zeroed in on her husband. "Perhaps she doesn't share your firstborn's predilection for killing children."

"Pearl died a few years ago," Cassie said. "She was only sixteen."

Jillian snapped her head to look at Cassie, her voice softer now. "That's terrible. What happened?" Then her eyes grew wide. "Was she here in Savannah? Did Douglas—"

"No—"

"What?" Jack glared at Cassie, clutching the armrests of the chair as if to launch himself out of it. "Yes, he did. He found out about her and—"

"No, he didn't." Cassie narrowed her eyes. "And I don't think you really believe he kidnapped her."

"Anastasia said—"

Jillian huffed out a laugh. "That woman tells lies like she breathes air."

Harris raised an eyebrow. It was as apt a description as she'd ever heard.

"You told Anastasia about the information Pearl had taken from your phone," Cassie said. "Not long after that, Pearl disappeared. Did you think that was a coincidence?"

"She found out about Douglas," Jack said, his voice solemn. "She wanted to meet him. I forbade it. But she had long since stopped listening to me at that point."

"Douglas didn't kill her," Cassie said. "Apex did. They made the problem disappear, just like they covered up everything Douglas did."

"I didn't know—"

"Stop lying, Jack," Jillian said, slashing her arm through the air like it was a blade ready to cut him. "There's no way you weren't informed. Apex would've made sure of it. They love holding these things over people's heads. That's how they got you to donate so much money to them, isn't it? How they used your seat in Congress to push their agenda forward. Were you too naïve to see that? Too stupid? Or did you just not care?"

Harris gave Jillian an appraising look. The woman was smart. She wasn't afraid to call it like she saw it. She may have been blindsided by the news that Jack had two children without her knowledge, but she had apparently connected the dots faster than they had.

"We have the evidence," Cassie said. "We found everything Pearl hid before she was murdered. The proof is all there, that you were aware of Douglas' actions and you knew Apex covered them up to keep your reputation clean."

"God, Jack. How could you be so stupid?" Jillian scoffed, then she stood. "I need a drink."

She crossed the room to the dry bar and pulled out a glass. She looked over her shoulder at Harris and Cassie, holding the ornate crystal tumbler out in a silent question. They both shook their heads. Jillian nodded and got to work making her cocktail.

"What do you want from me?" Jack asked.

"What you did was a terrible thing, Senator Hughes, and neither of us can guarantee you won't be punished for your crimes." Cassie held out her hand as though offering him a lifeline. "But it's clear that Anastasia Bolton and other members of Apex Publicity are the ones pulling all the strings here. I know they're planning something big. Your son becoming the next President of the United States is just one small cog in the machine they're building. I intend to dismantle that machine, and if you help me do that, I promise to advocate on your behalf to whichever authorities are brave enough to take them on."

"Nobody is that brave," Jack said, finally meeting Cassie's eyes. "Do you realize what kind of influence they have over people? I'm hardly the only senator with skeletons in his closet."

"No, but your skeletons are in the spotlight right now. You'll be their latest scapegoat, just like Richard Blackwood was. Do you really want that to happen, or do you want to get ahead of this while you can?"

"I-I—"

"For God's sake." Jillian slammed a bottle down onto the bar cart. The amber liquid sloshed around the inside. "For once in your life, Jack, grow a goddamn spine. Don't make me do something *dramatic*."

Harris glanced over at the senator's wife, expecting to see a glass full of liquor in her hand. Instead, she pointed a small silver gun directly at her husband.

31

Cassie's heart pounded at the sight of the small weapon.

Chris stared at her from beside the other woman, his lips forming words she couldn't hear.

When this was all over, she wasn't leaving her house for a month.

"Jillian," Jack croaked. "Sweetheart."

"Don't you *sweetheart* me." Jillian ground out the words through clenched teeth. "It's been a long time since your pet names meant anything to me."

"Ma'am," Harris said, her tone meant to deescalate. One hand rested near her hip as though she'd gone for her gun and remembered it wasn't there. "There's no need for this. Jack will tell us what we want to know, won't you, sir?"

"Y-Yes," Jack said. "Of course."

Jillian took several steps closer to her husband. "Yes, he will. Otherwise, he'll learn what it feels like to have a broken heart. Only his won't be because he realized the person he loves cares more about money and power than him." She waggled the gun as she pointed it at his chest, then spat out her next words. "How could you do this to me? To us? Did our marriage mean nothing to you?"

Jack's eyes were wide as he watched his wife tower over him. "Of course it did."

Jillian shook her head. "I wish I believed you."

Harris took a step toward them. "Jillian—"

"I don't want to hurt you. Either of you." Jillian's gaze flickered from Harris to Cassie, then to Bear and back to Harris again. "But this is the only way he'll talk. Proper motivation."

"Jillian," Jack said, holding his hands out in surrender, pressing back into his seat like he was trying to push right through it. "Please, listen to them. You don't have to do this."

"No, you listen to me! For once in your life, care about something —some*one*—other than yourself."

"I'm listening, Jillian." Jack's tone had gone softer. "I'm listening."

Through angry sobs, Jillian continued. "I wanted to be a doctor, do you remember? But I put that off to support *you* and *your* dreams. Once we had more money, you said I could go to school. Do whatever I wanted. But it was never quite enough. We were never *comfortable* enough. You always wanted more, more, more."

Jack cried now, too. "I'm sorry."

Jillian laughed, gesturing wildly with the gun as she glanced back at Cassie and Harris. "I think that's the first time he's ever apologized to me. Can you believe it?"

"Jillian," Harris tried again. "I'm sorry about what you've been through, but this is not the answer."

"But it is. I might not have gotten the fairytale life I was promised, but I'll be damned if his actions hurt anyone else." She stared down at her husband, disgust evident in the curl of her lip. "Tell them what you know."

"I-I don't even know where to start," he said. "I don't know how to help."

"Have you ever heard of the company Five Winds?" Cassie asked, keeping her gaze steady on the man. Maybe if she could get Jack to cooperate, if she could show Jillian they had gotten what they needed, she would lower the gun. She slipped her phone from her pocket and discreetly hit the record button. "Or the man who owns it, Zhang Wei?"

Jack startled, his eyes going wide. He glanced at his wife, then back at Cassie. When he opened his mouth, nothing came out.

"Don't even think about lying." Jillian waved the gun as if to remind everyone of its presence. "You made Ross donate money to that company. A lot of money. I never understood why when there were so many other places he could invest. Causes that were much closer to his heart."

"Zhang Wei made billions developing technology in China," Jack said, his voice quiet but steady. "When we spoke, he told me that, in many cases, China was years ahead of the United States, but in others, they were far behind. He wanted to come over here and learn from us, not for the good of one country over another, but for the good of the world. For the good of humanity."

"It was a load of bullshit," Jillian translated. "We both knew it."

Jack nodded, glancing up at her and away again. His voice was shakier this time. "There have been rumors that he had connections to the Chinese government. That he was much more politically minded than he's let on."

"What are you saying?" Harris asked. "He was spying on behalf of the Chinese government?"

"I don't know." Jack glanced up at the gun again and swallowed. "I mean, yes, probably. Again, there's no proof of this. I just know what I heard when I first met him."

"What about after?" Harris asked. "When Apex started asking you and your son to invest in his company?"

"It wasn't just Five Winds," Jillian said. "That man owns more than anyone realizes. And what he doesn't own, he's invested in. His reach extends to the United States, too."

"Jillian, please, we can't—" Jack cut off, searching for the right words. "Think of Ross. If we're not careful, he could get hurt."

"And whose fault is that?"

Jillian took a step forward, punctuating the end of her sentence with a stab of the gun.

"You knew what you were getting him into, and you still did it." Jillian's voice broke. "I love Ross as though I gave birth to him myself, but he's only ever been a tool to you. If he gets hurt, you have no one to blame but yourself." She was calmer now, but there was something brittle about her control. "Be honest for once, Jack. Maybe we can put an end to this and you can live out the rest of your miserable life in this house that never felt like a home to anyone but you."

Jack had to say the right thing here. If he didn't, would they all get caught in the crossfire?

"Apex introduced you to Zhang Wei, right?" Cassie asked. After a moment's hesitation, Jack nodded. "Do you know why? What they wanted you to do?"

"They wanted my money, mostly. Then I was tasked with introducing him to people he wanted to work with. Other politicians. People in the tech industry. It wasn't out of the ordinary. At least not at first."

"When did that shift?"

Jack ran a hand over his face. "I started noticing a pattern. He wasn't investing in the biggest companies or the ones that would make the most profit. They seemed random until I realized he was using them to gain information about the government that his contacts were not willing to volunteer."

"Like what?"

"Five Winds, for example, wants to produce solar panels and other green technology. All those products come with an app that you download on your phone, allowing you to access various information, like how much energy is stored, when you might need maintenance, that sort of thing. All of that connects to the internet, which means his company—and by extension, China itself—will be able to monitor the information coming through. They can control the data being transferred, and if they wanted to, they could even decide if the panel should be on or not."

Cassie knit her eyebrows together. "But how many people use solar panels, really? And how many would use the ones produced by Five Winds?"

"China has flooded the market in recent years. They control most of the supply chain to begin with. If it's not Five Winds, it's probably someone else who has the same connections as Zhang Wei. And we're not just talking about people out west looking to convert sunlight into power." Jack leaned forward, shaking his head. "He wants to sell to our military."

Harris shifted on her feet. "But there are restrictions in place. Certain foreign technology cannot be used in buildings occupied by the government or the military. That goes for security cameras, computer chips, probably solar panels, too."

"Which is why Apex wants politicians involved." Cassie's eye flickered to Jillian. She ignored the specter in the corner of the room. "Why they want Ross in the Oval Office. He can change some of those laws, make more exceptions to the rules."

"What else?" Jillian demanded of her husband. "It's not just Five Winds."

Jack shrugged, looking like this conversation was wearing on him.

"Everything. Smart TVs also connect to the internet, and the companies could leverage their products, whether through physical pieces of hardware or the technology for software. They can withhold those from corporations until they agree to stay silent about political issues important to China. They could stop ads from companies critical of China."

"Another way to influence politics," Harris muttered, her gaze traveling to a bare spot on the wall. "Influence campaigns."

Jack nodded. "He's also interested in the electric vehicle market, using the cars to collect details about their surroundings. They can use the sensors on subway trains and rail cars for espionage. Everything is connected these days. What's stopping China from taking over our cars and using them against us? Or selling this information to another country? The possibilities are endless."

Jillian seethed, her knuckles turning white as she gripped the gun. "And you helped make it happen."

"Apex has been around since the eighties," Jack replied, unbothered. "I'm hardly the first person they've used, and I won't be the last. What was I supposed to do?"

Cassie needed to keep Jack on track, so before Jillian could respond, she asked, "Is this information really that damaging?"

Jack looked at her like a naïve child. "China could flip a switch and power in half the country could go out. All our electric vehicles could act up. They could disrupt our supply chains."

"It'd be catastrophic," Harris said.

"That's not to mention the ramifications of artificial intelligence," Jack continued. "They could use all this information to train a program to find ways to dismantle us from the inside out. It would cause chaos, cost us billions of dollars to repair, and be enough of a distraction that maybe something much more important could slip through the cracks."

Harris' body thrummed with tension. "Like what?"

"Name it. There's plenty they could do while we're looking the other way. Plenty they could steal."

Cassie leaned forward, anticipation coursing through her body like a tidal wave. "There has to be something more specific."

"If I were you, I would look at what we have that China doesn't. Something we keep guarded by any means necessary."

Harris ran a hand over the top of her hair, smoothing down her ponytail. Seconds ticked by in relative silence. The candle on the coffee table continued to distribute its sweet swell. A cloud passed over the sun, darkening the room for a moment. Chris stood in sharp relief against the wall until the space brightened again.

"Military technology?" Harris asked. "Our air force. They've stolen aircraft technology before. Copied our designs. Our air superiority is not as great as it once was."

"And we're racing to stay ahead of them," Jack said, "but it's not easy. They'll do anything they can to get a leg up."

"And you helped them do that." Harris looked down her nose at him. "Was it worth it?"

"It's not like I set out to betray my country. I didn't know what

Apex was really after until it was too late. By then, I was in so deep, I didn't have any other choice."

"And now our son is in the same position," Jillian said. "How could you do this to him?"

Jack looked down at his shoes. "I didn't have a choice."

"You always have a choice," she replied, her voice hard. "I've endured so much because of you. I'm done."

Jack's eyes flared wide. "Jillian—"

"Relax." Jillian flicked open the chamber on the revolver, then tossed the gun down onto the chair next to her. "It was empty. You think I'm stupid enough to kill you? Please. You deserve so much worse than that."

32

Cassie hunkered down in the back of the vehicle while Harris exited the gates of Jack Hughes' estate. They drove for a few minutes before pulling over to the side of the road and parking. Cassie got out of the car and slid into the passenger seat. Neither one had spoken during the short trek, and even now, Cassie didn't know what to say. What to think. What to *do*.

"Well," Harris said, leaning back and balancing her elbow on the armrest. "Shit."

Cassie laughed, a maniacal noise escaping her mouth. "Yeah, that about sums it up."

"You think we did the right thing leaving them like that?"

"What other choice did we have? They're adults. They can figure their own shit out."

Harris rubbed a hand along her chin. "I expect one of them will file divorce papers after this."

Cassie nodded. The fury in Jillian's eyes had raged like an inferno.

"The bigger question," Harris continued, "is what to do with the information Jack gave us."

"It narrows down our search, at least. But I still don't know where to go from here."

"None of this is all that surprising. Espionage is a given. We've caught China and Russia with their hands in the cookie jar plenty of times."

"That might be changing," Cassie said. She stared out the window for a moment, watching the wind rustle the trees along the sidewalk. "Apex has a lot of pieces on the board still. Even if one falls, another can move."

"I know." Harris' shoulders slumped as she let her head fall back against the headrest. "Apex changed the game for China. Who knows what they're capable of with that kind of power?"

"I don't think we can afford to worry about that right now. We need to get our hands on hard evidence that Apex has orchestrated all this. We've got proof that Anastasia knew about Douglas and Pearl. Apex will sidestep that scandal and pin everything on her."

"Have you gone through Pearl's evidence?"

Cassie shook her head. "We couldn't access a couple encrypted folders. That's why we sent it to Lorraine and one of Omega's contacts."

Harris nodded, then her phone rang. "It's the station."

Cassie snorted. "Gonna tell them you were kidnapped?"

Harris gave her a sour look and ignored the question before bringing her phone to her ear. "This is Harris."

The car was silent as Harris listened to the other end of the line. Cassie could hear a muffled woman's voice but otherwise couldn't make out the words. Bear shifted in the backseat and Cassie scratched under his chin until he was settled again.

Amid the background noise, she let her mind drift. How the hell were they going to prove Apex was stealing military secrets from the U.S. government? How had she even ended up in this position?

Apex. They had orchestrated all of this, dragged her into a world of conspiracy theories and treason. Anger reared its ugly head inside her, darkening her thoughts with its poison. She'd never asked for any of this, but if she didn't do something about it, who would?

"*What*?" Harris's sharp tone cut through Cassie's thoughts. "Say that again?"

Harris' skin had gone pale. Her mouth was turned down into a frown. She glanced at Cassie with worry in her eyes. Cassie's heart raced.

"Thank you for letting me know." Harris paused and listened. "No, do what needs to be done. I'll check in when I can."

Cassie barely waited for Harris to hang up before she asked, "What happened?"

Harris stared down at her phone, gripping it like she contemplated throwing it out the window. When she looked up and met Cassie's eyes, they were wide with uncertainty. "Warden Wickham was found dead in his home this morning."

Shock coursed through Cassie's body. "How?"

"Bullet to the head. They're investigating for murder."

The man had his enemies, and Apex was at the top of the list. Maybe it had been a warning after the press conference. Anastasia had said Blackwood was still alive, for now. She'd been flippant about his public confession. Maybe he had something Apex wanted. Killing Wickham could've been enough to get Blackwood to fall into line.

Cassie's heart rate never slowed. Harris wouldn't be acting like her world had shattered if the only news was that Wickham was dead. Uncertainly clawed its way up Cassie's throat until she had trouble sucking in enough air to expand her lungs.

"What else?"

Harris met her eyes when she spoke. "Jason and Lorraine were arrested."

Cassie slammed her eyes shut. All she could see was the altered video Anastasia had threatened him with. But that didn't explain Lorraine's involvement. After a moment, she looked over at Harris again. "Why?"

"They were there when the police showed up. At Wickham's house." Harris shook her head, like she couldn't wrap her mind around it. "The police got an anonymous phone call about gunshots. When they arrived, Jason and Lorraine were inside. He had his gun on him." Harris looked out the window, her gaze distant. "It was logical for them to detain them."

Cassie sat up straight in her seat. "They didn't do this. Jason didn't shoot him. Lorraine would *never*—"

Harris held up her hand. "I know. But you can see what it looks like. They both have motive for revenge."

"We have to go back to Savannah," Cassie said. "We have to help them."

Harris grimaced as she looked away again. "I'm not sure that's a good idea."

Cassie leaned forward, trying to meet Harris' gaze again. Bear sat up in the back of the vehicle, all his focus on the tension radiating from the front seats. "Why not?"

"I think you were right," Harris said, finally looking back over, "and this has Apex written all over it. They're either sending a message or trimming loose ends. Maybe both. If Jason and Lorraine are in a cell down at the station, they're safe."

Cassie bit her tongue. Every fiber of her being was fighting for Harris to put the car in drive and floor it all the way back to Georgia. Jason and Lorraine being locked away for a crime they never would've committed sat like a rock in her stomach. And all the while they thought Cassie was dead and Harris didn't care enough to visit.

She forced logic to the forefront of her mind. Because Harris was right—they would be safer there, especially as Cassie made her final moves. Apex would retaliate, and the fewer targets on the field, the better.

After several moments, Cassie asked, "Can you do me a favor?"

Harris met her eyes again. "Of course."

"Can you get in touch with my sister and my parents? Tell them —" Cassie broke off, knowing the less they knew, the safer they were. "Tell them to get out of town for a while. That something connected to me and my death is going down and they might be in danger."

Harris nodded. "Laura hasn't been answering my calls for a while." She gave Cassie a small smile. "She blames me for letting you go off on your own. But your parents will pick up if I call. They'll believe me. They'll relay the message."

Cassie swallowed down the pain that bloomed in her chest. "Thank you."

Harris laid a hand on Cassie's arm. "We'll figure this out. Even if it's just the two of us against the world, we'll make sure Apex doesn't get away with this."

Cassie was grateful her phone pinged at that moment so she had an excuse to look away from Harris and discreetly wipe her eyes before looking at the screen of the burner. Her heart stilled while she read the message before it ratcheted up again. When her gaze settled back on Harris, she could feel hope pushing away the despair she'd felt just moments ago.

"Looks like we'll be heading back to Savannah anyway," Cassie said.

Harris pinched her eyebrows together, peering down at Cassie's phone. "Why?"

"Blackwood wants to meet." She didn't bother hiding her hope. "He found what he was looking for."

33

Jason didn't bother keeping the scowl from his face as an officer led him and Lorraine down the hall and toward the front doors of the station. They'd been forced to spend the night in a jail cell, and judging by the bags under Lorraine's eyes, he hadn't been the only one who'd gone without much sleep. The cot he'd been forced to lie on was stiff and lumpy, but that's not what had kept him from unconsciousness.

By all accounts, what had happened yesterday did not look good. But his gun was legal and registered, and they'd inspected it as soon as they'd reached the station and determined it had not been fired recently.

But what had really bothered Jason was the fact that these people knew him. He'd worked with the Savannah PD as a private investigator. Most of them knew he'd been involved with Cassie. If they hadn't known before her disappearance, then they'd found out after. He'd been in Harris' office more over the last few months than ever before.

And yet they still suspected him?

Jason met the eye of every officer who passed. Some averted their gaze as soon as they noticed him, but others openly sneered, as though there were any chance in hell he and Lorraine were responsible for the Warden's death.

Lorraine looked over her shoulder at him, wary as though she could feel the rage radiating off him in waves. He nodded once in a curt gesture that told her he wasn't okay, but that he would keep his shit together. She turned back around and continued to follow the officer who led them away from where they'd been held for the night.

How could she be so calm?

After spending the night in a jail cell, all the hope that had flooded his system following his meeting with Annette Campbell had washed away.

It felt like everything was crumbling down around him again.

As much as he didn't want to admit it, he'd let his anger get the better of him lately. They'd seen that every time he'd stormed through the front doors of the station and had it out with Harris. Usually, that was behind a closed door, but not always.

Did they think he'd finally gone off the deep end?

Jason's blood cooled as he saw the situation through their eyes. It hurt, but they were doing their job. It was worse that Harris hadn't even bothered to visit them. Every time he heard footsteps during the course of the night, he thought she'd emerge from the shadows with a worried expression on her face.

Did she know what had happened? Did she even care?

They reached the front of the station, and he and Lorraine collected their things. The officer who'd led them there—an older man with a bushy moustache—gave them a once-over, as though checking to make sure they hadn't pickpocketed a stapler.

"We'll have follow-up questions," he said. "Don't go anywhere."

"Of course," Lorraine said, playing with the hem of her shirt. "We understand."

She looked at Jason, as though encouraging him to play nice. He resisted rolling his eyes but couldn't keep the bite out of his voice. "Wouldn't dream of it."

The officer narrowed his gaze. "You got something you want to say, son?"

"He doesn't," Lorraine said, tugging on Jason's arm.

"Is my car in the parking lot?" Jason asked. "How are we supposed to get home?"

"You've got someone out there waiting to pick you up. We're still inspecting your car."

"When can I have it back?"

"When we're done."

"Which will be when?"

"When we're done."

"Thanks for the clarification."

"You're welcome," the officer said, and gestured for them to go out through the front doors.

"Thank you," Lorraine said, pulling on Jason's arm a lot harder now. "Have a nice day."

Jason looked down at her but allowed her to pull him through the front doors of the station. "You always this nice to people who accuse you of murder?"

"Are you always this rude to police officers?"

"Usually."

Lorraine looked around the parking lot. "I wonder who's picking us up?"

"I don't know," he said, casting his eyes around the full lot, too. He didn't recognize any of the cars. "If it's Harris, I think I'd rather walk."

"She's the last person you should be pissing off," Lorraine said. A horn beeped from the far side of the lot, where a white SUV idled. "That for us?"

The sun glinted off the windshield, and Jason couldn't see whoever was inside. They honked again, this time flashing their lights. "I guess so. Come on."

The sun was hot on the back of Jason's neck, but Lorraine wrapped her arms around herself like she was cold. Another car pulled into the parking lot and drove past them, circling to find an open spot. Kids shouted from somewhere nearby, but Jason didn't bother locating them.

"What are we going to do?" she asked. "The Warden is dead. He was murdered. That can't be a coincidence."

"It's not." If he was sure of anything, it was that. "The bigger question is whether anyone knew we were heading there yesterday morning. If they set this up for us, or if it was a complete coincidence."

"When it comes to Apex, I don't think they deal in coincidences."

"Neither do I," Jason said. He squinted against the sun, trying to figure out if he recognized the car. "You see who it is yet?"

Lorraine was squinting, too. "No."

The door to the SUV swung open and a woman stepped out, her face still hidden from view. She wasn't dressed like Harris, but maybe it was a friend? Jason wracked his brain, wondering who would have known where they were and had been willing to come get them.

Lorraine gasped. The woman still had the haughty look he was accustomed to, but she was looking a little worse for wear. Her eyeliner had been smudged and lipstick wiped clean from her face. The edges of her mouth were stained dark red, giving her the look of a vampire.

Not far from the truth, really.

"Anastasia," he gritted out between clenched teeth.

"Mr. Broussard," she said, her trademark tone as clipped as ever. "And Miss Krasinski. It's good to see you both."

Jason crossed his arms, his tense muscles bulging. "Is it?"

"It is. We have a lot to discuss."

"Unless you're here to tell me exactly what you did with Cassie, then we have nothing to discuss."

Anastasia's eyes brightened and her lips twitched up into an almost-smile. Then her gaze slid over to Lorraine. "I heard about what happened to the Warden."

"We had nothing to do with that," Lorraine said.

"I know," Anastasia said, shaking a strand of hair out of her face. "You might not believe this, but neither did I."

"You're right," Jason bit out. "I don't believe it."

"I was a little preoccupied." Anastasia took a small step to the side. Some of her body was still hidden behind the door of her SUV, as though worried that if she drifted too far from it, they might take advantage of her exposure. "Had a little run-in with Omega and some of his friends."

"Omega?" Jason asked, his gaze dropping to Anastasia's side where blood had soaked into her clothes.

"We had a disagreement." Anastasia shifted again, wincing from pain. "I got lucky."

"If you're expecting sympathy from either of us, you'll be waiting a long time."

"Not sympathy." Anastasia paused, as though searching for the right word. "Understanding."

"We want nothing to do with you or Apex. Cassie made that very clear, both before and after you dragged her to Nashville. Nothing's changed now that she's not here."

Anastasia's smile was wide and wicked. Her tone dripped with condescension. "Oh, Jason. Everything's changed. And it's about time you figured that out."

Lorraine looked over her shoulder at the station behind them, then back at the woman beside the vehicle.

She spoke slowly, like she'd put everything together as the words spilled from her mouth. "Adelaide would have been here. She should've been here. Where is she?"

Anastasia lifted and dropped one of her shoulders. "I don't know."

Something in her voice made Jason's hackles rise. "But you've seen her, haven't you? Recently?"

"Yes." Anastasia stared them down, neither apologetic nor guilty. "As capable as she is, she's been too distracted. Never saw it coming. I'd been hoping for more of a challenge, honestly."

Jason stepped forward. "If you've done anything to her—"

"Nothing she won't recover from." Anastasia waved away his words. "Besides, I've decided to pivot."

Jason seethed, anger consuming any sentences forming in his throat.

Lorraine asked the obvious question. "Pivot?"

"Loyalty only goes so far, I suppose."

For the first time, Anastasia spoke with true emotion. Jason recognized the bitter taste of anger all too well.

"Apex and I are no longer aligned in our goals. So, here I am." It looked like the next words caused her physical pain. "Asking for your help."

Jason stared at the woman. Then tipped his head back and laughed. It was long and loud, and despite the tension gathered around the three of them, it loosened some of his muscles. "You've got to be kidding."

"I'm not."

Jason shook his head, his smile still in place when he said. "No."

"Trust me—"

"Trust you? What have you done for us to trust you? There's no way in hell we're helping you."

"I thought you'd say that." Anastasia shifted, but this time it was to reveal the gun she'd had in her hand the whole time, hidden behind the door to her SUV.

Jason shook his head. "You're an idiot. Even if you killed us both right here, there are so many cameras around the police station, you'd never get away with it."

"You underestimate my abilities, Mr. Broussard. Even without Apex's considerable resources, I can get away with more in an hour than you could in an entire lifetime. But that's irrelevant." She loosened her grip on the gun until it hung limply from just a few fingers. "Because it turns out, I don't need this."

Jason took three large steps forward, narrowing the distance between him and Anastasia. Closing his hand around her throat, he pushed her back until she slammed against the side of her vehicle, eliciting a grunt of pain and knocking the gun from her hand. Lorraine scrambled forward and picked it up.

He tightened his fingers around the woman's neck until Anastasia let out a whimper.

"I've waited a long time to watch Apex fall. I'd hoped it would start with you. Guess it's my lucky day."

"It is," Anastasia gasped, trying to maintain composure even as Jason restricted the oxygen to her brain. This close to her face, he could see just how exhausted she was. "Just not in the way you think."

"I don't want any more of your bullshit."

"Not bullshit," she choked out. "We both know I'm a self-serving bitch, which is the only reason why I let down my guard long enough for you to get this close. I have something you want."

"You said you didn't know where Harris was," Lorraine said, still holding the gun.

Jason's mind had moved beyond Harris, but he couldn't begin to hope—

"I know where she's going," Anastasia said, struggling against Jason's grip. "And I know who she's with."

"Say it."

"Cassie. She's with Cassie."

34

Cassie didn't sleep much on the way back to Savannah, her mind spinning. Amidst the turmoil, she clung to Blackwood's message like a lifeline.

Would Omega be there? The message hadn't come through in a group text. Blackwood trusted her more than Omega, but she had conflicted feelings. Especially after their run-in with Anastasia.

Amid Cassie's fits of restless sleep, Harris kept driving, her determination never wavering as they returned to Georgia. The two of them remained quiet on the way back, listening to the soft music playing from the car's speakers.

The sun peeked out from the horizon by the time they made it back to Savannah. Harris stopped long enough to get her backup weapon and a change of clothes for each of them from her house. Then she grabbed them both a coffee with extra shots of espresso on the way out of her neighborhood.

Blackwood had requested they meet at an abandoned office building. Somewhere they could meet in private with no interruptions. Harris knew the place and said it'd been derelict for years. Was this one of Blackwood's clandestine meeting places? How often did he do business there?

With half their coffees gone, Harris pulled around the back of the building and shifted the car into park. The structure looked to be a relic from the '50s but still sound as far as Cassie's amateur eyes could tell. It was only two stories, but still spacious. Not the type of place Mayor Blackwood would be caught having meetings with anyone of importance.

Neither of them moved to climb out of the car. Harris broke the silence first.

"Are we sure we trust him?"

"I don't trust him to help us out of the goodness of his own heart," Cassie said, "but I do trust him to do what's best for him. Taking down Apex means he can get some semblance of his life back. He's already tried begging for forgiveness, and that didn't work. Calling them out like he did over the Jack Hughes situation put a target on his back. He needs us as much as we need him."

Harris pushed open her door. "Let's hope that's true."

Cassie followed suit, then opened the back door to let Bear out. He sniffed the air for a moment, then brought his head down to the gravel underfoot, snuffling against the dirt and stone until his nose turned gray. When he wandered off to do his business in a patch of grass, Cassie turned her attention back to the building in front of her.

It was utterly ordinary, but the abandoned quality made it look haunted in a way that had nothing to do with spirits, though at least one was likely to show up once she entered the premises. Something told her that Blackwood had made deals with several devils in his time, and most of those conversations had probably happened within these walls.

When Bear returned to her side, pressing against her leg in reassurance, she followed Harris up a handful of concrete steps and through the door. As soon as Cassie crossed the threshold, the smell of mold and mildew assaulted her nose. The stale air wrapped its stubby fingers around her throat and squeezed. She choked on the sensation, bringing a hand to her mouth to stifle the sound.

"Jesus," Harris cursed.

Bear sneezed twice and shook his head, his collar rattling. When he pressed closer to her, she buried her fingers in the thick fur along the back of his neck.

"Can't see a damn thing," Harris said, feeling along the wall. She flipped a switch, and nothing happened.

Cassie didn't need her abilities to know what Harris would say next. "No power. Awesome." She pulled a small, high-powered flashlight from her pocket and clicked it on. It illuminated the whole space in front of them.

"Guess you're leading the way."

"If you're scared, all you had to do was say so."

Cassie scoffed, but Harris' words hit home. This was a make-or-break moment. Her intuition swirled in her gut, but she had no idea what it wanted to tell her.

Harris pulled her gun from her holster and held it in front of her, resting it on top of the hand holding the flashlight. Moving forward, Harris opened the first door on their right, entering an abandoned waiting room. Dusty coffee tables and dingy armchairs filled the space, as did several dead potted plants. Another door on the opposite side of the room led to a pair of secretary desks and a long hallway. Blackwood had told them this would take them to a back meeting room where he'd be waiting.

"Think this used to be a dentist's office," Harris muttered.

Cassie focused on the door directly in front of them. An invisible tug pulled her forward at the same time it told her to stay back. Bear pressed more firmly against her legs, letting out a quiet whine before his mouth opened and he started panting.

"He okay?" Harris asked, reaching the door but stopping short of opening it.

"If you think it smells bad in here, imagine what he's going through."

"He deserves a steak dinner when we get home."

Cassie patted Bear's head. "It's the least we can do."

Checking the window set in the door first, Harris twisted the knob and stepped through, clearing the room from left to right. But other than some sizeable dust bunnies and mice droppings, there was nothing much to be concerned with.

Both Cassie and Bear stayed close as they made their way down the hall. Harris tried the handle on every door they passed, but all of them were locked. Cassie didn't like not knowing what was on the other side of each one, and if the tenseness of Harris' shoulders meant anything, she felt the same way.

Coming to the end of the hall, Harris looked over her shoulder long enough to catch Cassie's gaze. The light from the flashlight was enough to see the question in the former detective's eyes. With a nod, Cassie confirmed she was ready to get this over with. They were so close she could almost taste it—if it weren't for the bile rising in her throat from the stagnant air around them.

Nodding back, Harris pulled open the door and swept her gaze and her gun in an arc around the room. Going up on her tiptoes, Cassie peered over Harris' shoulder to get a better look at the conference room ahead of them. Dim light filtered through dusty windows to illuminate the space. This room was more modern than the rest of the building, like it had been recently renovated.

Even still, dust coated every surface. Several long tables had been placed together until they formed the shape of a rectangle with the center left open. Office chairs lined the outside, cheap but not moth-eaten like the others. Cassie imagined Blackwood standing in the open center, reveling in the attention when all eyes were on him.

The man in question sat at the far end of the table in the only chair with a high back. The only other door in the room was behind him and to the left. Clutched in one hand was a glass of amber liquid filled three-quarters of the way to the top. He stroked his finger along the rim as though the glass were made of diamond.

"Not to be rude," Harris said, continuing her scan of the room even as she made her way toward him. "But I think you're in desperate need of a maid service."

Cassie finally met Blackwood's gaze, surprised to see the usual arrogance gone. His eyes narrowed at Harris, then Cassie, and finally searched behind her as though waiting for someone else to walk into the room.

"Assistant Chief of Police Adelaide Harris," Blackwood said by way of greeting. He lifted the glass of amber liquid to his mouth and took a long sip. "I'd say it's good to see you again, but that's not a lie worth telling."

Harris lowered her gun a fraction. "And here I thought lying was as easy as breathing for you. Maybe all the mold in the air is making it difficult."

Blackwood sneered, but his gaze shifted to Cassie. "You came."

"You said you had information for us." Cassie felt like there was a football field's worth of space between the two of them and the former mayor. She resisted the urge to cup her hands around her mouth and shout to make sure she was heard. "We're here."

"But Omega isn't. Why not?"

Cassie exchanged a glance with Harris. Telling Blackwood about their confrontation with Omega and Anastasia felt like showing their hand, but Cassie didn't want to ruin the tentative alliance they'd built with Blackwood by lying. "We got separated. I assumed you texted him too."

Blackwood's frown deepened. He took another sip of his drink. His gaze flickered to Bear, then to Harris. "I expected you to bring one bitch. Not two. This isn't what we agreed on."

Harris didn't bat an eye. "Bear is a male dog, *Dick*."

"You'll get the protection Omega promised," Cassie said, "as long as you deliver on your half. Do you have the information we need?"

Blackwood looked like he wanted to argue. Instead, he reached down next to him and produced a stack of papers, slapping them down on the table. "It's all here. Come check it out."

When both Cassie and Harris moved to cross the room, he held up his free hand. "My deal is with Cassie, not you, Assistant Chief. And put your gun away. I don't relish being made to feel like a hostage."

Harris didn't move. "Not going to happen."

"It's fine," Cassie said. "He's not going to do anything to me, not when he needs our protection. Besides, I have Bear."

"He could be armed," Harris argued.

"I'm not armed." Blackwood stood and turned on the spot, patting his pockets with his free hand. "My leverage comes in the form of information. Not scare tactics."

Cassie locked eyes with Harris. "Let's just get this over with. Once we confirm he has what we need, we'll contact Omega."

Harris scanned the room once more before she put her gun back in her holster, leaving the clasp open. Standing there with her hands on her hips—close enough to her gun that she could draw it quickly if needed—she nodded for Cassie to proceed.

Cassie nodded back, then made her way to the other end of the room.

Chris materialized against the wall behind Blackwood, a pale imitation of the man he'd once been. She'd never get used to the bloody mess of his chest or the vacancy in his eyes. His mouth moved, screaming at her. But she still couldn't understand.

Pulling her gaze from Chris, she kept walking. Once she passed the halfway mark, Cassie couldn't keep her eyes from the papers on the table. Next to her, Bear came to a halt, using his body to block her way forward. She looked down at him, but his gaze was trained on Blackwood. Or was it on the door just beyond him?

"Cassie?" Harris called.

"Shit," Blackwood said, setting his tumbler down. "I knew I should've told you to keep the mutt in the car."

The door behind him opened to a staircase. A figure stepped through, the pencil skirt and silk blouse surely belonging to Anastasia Bolton. But the blonde hair and porcelain skin did not.

Harris drew her weapon, and it was only then that Cassie noticed the newcomer had her own handgun raised, pointing straight at her. Bear released a growl low in his chest, and the woman lifted an eyebrow in amusement.

But then Bear's head whipped around, looking back at Harris and in the direction from which they'd entered the room. A moment later, the door swung open and two men dressed in black entered, their own guns raised and ready.

"Where are my manners?" Blackwood said, pausing to take a long sip of his drink. He smacked his lips in delight before he continued. "Please allow me to introduce my new representation, Apex's very own Sienna Vogel."

35

Cassie froze, not wanting to admit what she'd feared all along had come true. But there was no denying it. Blackwood had betrayed them and gone crawling back to Apex.

"Never heard of you," Harris said. She glanced at the men behind her but remained unfazed. "But you look like Anastasia. Which tells me all I need to know. You're just one of her lap dogs."

Anger flashed in the other woman's eyes and she bared her teeth at them like a feral animal. "I am no one's lap dog, least of all hers. She had plenty of chances to do what needed to be done and failed at every turn. I won't make the same mistakes she did."

"You already have," Harris said. "Underestimating us has never gone well for Apex."

Sienna laughed, a pretty sound despite the fire in her eyes. "Look around. You're outnumbered. I think you should put your weapon down and be grateful I haven't killed you yet."

"Not gonna happen."

"Adelaide," Cassie said, her voice shaking. She'd just gotten her friend back. She couldn't lose her again. "Please. We'll figure something out."

Harris gritted her teeth, but she turned her head just enough to eye the two men standing behind her, one gun pointed at her and the other pointed at Cassie. There was no way they'd both make it out unscathed if she remained stubborn.

Cassie watched as Harris held her hands up in surrender, then bent down and placed the gun on the floor. As she straightened, she kicked it away from her until it slid across the carpet and thudded against the wall. It was halfway between her and Cassie now, but too far for either of them to go for it before one of the others got off a shot.

Turning her gaze back to Blackwood, Cassie couldn't keep the hurt out of her voice. "How could you do this? Omega would've done everything in his power to protect you. Apex doesn't care whether you live or die." She shook her head in disgust. "How can you trust anything they've promised you?"

Blackwood shrugged, looking unaffected by her pleading tone. "When I couldn't find the information I was looking for, I had to go in another direction." He gave her a sad smile like she was a promising candidate he'd decided not to hire. "Besides, Sienna here was quite convincing."

"About that," Sienna said. There was no sad smile on her face as Blackwood looked up at her. "You failed to deliver Omega like you said you would."

Blackwood's body went rigid, and Cassie saw panic flare across his face. "There's still time. He'll come for Cassie, I'm sure of it."

"Oh, I'm sure of it too," Sienna said. "She's a much better hostage than you are. Which means we're no longer in need of your services."

Sienna shifted her gun from Cassie's head to Blackwood's and pulled the trigger. A loud *bang* erupted and his body slumped over the table, the glass tumbler falling from his fingertips as blood poured out of the hole in his head.

"Now, where were we?"

Cassie let out a strangled cry at the same time Harris cursed. Bear's growls grew louder. He pressed against Cassie's legs, forcing her back a step. That was the wrong move. Sienna lifted her gun back to Cassie.

"I wouldn't do that if I were you."

More than anyone, Cassie was familiar with death. The way a body went limp. How it grew cold and felt empty. She knew a person's spirit could either move on or stay behind. Chris had chosen to remain, but it had taken some time before he'd appeared that first time. Would Blackwood be the same, or would he pass into whatever afterlife he'd earned while he was still alive?

The image of her trailing spirits like they were nothing more than a line of macabre ducklings made a bubble of hysterical laughter rise in her throat, but she tamped it down with whatever willpower she had left. Now was not the time to lose her shit.

"Cassie, Cassie, Cassie." Sienna's voice was chiding, almost playful, and it cut through the grief of having one more person's death on her conscience. "You should've just fallen in line like Agent Viotto. You would've proven even more useful."

"Chris never *fell in line*," Cassie said, anger flaring white-hot in her chest. "He never worked for you. Not really."

Sienna tipped her head back and laughed. It was a bright, cheerful sound. "Are you sure about that?" She nodded toward Blackwood. "Perhaps his friend in the NSA would beg to differ."

Cassie's head spun at the same time her stomach churned. She didn't want to acknowledge the woman's words. The thought of Sienna's implication made bile rise in Cassie's throat until it burned at the back of her mouth. She swallowed, but it didn't go away.

"Oh," Sienna said, bringing a hand to her mouth in mock shock. The gun in her other hand never wavered. "Did he not tell you? What, you thought we just needed him for his credentials? Did it never occur to you that we'd force him to prove his loyalty? God, you're even more naïve than I thought."

"You're lying. He would never do that."

But when she looked to the faded specter of her friend, his gaze was steady and his mouth was clamped shut.

"Believe me or not, I don't really care." Sienna shrugged, dropping the falsities. "But Blackwood was never going to get his hands on that information. Agent Viotto destroyed it, like a good little *lap dog*. The question is whether you'll be a more obedient one than he was."

"Never," Cassie seethed.

"We'll see about that." Sienna glanced around the room with a calculating stare that could only mean the cogs of her mind were turning. "You have something I want. I'll get it one way or another, Cassie. The question is whether I shoot your friend or your dog first. Decisions, decisions."

The squeak of a hinge preceded two quick bangs. Cassie whirled as Sienna's two men crumpled to the floor, both dead. Harris dove toward Cassie, hitting the wall in her panic to get down to the floor. Bear pushed against the back of Cassie's legs, forcing her down onto the carpet too.

But not before she saw the newcomer's sleek hair cascading over one shoulder and her crimson-tipped nails wrapping around the butt of her gun.

"Are you insane?" Sienna screeched.

Cassie rose up on her haunches just enough to catch a glimpse of the two women facing off against each other before Harris dragged her back down.

"Hello, Sienna," Anastasia said, her voice like a dagger wrapped in silk. "Fancy meeting you here."

"You just killed two of our men."

"Now they're *our* men?"

Sienna scoffed. "You think bringing them Cassie will make them forgive the mess you've made?"

Anastasia's voice remained steady. "I know better than that."

"Then what's your play here, Anastasia? You're out of moves."

"That's where you're wrong. And why you were never going to climb the ranks higher than me, Sienna." There was a pause, then she said, "I'm here to make a deal."

"You have nothing I want," Sienna said.

Her sentence was punctuated by the sound of a gunshot.

For a brief second, no one moved. No one breathed.

Then a body crumpled to the floor.

"Funny," Anastasia said. "I was about to say the same to you."

36

ANASTASIA ALLOWED HERSELF A FULL FIVE SECONDS TO REVEL IN THE fact that Sienna Vogel was dead. And Anastasia had been the one to pull the trigger. It was a bittersweet moment—she would've preferred a slower death for that bitch—but one she wouldn't linger on.

Not when Adelaide Harris was standing two feet away, her gun pointed at Anastasia's head.

"Drop it," Harris snarled.

Anastasia didn't move an inch. "You have no idea how long I've wanted to do that."

"*Drop the gun*," Harris repeated, tightening her grip on her own weapon.

"I'd rather not," Anastasia said. "I have no interest in killing either one of you, but something tells me that doesn't go both ways."

"You've already tried killing me once," Cassie said, clawing to her feet.

"So you'll excuse us if we don't take you at your word," Harris finished.

Anastasia shrugged, careful to keep the movement slow. "Things changed."

When Harris didn't move to lower her weapon, Anastasia bit her tongue to tamp down on her impatience. It felt like a horde of ants crawled across her skin. She itched to do *something*. They needed to get out of this building and keep moving forward.

Besides, she didn't need her gun to get what she wanted from them.

"Fine," Anastasia said, letting the gun slip from her hand until it dangled from her finger by the trigger guard. "Have it your way."

Harris leaned forward and snatched the gun from Anastasia's hand. Without looking away, she passed it back to Cassie, who inspected it and then held it at the ready. She wasn't a natural. Anastasia didn't need to ask to know she'd never killed. But Cassie was competent enough. She'd make a formidable opponent.

But it wouldn't come to that.

"I'm not your enemy," Anastasia said, holding her hands up.

Harris snorted. "Since when?"

"Since yesterday, actually."

"Great argument. Real convincing."

Anastasia turned to face Harris, looking down the barrel of the gun pointed at her head.

"Apex and I are not seeing eye to eye at the moment." She didn't want to admit this next part, but it was the only way these two would listen to her. "They're not happy with my recent performance. I've made too many mistakes. It's unacceptable."

"So, what, you got a poor quarterly review, and all of a sudden you're switching sides?"

Anastasia couldn't decide if she wanted to grin or grit her teeth. Harris had always been snappy with her retorts, and in a different life she would've made a hell of an Apex employee. But this was the circumstance they'd been given, and there was no changing that now.

"Sienna over there called me to gloat, telling me Apex was going to have me transferred. I've been around long enough to know what that really means." She leveled a look at the two women. "Besides, I'm not switching sides. There's only ever been one side for me—my own. Apex no longer serves that purpose, and so here I am."

"And what?" Cassie asked. "We're just supposed to believe you? Blackwood made a similar argument and look where he ended up."

"Blackwood was an idiot to come to you empty-handed. I've made moves to ensure you can't refuse what I have to offer."

Harris' face drained of color. It sent a thrill of excitement through Anastasia whenever she could throw someone off-balance with a few well-placed words. As stalwart as Harris had always been, she was still human.

But it was Cassie who took a step closer. "What have you done?"

"Nothing. Yet."

Harris stepped closer, too. She was near enough now that if Anastasia was quick, she'd be able to disarm the other woman and use her as leverage against Cassie, who would still hesitate to pull the trigger. And that was all Anastasia would need to get the upper hand.

But that was the old Anastasia. She couldn't be that person anymore. Not if she wanted to gain Cassie and Harris' trust and take down Apex.

"Spit it out," Harris demanded.

Anastasia sighed. They had no flair for the dramatic.

"If you must know, I had a little run-in with Jason and Lorraine yesterday." She put her hands up and hurried on before either of them could do something rash. "They're both in perfect health. I haven't touched a hair on their heads."

"Prove it," Cassie demanded.

The dog by Cassie's side let out a rumbling growl as though he could understand the conversation they were having. Or maybe he could just taste the tension in the air. Her arm throbbed as she remembered he'd already gotten a taste of *her*.

"I swear to God, Anastasia, if you've hurt either of them—"

"I have no interest in doing that unless you try to double-cross me."

Harris looked like she was doing a better job of keeping her shit together, albeit marginally. "What do you want?"

"I'm so glad you asked." Anastasia clasped her hands in front of her in an attempt to look at ease and not like she'd just crossed the point of no return. "I know you have Pearl's journals and whatever information she took from Jack's phone, which means you have proof that I helped cover up the Ash Wednesday murders. I'm guessing you went to Blackwood because you knew that wouldn't be enough to take down Apex as a whole. They'd throw me under the bus and then bide their time before they made their next move."

"Your point?" Harris ground out.

"My *point* is that I'm nobody's scapegoat. I want full amnesty, and in exchange I'll give you my full cooperation. I know more about what Apex has done and what they're willing to do than you could possibly imagine. As much as you see me as your enemy, I make for a better ally. Trust me."

Cassie scoffed. "And you thought kidnapping Jason and Lorraine was the way to get us to trust you?"

"I didn't kidnap them," Anastasia replied. "They came willingly once I told them where Harris was. Rather, *who* she was with."

Cassie blanched, her mouth opening on a little gasp. "You told them I was alive?" She looked around the room like they'd step out of the shadows at any second. "Where are they?"

"Safe. At least until I can guarantee you'll keep your word."

"We're not the ones with the shaky track record," Harris said.

Anastasia shrugged. She wasn't wrong. "If you kill me, you'll never find them. Consider that my insurance policy. But I didn't come empty-handed. I'll give you something else you've been wanting to know for quite some time."

"What's that?" Cassie asked, though she sounded like it pained her to do so.

The evidence Cassie had was much more damaging than this piece of information, but it was still important to the other woman. What Anastasia was offering equated to a sentimental olive branch.

"The location of Pearl Everly's body. She's buried beneath the newest cabin at Camp Fortuna."

Cassie sucked in a breath. "She was there all along?"

Anastasia had half-expected Cassie to stumble upon Pearl's spirit when she'd gone to Camp Fortuna while investigating Henry Holliday's disappearance. That was a risk worth taking at the time, and here she was, now giving away the information for free.

Anastasia nodded. "Henry's murder threatened to uncover more than what Joy Abbott got up to in her spare time. We needed you to take care of that case quickly without finding out what other skeletons lay hidden in that particular closet."

Somehow, Cassie paled even further. If any more blood drained from her face, she'd start swaying on the spot. "Do the Abbotts know? The Pastor—"

"No." Anastasia huffed out an annoyed breath. "Pastor Abbott is a good man. If he had any idea, he would've ruined the whole scheme."

"Did you kill her?" Harris asked.

"No," Anastasia replied, "but I killed the man who did, if that's any consolation."

"It's not."

"That's too bad."

"Okay," Cassie said, her eyes distant as though she could see her options hanging in the air before her. "Then what do we do now? Something tells me you already have a plan."

"It's simple, really." Goosebumps erupted along Anastasia's arms as she edged closer to putting her plan into action. "You'll contact Omega and tell him you want to meet. Don't tell him I'm with you or he won't agree to it."

"He's going to be pissed off when you show up anyway," Harris said. "He might shoot first and ask questions later."

"He won't. He'll be too intrigued about the prospect of me becoming a turncoat. I assume he's still with Ross?"

"As far as we know," Cassie said.

Anastasia nodded. She'd thought as much. "The two of them show up and we pool our resources. Once I'm convinced we have enough to take down Apex and that I'll have full immunity, we'll make our next move."

"Which is?" Harris asked.

"One step at a time, Adelaide." Anastasia turned the other

woman's name into a purr, just to see how the familiarity hardened Harris' gaze. "Let's not get ahead of ourselves here."

A buzz from Cassie's pocket kept Harris from making a retort. When she pulled her phone out and read the message she'd received, Cassie broke out into a grin.

"Looks like Omega had the same thought," she said.

Harris scowled at the mention of the man, but she never took her eyes off Anastasia. "What'd he say?"

"He wants to meet." Cassie sucked in a deep breath. "He said he's found what we've been looking for."

37

It'd only been a few months since Cassie had last been to Camp Fortuna, but it felt like a lifetime ago. It was no wonder, given everything that had happened since she'd last been here, but the shiver that ran down her spine had little to do with that.

Camp Fortuna felt like a ghost town.

The wrought iron gate had been left open, the security booth vacant. Cassie had driven so Harris could keep her gun on Anastasia from the backseat. Bear occupied the other seat in the rear, body taut with the tension swirling around the interior of the vehicle. His eyes remained on Anastasia, too.

The enemy-turned-ally in the passenger seat was the least of Cassie's worries as she slowed the car to a crawl.

It was late afternoon now, the sun bright overhead, but you never would've known it by the shade the trees cast over the long driveway. The path was rough and overgrown, branches scraping along the sides of the car and weeds brushing the undercarriage.

After Joy Abbott had been arrested for her role in Douglas Hughes' sick machinations, her parents stepped down from their roles at the camp. A pair of trusted associates had kept it open in an attempt to take care of the troubled teens who had nowhere else to go, but according to Harris, that hadn't lasted long. It was Pastor Abbott who had put his time and effort into making this place shine, and without him, it'd fallen apart.

Someone had bought the land but hadn't made any moves to reopen the camp. Most of the kids had been placed in alternative living situations, but a few had run away. Cassie had asked after Madison, the young girl who'd been friends with Henry and had nearly died at Joy's hands, but Harris didn't know where she'd ended up. It shattered Cassie's heart to think Madison had to start over somewhere new without her closest friend by her side.

"Remind me again why Omega wanted to meet here," Harris said. Next to her, Bear's ears pointed forward and his nose worked overtime as he took in the new scenery. "And why we agreed to it after he threatened to shoot me?"

Cassie glanced at Anastasia, but the woman just shrugged.

"Don't look at me," she said. "He's your friend."

Friend put a little too much emphasis on the relationship they'd cultivated over the last few months.

But if he'd really found everything they'd been looking for...

"If Pearl's body is here," Cassie said, "maybe there's something else we missed. Something we can use against Apex. We're not going in blind. And he has no idea Anastasia is with us, so we'll have numbers on our side. We won't be caught off-guard again."

Silence invaded the car as they emerged from the tree-lined driveway. Cassie wasn't surprised to see the parking lot empty except for a single car. She recognized it, even before she noticed the back window that had been smashed out and was now replaced with plastic and duct tape.

"That's Omega's. Doesn't look like anyone else is here."

"I don't trust it," Harris said.

"What choice do we have?" Cassie asked, stopping a few spots away from the other vehicle and shifting the car into park.

"I don't suppose you'd give me my gun back?" Anastasia asked.

Cassie shot her a look that she hoped conveyed everything she felt about that particular idea.

Anastasia held up her hands. "Had to ask."

"Let's get this over with," Harris said, throwing her door open.

In unison, they stepped out of the car, heads on a swivel as they crossed the parking lot. Weeds had sprouted up wherever they could find purchase, the grass overgrown. When she was last here, Camp Fortuna had looked neat and tidy. Idyllic.

Now, it looked wild and forgotten.

Cassie kept Bear off his leash but close. She also kept a grip on Anastasia's gun as she led the way down the path toward the Abbotts' abandoned house. The weapon's weight was a constant reminder of what she was capable of if she chose to point it at someone's chest. She had no reason to believe Omega wanted to hurt her, not if he had evidence of his own, but he always had a trick up his sleeve.

Other than the tall grass rustling in the leaves and the sweet chirps of the birds overhead, Camp Fortuna remained silent. Cassie couldn't help but feel the loss of all those kids, talking and laughing as they completed their chores and spent their downtime under the shade of the larger trees that dotted the property.

They approached the big house off to the right. The white colonial with blue shutters still stood tall in front of them, but the big wraparound porch was devoid of the furniture that had once made it look so inviting. Paint peeled from the bannisters and leaves skittered across the worn floorboards. It was barren of any of the warmth she'd felt all those months ago.

"This is where he said to meet, right?" Harris asked.

"Yeah," Cassie answered, keeping her voice hushed. The wind lifted the hair off her shoulders and tousled it before dropping it back down. "He said he'd come out when we—"

The door to the front of the house opened. Harris raised her gun. Cassie did the same, chastising herself for hesitating. But when the figure emerged, she forgot all about keeping him in her sights.

"Ross?"

Ross Hughes looked haggard. His hair was disheveled, dark circles under his eyes. His clothes remained unchanged from the last time Cassie had seen him. Stains darkened his shirt and pants from when he'd been forced down to the ground during their shootout. A crimson streak along his biceps indicated he might not have gotten out of there unscathed.

But the smile on his face was full of relief.

"Thank God you're here, Cassie." Ross rushed down the steps, not even bothering to look at anyone else. "We were afraid you wouldn't come."

"Of course I came." She tracked his movements and the way he favored one leg. "Are you okay?"

"I've been better." Ross laughed, but it sounded strained. "Not as young as I once was, I guess. I don't bounce back as quickly as I used to."

"You've been with Omega this whole time?" Harris asked.

Ross startled, like he just remembered Cassie wasn't alone. "Yes, I —" He stopped when his gaze landed on Anastasia, his expression turning dark. "What is *she* doing here?"

"Being helpful," Anastasia replied, her sweet smile still poisonous.

"I'll believe it when I see it."

"Us too," Harris said, "but she knows what will happen if she stops behaving."

"You act like I didn't kill several of my colleagues in order to save your lives."

Ross' mouth dropped open. "What?" His wide eyes focused on Cassie. "Is that true?"

Cassie nodded. "It's a long story, but we went to meet Blackwood. Someone named Sienna Vogel was there waiting for us."

"Sienna was there?" He shifted from one foot to the other, pain crossing his face when he put too much weight on the bad one. "I got a message that she was taking over as my publicist. I thought that meant—" He shook his head. "I haven't been taking any calls from Apex for obvious reasons." He hesitated. "But she's dead?"

Cassie's stomach turned as she remembered how many bodies they'd left behind in that battered building. Would anyone care? Did they have anyone to bury their bodies when they were finally discovered?

"She had a couple men with her," Cassie said. "She killed Blackwood. Then Anastasia came in and shot the three of them. She says Apex cut ties with her, so for now, she's on our side."

Ross scoffed. "And you believe her?"

Cassie shrugged. Several doubts had occurred to her during the two-hour drive to Camp Fortuna, but they weren't going into this alliance blindly.

"There was no love lost between her and Sienna, I can tell you that much. She's promised to help us if we give her immunity."

"After everything she's done? Everything she's helped cover up?" Ross asked. His gaze landed on Harris. "After what she did to you?"

"This is bigger than me," Harris replied. "I don't like the idea of her not dealing with the consequences of her actions, but if we bring Apex down, then her life as she knows it is over. Even if she doesn't go to jail, she'll never be able to do what she's been doing for all these years."

Anastasia scoffed. "I love being talked about like I'm not even here."

Cassie ignored her. "Where's Omega?"

Ross glanced around like he just remembered where they were and what they were doing here.

"He's checking out the rest of the camp to make sure we don't run into any surprises. He should be back any minute. Did you bring all of Pearl's stuff?"

"I've got it all here." Cassie patted her pockets, where she'd stuffed the small journal and USB drives. "Omega said he uncovered some new information?"

"He did," Ross said, hope finally illuminating his eyes. "Let's go inside where it's safer."

38

THE FOYER WAS HOW CASSIE REMEMBERED IT. NOW, HOWEVER, IT lacked the familial touch that it'd had when the Abbotts' pictures were still hanging on the walls. A pair of couches and some chairs were still set up to make it look like a waiting room. They had been outdated but clean before, and now they were all covered in a fine layer of dust. The curtains had all been drawn too, making the room look dark and desolate.

The Abbotts' loss weighed heavily on Cassie's shoulders. They'd loved this place. Loved those kids.

"How could they just abandon it?" she asked, wrapping her arms around her torso.

"I don't think the Abbotts had much of a choice," Harris said, glancing around. "A lot of this had been donated to Camp Fortuna for the express purpose of taking care of the children. When it all shut down, the new owner decided not to auction off the items right away."

"A new owner, huh?" Anastasia locked eyes with Ross. "Who could that have possibly been?"

Ross frowned under her scrutiny. "You know as well as I do that it was my father."

He looked to the others, something like embarrassment crossing over his face. "He said he didn't want someone excavating it and ruining everything the Abbotts built here. He'd been donating to the camp for a long time, knowing not every kid was as lucky as I was to get adopted. Let alone into a wealthy family."

Anastasia scoffed. "He was covering his own ass."

"What's that supposed to mean?"

Cassie stepped in between them, Bear sticking close to her side. She cast a glare at Anastasia, then turned to Ross. "Anastasia says Pearl Everly's body is buried here."

Ross paled at the news, his mouth opening and closing like he wanted to deny it but found no evidence to support that claim. Finally, in a crackling whisper, he asked, "Do you know who killed her?"

"No one you know," Anastasia said in a tone that was far from reassuring. "And no one who will be able to confirm or deny that information."

"But she's here?" Ross asked Cassie. "You're sure?"

"As sure as I can be."

Cassie swallowed, remembering Anastasia gave them that information for free because she still held the location of Jason and Lorraine under lock and key. "Anastasia had no reason to lie to us about that. This was even before Omega reached out to meet here."

Ross sank down onto one of the couches, a plume of dust rising around him. He coughed and waved away the cloud. Then he looked up sharply at Anastasia. "Did my father know?"

"That's debatable," she said.

Ross ground his teeth together. "Are you incapable of giving a straight answer? Is everything a game to you? That young girl was murdered because of what she knew. You may not have pulled the trigger, but you pointed the gun in her direction. How can you live your life knowing that?"

"We all do what we have to in order to survive."

Cassie wondered how Anastasia had ended up at Apex. Had she always been this cold and callous, or had they created that monster? What had made her so desperate to be a part of their cause that she'd be willing to turn the other cheek while kids went missing?

Whatever it was, it was no excuse for all she'd done while in Apex's employ.

"When we talked to him," Cassie said, "your father seemed to believe Douglas killed Pearl. He was pretty shocked when we suggested that wasn't quite the truth."

Anastasia laughed. "He was always very good at understanding the importance of plausible deniability."

"What happened after we left the park yesterday?" Harris asked. "What have you and Omega been up to?"

"Once Anastasia left, he calmed down. Explained everything to me. I've been in the dark about so much."

Ross ran a hand through his hair. His voice broke, and he had to swallow a few times before he could continue.

"At first, I didn't want to believe him, but everything started lining up. Started making sense. The things Apex told me. The things my father said over the years. I knew they were pushing me to invest in certain companies, go to bat for certain legislation, but I never saw the whole picture." It looked like his next words caused him physical pain. "Maybe I didn't want to."

"Don't be so hard on yourself," Anastasia said, her tone still without a trace of empathy. "You were never meant to find out."

"What information did Omega find?" Cassie asked, cutting a glare at the other woman before returning her gaze to Ross. "What does it have to do with Camp Fortuna?"

"Agent Viotto's sister called him. Said she'd gone to Michigan to open that safety deposit box."

Cassie startled. She'd forgotten about Christina and her kids. "Is she okay?"

"As far as I know, she's fine," Ross said. "But she found some stuff she didn't understand. Made copies and sent it to him. After he looked at it, he wouldn't say anything else. We came straight here."

"Where is Omega?" Harris asked, looking around like he might step out of the shadows at any second. "Shouldn't he be here by now?"

"This place is pretty big," Ross said, standing again. "I'm sure he'll be back soon."

He turned to Cassie, his eyes wide and pleading. "Can I see Pearl's journal? It's not that I don't believe what you've said about my father. He deserves what's coming for him. I just—" He shook his head. "I think I need to see it for myself, to really understand how it happened."

Cassie nodded, her heart breaking for him. She pulled the journal from her pocket and passed it over. Ross took it with reverence, like it might disintegrate if he handled it too roughly. "Let's go in the kitchen. The lighting's a little better in there."

Cassie followed Ross into the next room. The cheery yellow walls glowed in the afternoon sunlight, enlarging the space. Dust motes swirled in eddies of air as they entered the space.

The group moved around the room, all of them too agitated to sit. Harris peered out one of the dirty windows to survey the backyard. Bear joined her, standing on his hind legs and placing his front paws on the sill to look through the glass next to her.

Anastasia opened cupboards and drawers with a curious expression. Was she looking for something specific? The thought had Cassie searching for the kitchen knives. When her gaze landed on the knife block, she was relieved to find it empty. Anastasia caught her eye and grinned.

Ross hunched over the table, flipping through the pages of Pearl's journal and soaking in every word. His expression grew darker with each passing moment, and more than once, Cassie saw him glower at the book. Cassie remembered the reverent way Ross had spoken about Jack and wondered what he thought of Pearl's strained relationship.

As if reading her thoughts, Ross looked up and met her eyes. It struck her how resigned he looked in that moment.

"My father wasn't always the easiest to live with. He was the disciplinarian and had high expectations for me, but since learning about

Douglas and Pearl?" Ross clenched his jaw. "It's like I don't even know him. I spent my whole childhood feeling like he saved my life when he adopted me, but when I think about it now, it's like I barely dodged the bullet. Both of them deserved so much more than this."

"We've got the USB drives with all the information from his phone, too," Cassie said. "Between that and Anastasia's testimony, your father will pay for his part in all of this."

Cassie didn't know how much of a comfort that was, but Jack hadn't been in the dark like Ross, and he had to face the consequences of his actions.

She kept an eye on Bear, noting that he wasn't on edge any more than the rest of them. "But it's Apex we're really after. We need to make sure the company is dismantled once and for all. We can't take any chances here."

"Whatever Omega has better be big then," Anastasia said, leaning against the kitchen counter and crossing her arms. "You'll need to hit them with everything you've got all at once if you don't want them to slip away in the middle of the night."

Ross scowled at her. "You say that like you're not a star witness in all of this."

"Without evidence, I'm just a pretty face with an interesting story."

Cassie glanced over at Harris, who still stood by the window. "Any sign of him yet?"

She looked again but shook her head. "Not from this angle. Let me go check the other side of the house."

"Take Bear with you."

Harris rolled her eyes, then held up her gun. "I'll be fine. He should stay here with you."

Cassie wanted to argue, but as Harris left the room, Ross placed a reassuring hand on her shoulder. "She'll be fine. We already checked the house. No one else is here."

"I know," Cassie said. "It's just hard not to feel paranoid when you're dealing with Apex."

"I know what you mean." Ross laughed, but it came out a little strained. "God, all of this feels like it's out of some blockbuster action movie, doesn't it? How did we get wrapped up in all of this?" His mouth twisted to the side in some semblance of a wry smile. "Well, I know how I did, but what about you? How do you fit into all this?"

"That's a long story." Cassie looked to Anastasia, allowing the question to settle in her eyes. "Why did Apex choose me out of everyone?"

"Right place, right time. For us, at least." She grinned. "Once they set their sights on someone, they don't take no for an answer."

"Still, you're not in politics," Ross said. "You're not a police officer or a detective. Say what you want about my father, but he prepared me for a life working for the government. You meet a lot of two-faced people and soon find out that you have to become one of them to just keep your head above the water."

He studied Cassie for a moment, his eyes roaming her face as though trying to find even a hint of that nature in her expression. "But you're not like that at all, are you?"

"I try not to be."

"If we pull this off," Ross said, "your whole life is going to change."

Cassie furrowed her brows. "What do you mean?"

"People already know your name from the headlines. Then, you come back from the dead? If they find out you helped take down Apex, everyone will know who you are."

Cassie's heart dropped into her stomach.

"What about you?" she asked him. "You wanted to be president. Aren't you worried about how this will impact your career? Your family?"

Ross opened his mouth to respond but closed it again. His brows pinched together like he was in pain. His eyes begged for forgiveness. But why? He hadn't done anything wrong.

She didn't realize she'd taken a step backward until the bottom of her back hit the table. "Ross?"

"I'm sorry, Cassie—"

"There's no point apologizing to a dead woman," a voice said from the doorway.

Cassie whipped around, her weapon heavy as she raised it. But just as soon as she did, she felt herself falter.

Two people stood in the doorway.

Harris, anger and concern warring with each other across her face.

And Jack Hughes, his eyes hard as he held a gun to her friend's head.

39

People think when you're used to handling guns, accustomed to dodging bullets, you become numb to fear. But that's not true at all. Sure, Harris had honed her instincts over the years and learned when and how to react to these types of situations, but that didn't magically negate the terror she felt each time she looked down the barrel of a gun. She'd felt it when Anastasia had kidnapped her, and she felt it now. Her scalp burned where Jack had a fistful of her hair.

Her head throbbed as she took a steadying breath, still dizzy from what had just happened in the other room. After she'd left the kitchen, she'd crossed to the other side of the house to peer through the windows. She'd let her guard down, believing the house empty. If she'd taken Cassie's advice to take Bear with her, she wouldn't be in this predicament. Anger surged through her system, white-hot and blinding—the only logical reaction to being held at gunpoint with her own weapon.

Jack had crept from the shadows and blindsided her, using the butt of his gun to temporarily incapacitate her. All she remembered was the squeak of a floorboard and a sharp pain at her temple before everything went black. When she'd regained consciousness, Jack was fitting zip-ties around her wrists and then pointing her gun at her face. He'd instructed her to keep quiet and stand up, then shoved her back toward the kitchen.

"First thing's first," Jack said. His commanding voice didn't sound uncertain at all. Whatever he planned to do now, he was all in. "Drop your gun."

"No," Cassie said. Even though her voice shook, Harris was proud of the way her arm remained steady.

"I won't ask twice. Your friend here means nothing to me. I have no interest in killing indiscriminately, but do not test me. I've come too far to turn back now."

Bear let out a low growl and pressed into Cassie's leg. Jack's fist tightened in Harris' hair, but he otherwise had no reaction to the dog's warning. Harris kept her eyes steady, watering as they locked in on Cassie's anguished gaze again.

"It's okay," Harris said, forcing herself to believe the words. "We'll be okay."

Cassie hesitated, every micro-expression flickering across her face mirroring the thoughts bouncing around in Harris' own head.

Cassie gritted her teeth and lowered her weapon at a snail's pace, as though hoping an alternative solution might fall from the sky and land at their feet. Panic coursed through Harris' body, spiking her adrenaline and increasing her heartrate until it roared through her ears.

Ross stepped forward and slipped the gun from Cassie's grasp with a whispered, "I'm sorry."

Cassie glowered at him.

"The dog. Put it outside," Jack commanded.

Cassie stiffened as she glanced back at him but didn't move. Harris could hear the way Jack bared his teeth as he spoke.

"Put it outside, or I'll put it down."

Cassie put a protective hand on Bear's head, then slipped her finger beneath his harness and led him to the back door. When she opened it, he looked up at her and whined, then glanced back to Harris as though she might talk some sense into his owner. Harris was silent as she pleaded for him to do as he was told. He whined again, sensing the tension in the room and understanding their reluctance to see him go. With a little nudge from Cassie, he trundled down the back steps, then turned and watched as Cassie closed the door between them.

As soon as it shut, he let out a high-pitched bark full of desperation, and a fist wrapped around Harris' lungs and squeezed until she felt lightheaded. She'd loved that dog even before he'd saved her life.

"Good riddance," Anastasia muttered, and Harris glanced over in time to see her running a hand along the bandage on her forearm.

"Come back over here," Jack said, nodding at Cassie. "Keep your eye on her, son."

Cassie followed Jack's instructions, and Ross took a step back before he lifted the gun in her direction, his aim not intended to kill. Maybe it was the opening they needed.

Jack yanked on Harris' hair, maneuvering her away from the doorway so that the wall was to their backs. The five of them now stood in a rough triangular formation, and it seemed a cruel twist of fate that the one person in the room who'd caused the most trouble, killed the most people, and covered up the most crimes was the one without a gun trained on her.

"It's good to see you, Jack," Anastasia said, that telltale purr back in her voice, but her body was coiled tight like a bowstring ready to snap.

"Anastasia. I was surprised when you reached out. Last I heard, Apex had replaced you."

Anastasia had spoken to Jack? Was this before or after she and Cassie had spoken to him in his home?

"By Sienna?" Anastasia's laugh sounded perfect and practiced. "She tried her best, but she wasn't up to the task."

"No, I suppose not." Jack sighed. "Your suggestion to meet here felt like kismet. I know we haven't always seen eye to eye over the years, but I hope you know I appreciate everything you've done to help me through my most difficult times."

Anastasia tilted her head in acknowledgement, but her eyes remained sharp.

Harris schooled her features, but she still felt a shock of surprise like a jolt of electricity up her spine. It had been Anastasia's idea to meet at Camp Fortuna? How many sides was she playing?

Jack shifted his stance.

"Is that the journal?" he asked. Ross nodded, and his muscles relaxed. "And the rest of the evidence?"

"Cassie has the USB drives," Ross said. His voice was different now. His answers were rote.

"Place them on the table."

"What are you going to do with them?" Cassie asked, clenching her fists at her side.

"Destroy them. Obviously." Jack's laugh was humorless. "I won't be able to deny that Douglas was my son, but without Pearl's evidence, no one will have anything that can prove I knew what sins he committed while he was still alive. And no one will know she was my daughter. I can still get out of this unscathed."

"We've already sent the evidence off to two different people. It's too late for that, Jack."

Harris held her breath. When Jack spoke, it was through clenched teeth. "Who?"

"I-I don't know."

Harris hoped Jack mistook the shake in her friend's voice for fear and not the lie it was.

"They were Omega's contacts. You'll have to ask him."

"I need you to think long and hard about that answer and try again. Omega's in no shape to answer questions."

Cassie held her hands out as if to show they were empty. "I can think about it for as long as you want, but I never saw who he emailed them to."

"Did he have a computer on him?"

Ross answered. "Yes. It's still in the car."

"Good. We'll get that later."

"What did you do to him?" Harris asked. She hadn't written off Omega just yet.

"I would be more worried about what I'm going to do to you, sweetheart."

Harris cringed away from Jack's hot breath on the back of her neck, but she infused as much venom into her voice as possible. She wanted him to know she wasn't afraid. "What's your play here, Jack?"

Jack shook her head from where he held her hair. "That's for me to worry about."

A headache blossomed across the top of her scalp. "You *should* be worried about it. The evidence is piling up against you, Senator Hughes. Thanks to that press conference, everyone knows about your connection to Douglas, and now Blackwood is dead. How do you think that's going to look?"

"It's not like I killed him."

"Yeah, but do you have an alibi? I don't think you can say you were holed up at Camp Fortuna, waiting to ambush Savannah's Assistant Chief of Police and her colleague."

Harris wasn't sure how long she could keep pushing Jack's buttons before he snapped, but every moment she wasted was another moment they were alive. "A camp that you now own, I might add. Someone out there is going to see how invested you are in this property and start asking questions. Start connecting the dots."

"That's what I pay Apex for." Jack's voice oozed confidence, his smug smile audible.

She wanted to slap it right off his face.

Harris met Anastasia's eyes, seeing that the woman's expression mirrored Harris' thoughts. Anastasia's anger turned to contemplation. She was calculating her next move, but would it be in Harris and Cassie's favor, or against?

"They've done their job for this long," he said. "We're in the home stretch now. I just need to wait until my son becomes the next president of the United States, and then I'm untouchable."

"I don't know about that. You've got a lot of blood on your hands, Senator. You knew Douglas was killing all those kids, and you did nothing to stop it. You knew Apex sent someone after Pearl. They killed two of your children for you. Did you even mourn them? Did you even care?"

"Do *you* care that I'm about to put a bullet in your brain?"

"If you killed Omega, that's another body to add to your count. If you kill us, that's more blood on your hands."

As scared as Harris was, there was one person in the room who might still listen to reason.

She locked eyes with Ross. "He's killed two of his children. His *biological* children. I know you think you owe him everything, but you don't. *He* chose to adopt you. *He's* the one who owes *you* the world, Ross."

"What do you think I'm giving him?" Jack said, growling. "Handed him the presidency on a silver platter. *My* name did that. *My* money paid for that."

Harris shook her head, and Jack's grip tightened at the movement, making her wince. Still, she didn't dare close her eyes and lose the connection with Ross. "All he's given you is a pile of skeletons to hide in your closet. Secrets and lies and bloodshed. That's his legacy, Ross. But it doesn't have to be yours."

Jack pressed the gun deeper against her scalp. "Shut up."

"If you won't listen to me, listen to her." Harris used her bound hands to gesture to Anastasia, who still stood near the cabinets across the room. Her shoulders were relaxed, and she had one hip jutted out to the side like they were all just standing around the water cooler and talking. "The most ruthless person in this room was ready to cut ties with Apex just a few hours ago."

While Anastasia had reached out to Jack, Harris still believed her initial offer was real. She'd killed three people to prove it, and Sienna Vogel hadn't been a nameless, faceless soldier, either.

"She was willing to flip on the company she dedicated her career to in order to escape the mess *your* father created. If that doesn't speak volumes, I don't know what does."

Every gaze in the room landed on Anastasia, and for the first time since Harris had met the woman, she seemed at a loss for words. It only lasted the span of two heartbeats, but it was enough time for everyone in the room to understand that Harris' words rang true.

"I am who I am," Anastasia said, her shoulders rising in a lazy shrug despite the stiffness invading her limbs. "And I'm no one's scapegoat."

"And what?" Jack's laugh bordered on outrage. "You expected to walk away with a clear name?"

"Yes." Anastasia blinked up at him, the picture of innocence. "That's exactly what I expected. I'm a big enough person to admit that Blackwood had the idea first, but since he's dead, there was no point in the deal going to waste."

"And if my son isn't president, who do you think would have the power to let you off the hook for everything you've done over the years?"

"Omega." Anastasia's brows furrowed and her bottom lip jutted out. If Jack's stiffening body was anything to go by, then the patronizing look had its intended effect. "You really have no idea who he is, do you?"

"Do you?" Jack asked. "Last I heard, you thought he worked for you."

"Unlike you, I learn from my mistakes."

Ross stared at Anastasia. "You were going to throw us to the wolves?"

Anastasia threw up her hands. "What would you have me do? Your father carved a mile-wide trail in the dirt and spelled his name out in blood. I've done my fair share of covering it up. I figured it was time to make it someone else's problem."

The smile that graced her face was as close to the old Anastasia as Harris had seen in a long time. "But you know me. I always leave my options open, and I'm nothing if not amenable to a new plan."

"How's this for a new plan," Jack said. "I think it's time my son had some skin in the game."

Ross stilled. "What?"

Dead silence filled the room.

"Shoot her."

40

Cassie's gaze swung to Ross, taking in his pale skin and his sweaty brow. He still had the gun he'd taken from her, but his arm hung limply at his hip, his body listing to the side as though the weapon threw him off-balance. She understood that feeling, knew on an intimate level the weight of responsibility pressing down on your body when you chose to point a gun at someone and place your finger on the trigger. Ross wasn't ready to carry that burden.

But his father didn't care.

Cassie sucked in a sharp breath, then promptly forgot how to let it back out.

There was no love lost between her and Anastasia, but so many lives had ended in the past few days, it made Cassie sick. And for what? Because billionaires wanted more money, and politicians wanted more power? The cycle had to end or the whole world would go up in flames.

As her lungs burned from a lack of oxygen, Cassie's gaze fell on Jack and the way his lips peeled back from his teeth in a grotesque imitation of a smile. His eyes were narrowed on Anastasia, reveling in the power he was taking from her. After so many years of needing to follow her every instruction to get himself out of the tangled web his own actions had weaved, it must have felt revolutionary to sever the cord between them. How long had he been waiting to do that?

Harris shifted her weight, catching Cassie's eye. Jack's buttons had been easy to press. The longer Harris kept him talking, the higher their chances of figuring a way out of this mess.

When Cassie's vision started going spotty, she remembered to blow out the breath she'd held in. Her stomach roiled. When had she last had a decent meal? She couldn't remember, but there was enough in there to come back up.

"I can't shoot her," Ross said in a shaking voice. "You know I can't."

"You can," Jack said. "And you will."

Anastasia backed up a step, pressing her hip into the kitchen counter as though if she tried hard enough, she could walk through the solid material and disappear. It was ironic, really. She'd been the one to suggest they meet at Camp Fortuna. Now it threatened to be her final resting place.

Anastasia met Cassie's gaze, and for the briefest moment, fear flared in the other woman's eyes. The woman who'd committed unspeakable crimes and could walk into any room with her head held high, not an ounce of doubt or concern weighing her down. But she must've heard the conviction in Jack's voice because she couldn't hide the terror on her face.

Cassie shouldn't care if the woman lived or died. But she still had her basic human decency. If Anastasia paid for her crimes, Cassie wanted it to be in the light of day, in a court of law, where everyone would know what she'd done. Whether Cassie liked it or not, Anastasia was their star witness against Apex.

And beyond that, she was the only one who knew where Jason and Lorraine were.

True to character, Anastasia refused to go down without a fight. "Look around, Jack. You've got the upper hand here. And who do you have to thank for that?"

Jack rolled his eyes. "You act like coming here was a stroke of genius. That getting my son to send that message was some great ploy. You've always oversold yourself. I understand why Apex couldn't wait to get rid of you at the first possible chance."

Ross had sent that message from Omega's phone. Despite her recent misgivings, she'd give anything to see Omega bust through the front door and take matters into his own hands right now.

"Dad—"

"You'll do as you're told, Ross." He leaned forward, like an animal ready to attack. "I sacrificed everything for you, and this is how you repay me?" His expression was full of loathing as he looked at his only remaining child. "You'd be nothing without me, Ross. You understand that, right? Nothing."

Ross shrank in on himself. "I know. I know that. But—"

"But nothing."

Jack paused, but his voice came out gentler now. "You're on the precipice of everything you ever dreamed of. Your name—*our* name—will go down in history. We can change the world. Make it work for *us*. You can have everything you've ever wanted. All you have to do is point the gun at the person who wants to take all of that away from you. *And pull the trigger*."

Ross' brows pinched together as if his father's words caused him physical pain, but Cassie saw the moment he resigned himself to his fate. After all, what other choice did he have? If he stood his ground, they'd all go down together. At least this way, he'd come out on top. Even if it meant losing his humanity along the way.

The second Ross raised the gun at Anastasia, Cassie stumbled forward. She placed her body between the two of them, holding her arms out to the side. It was a stupid, reckless thing to do. She didn't want to relive the pain of being shot again. She had no interest in sacrificing herself for Anastasia.

But she would for Lorraine. She would for Jason.

"Cassie," Harris cried out, her voice raw, struggling against Jack's grip.

Ross looked as wounded as Harris sounded. "Please," he told Cassie. "Please move."

The air shimmered next to him. The world spun as adrenaline

surged through Cassie's system. The room tilted as her heart pounded against her ribs. She had to be hallucinating. A second later, Chris' spectral form appeared.

Every part of this version of him was familiar now, from his blood-stained chest to his pale eyes, but he was closer than usual and she could see it all in sharp relief. The way the drops of blood stood frozen in time. The blue-gray pallor of his skin. The milk-white layer covering his irises, making them look several shades lighter than they had in life.

His mouth moved, and she could make out the faint murmur of his words. He was so close, enough that she could *almost* hear him. Chris spoke no louder than a breathless whisper.

She stepped forward without thinking.

Ross' voice was strangled. "Cassie, don't."

Reality crashed down around her, the room slamming back into place. Ross pointing the gun. Anastasia behind her. Harris' panting as she struggled. Jack seething under the crease between his brows that formed a canyon. The faint whisper of Chris' words was a siren's call to her ears.

Shaking her head free of the sound, Cassie found her words again. "Ross, you can't do this."

"You heard him." Ross' voice was tight, and his arm shook, the weight of the pistol threatening to pull him forward. "She'll ruin everything we worked for."

"You mean everything *he* worked for," Cassie said. She willed her heart rate to slow as she wiped the sweat from her palms. "Did your father ever stop to ask what you wanted? Think about your wife. Your kids. How will you ever go home to them knowing what you've done here?"

Ross' face crumpled. He covered his mouth with a fist and let out a strangled sob, the gun still shaking in his other hand.

"You're playing a dangerous game, Miss Quinn," Jack called out.

Cassie wanted to look over at him to make sure Harris was still okay, but she had to keep her eyes on Ross. He would listen to her. She had to believe that.

"You've been manipulated as much as the rest of us. You walked into this arena thinking you knew the rules of the game, but you were as blindsided as I was. You had good intentions, Ross. I know that. But if you pull that trigger, those good intentions mean nothing."

Ross stared at her for the span of several heartbeats. His eyes were distant. His face went slack. As he stood there, his body swayed as his mind spun.

When he finally spoke, there was a hollowness to his voice, like the realization had carved a hole in his chest. "My life is over."

"It doesn't have to be," Cassie said, her voice gentle even as her heart drummed against her ribcage. "Your father manipulated you just like Apex did. If you pull that trigger, you'll be no better than him. Look at all the secrets he's been running from and how they've impacted you over the years, how they're impacting you now. Do you want that for your own kids? Do you want your son or your daughter to be in this position some day?"

Ross shook his head, tears streaming down his face.

"I know you don't. Because you're nothing like him, Ross. You never were. And he doesn't have the power to change that."

"Maybe not," Jack replied. "But I'll be damned if I let anyone get in the way of everything I've worked for. Not even my own son."

The senator moved his gun away from Harris' head and swung it toward Cassie. She froze as terror held her in place, her feet like lead weights attached to the ends of her legs. With two guns trained on her, she had nowhere to go. No options left.

It was like she'd been transported right back to that garage three months ago, her body understanding what her brain couldn't comprehend. But that had been Chris with the gun in his hand, his eyes desperate and pleading. Jack's gaze held nothing but contempt for her as his finger squeezed back the trigger. Harris' mouth opened in a primal scream that Cassie could hardly hear over the sound of the bullet exploding from the end of the barrel, her bound hands coming up too slowly to change the trajectory of the shot.

Chris stood in front of her, so close she could see the laugh lines around the edges of his eyes.

His hands were on her shoulders, ice-cold but firm as he shoved her backwards.

She stumbled, tripping over her own feet as she crashed into the wall behind her.

The heat of the bullet seared the air before it found its mark in the center of Anastasia's chest.

41

CHAOS ERUPTED AROUND HER, BUT CASSIE COULDN'T TEAR HER GAZE away from Chris' penetrating stare.

Despite his outward appearance, there was a warmth to his pale gaze that reminded her of the way he'd looked at her when one of them cracked a joke. One corner of his mouth tipped up as though he were about to laugh. His glacial hand squeezed down on her shoulder once more, as if in reassurance.

And for the first time since he'd appeared to her, she could hear his voice.

It was nothing more than a broken rasp, as though he couldn't pull enough air into his shattered lungs, but there was no mistaking what he said.

"*Trust him.*"

He looked at her so expectantly that she nodded. Later, she'd figure out who he was talking about. A smile stretched over his face at her response. It reached his eyes, which sparkled with the same hint of mischief he'd had in life.

And then he vanished.

Someone wheezed to her left. Anastasia sat near Cassie, her legs folded under her as though she'd chosen to sink down to the dirty kitchen floor, leaning back against the lower cabinets to catch her breath. Her eyes were focused on the space Chris had just occupied, her brows pinched together in confusion.

When Anastasia's gaze slid to Cassie's, the confusion turned to understanding before a thick cough wracked her body. Blood trickled out of the woman's mouth, staining her lips the exact shade of crimson she'd preferred. Shock coursed through Cassie like lightning. Her gaze fell to the wound in Anastasia's chest. By the time Cassie looked up again, the light in the other woman's eyes had faded to nothing more than a dull glimmer.

Then Anastasia Bolton's life drained from her body with one final exhale.

A second gunshot rang out. Cassie tore her focus from Anastasia's lifeless form. Harris grappled for Jack's gun, which he held above his head like a toddler trying to keep a toy to himself. Bits of plaster dusted the tops of their heads, raining down from where he'd fired into the ceiling.

A crash sounded from the entryway. Cassie scrambled to her feet. Deep, guttural barking followed as Bear barreled into the room and zoomed past Cassie. When the dog clamped down on the back of Jack's calf, the man let out an agonized scream. He let the gun drop to the floor. Harris wrestled the weapon between her bound hands. She took two large steps backwards and kept the gun trained on him while she called out to Cassie.

"Are you okay? Are you hurt?"

"I'm fine," Cassie answered, breathless.

"Anastasia?"

Cassie looked back down at the woman. "Dead."

Harris swore. Another figure stumbled into the room, having come from the same direction as Bear. He leaned heavily against the doorframe.

Omega's cheeks and forehead were smeared with blood and dirt. He gripped his gun in one hand and clutched the side of his torso with the other.

Omega's voice was steady as his own gaze landed on Ross.

"Drop it."

Cassie turned. Ross still held his gun out in front of him but no longer pointed at her. Now, he faced his father, the weapon steadier in his hands. Wet tear tracks lined his face, but his eyes were hard now. Unforgiving. Spiteful.

"Don't," Cassie said, taking a slow step forward. "He's not worth it."

"He doesn't deserve to live. Not when he's the reason so many people—children—are dead."

Cassie reached a hand out, her palm up. "That's not your choice to make."

Ross met her eyes. "He's a monster."

"Maybe that's true." She stretched her hand out farther. "But you're not."

Ross took in her words as everyone in the room held their breath. He shook his head. The resolve in his eyes wavered but held steady. Nausea rose in Cassie's throat, burning its way through her body. But then Ross' shoulders slumped.

A moment later, the weight of the gun settled in Cassie's open palm and she freed the air from her lungs. Ross sank into one of the kitchen chairs and buried his face in his hands. Cassie turned to Jack. He'd fallen to the floor, pale and sweating from where her dog had latched onto him.

"Bear," she called. "Come."

Immediately, Bear let go of the man and trotted over to Cassie's side, circling her as he sniffed her up and down as though looking for injuries. Satisfied she was in one piece, he sat beside her and looked up, his tongue lolling from his mouth in a goofy grin.

"Good boy," she said, reaching down to scratch his head.

"You okay?" Harris asked, the question directed at Omega. "You look like you're about to pass out."

"Nah," he said, waving the hand that held his gun. "Just a flesh wound. I've had worse."

"Then why'd it take you so long to show up?"

Omega grunted and gave her a sour look, but there was no real heat to his anger. He adjusted himself against the doorframe, using it to hold himself upright. "They tied me up."

He looked at Cassie for the first time since he'd entered the room. "That dog of yours found me. Chewed through the ropes. Brought me back here. He's one smart pup."

Emotion clogged her throat. "He is."

"Are you kidding me?" Jack clutched at his leg as he seethed on the floor. "I need a hospital. Someone needs to call an ambulance."

"As far as I'm concerned," Omega said, "you got off easy. But if you really want a reason to complain, I could put a few bullets in you. Nothing fatal." He looked down at the senator in disgust. "Just something to remember me by."

Jack wrapped a hand around his bite wound to staunch the bleeding, but clamped his mouth shut.

Omega's mouth widened in a hungry grin. "That's what I thought."

He slid his gun back into its holster and pulled a knife from his hip as he moved toward Harris.

Adelaide tore her gaze from Jack and retreated a step, swinging her gun around until it pointed at Omega. "Stay back."

Omega halted. He glanced between Harris and Cassie, who stood ready with her gun, and slowly lifted his hands in the air.

"Sorry. Should've anticipated you're a bit on edge. I blame it on the blood loss. Brain isn't working at full capacity at the moment." He looked back to Harris then gestured with his chin at the zip ties around her wrists. "Just wanted to cut you free. That's all."

Harris didn't look away from him. "Cassie?"

Trust him.

After doubting Omega's motivations for so long, she'd started to think of him as more of an opponent than an ally. Although their methods had differed, Omega had always made it clear that his mission had been to take down Apex Publicity.

"Cassie?" Harris asked again.

"We can trust him. He's on our side."

Omega glanced at her with a nod. He waited for Harris to lower her gun before hobbling forward and sliding the blade between her wrists, freeing her from the bonds. Then he took two steps back and put the knife away.

"Thank you," Harris said, rubbing at the raw skin where the plastic had dug into her.

"I should be thanking you," Omega said. "Not sure I'd be standing here if it wasn't for the two of you." His gaze slid to Bear. "The three of you."

Cassie's smile lasted no longer than a heartbeat before it turned into a frown. "Anastasia's dead. She was going to testify against Apex in exchange for full immunity. Without her, we might not have enough."

"I wouldn't be so sure," Omega said. "Chris had copies of everything Blackwood's friend in the NSA had found, plus some stuff he'd dug up on his own about Five Winds and Zhang Wei. We won't be able to hold everyone accountable for all their crimes—I doubt we'll ever know the full extent of Apex's plans—but what we have will stop them for now."

"Is that good enough? Won't they just come back?"

"Maybe. But that's how these things go. There's always someone who wants to see your downfall. We stop them now, and they try again. And we stop them again. If we're lucky, we learn from our past mistakes and they don't get as far next time."

It seemed bittersweet to Cassie. An imperfect ending. But reality was rarely as simple and straightforward as it was in the movies.

"It's not ideal," Omega said, as though reading Cassie's thoughts. "But we do the best we can with what we have. Besides, it keeps me employed." He shifted his weight and grunted, gripping his side. "But I think I'm due for a vacation after this."

Cassie wasn't used to Omega's smiles. They brightened his eyes. Made him look younger. Even injured and bleeding, he looked like a completely different person.

With a jolt of understanding, she realized that's exactly what it was.

The man in front of her was no longer playing a character. This wasn't Omega. He also wasn't Robert. He had removed the various masks that he'd worn since the second she'd laid eyes on him, revealing the person underneath. Despite the grime caked along the lines of his face, he looked younger than he ever had.

"You're an undercover agent, aren't you?" Cassie asked.

Omega's eyes twinkled. "FBI. Counterintelligence."

Her heart stuttered. "Did Chris know?"

Omega shook his head, the light in his eyes dimming as he took a step forward. "I'm sorry, Cassie. For how that went down. If your life hadn't been at risk, I would've found another way."

"I know." Cassie rubbed her chest, the pain too far below her old wound to be anything other than her heart breaking all over again. "Chris knew what would happen when he pulled that trigger. He gave us the best chance at stopping Apex."

"Wish he could've been here to see that."

"He was," Cassie said, looking down at Anastasia's lifeless form. "He saved me."

Silence descended over the room like a thick blanket, heavy and comforting.

Harris broke it first. "What are you talking about?"

"Chris was here," Cassie said. "He's been with me for a while, but he'd never get close enough for me to hear him. When Jack pulled the trigger, Chris pushed me out of the way. I felt his hands on my shoulders."

A hard, disbelieving laugh tore through the air, and everyone looked at Jack as though they'd forgotten he was in the room. Cassie certainly had.

He stared at her. "You're batshit insane, aren't you?"

She didn't dignify that with an answer. Cassie turned back to Omega. "He's been trying to tell me something this whole time. I could never hear the words coming out of his mouth. Not until today."

"What did he say?" Omega asked.

"To trust you."

Omega nodded, looking down at Anastasia. "Hope he got the closure he wanted."

"He did," Cassie said. "I just wish Anastasia hadn't died."

"Like I said, we don't need her—"

Cassie shook her head. "She had Jason and Lorraine. She was keeping them somewhere for leverage. I figured once we confirmed she'd get immunity, she'd tell me—"

A shrill bark cut off Cassie's words. Bear had jumped up when she'd mentioned Jason and Lorraine. She'd ignored him when he'd nudged her knee. Now, he was barking so loud that her head vibrated.

She looked down at him, stroking the fur between his ears. "What is it?"

Bear backed up toward the door that led outside, barking some more.

"What?" she asked again, thinking back over what could've triggered this reaction. Her heart stopped when she realized what had gotten his attention, then started beating wildly again. "Jason and Lorraine?" He barked his response, and Cassie felt lightheaded. "You know where they are?"

Bear barked and raced over to the back door, wagging his tail.

Cassie looked over her shoulder at the other two.

"Go," Omega said. "I'll call for backup and keep an eye on these two."

Cassie caught Harris' wide, eager gaze, and they moved at the same time, crossing the room and throwing open the back door. Bear bounded down the steps, his barks turning feverish as he took off across the field like a bullet.

They raced after him, hope pumping through Cassie's veins like a shot of pure adrenaline.

42

JASON'S ARMS ACHED AND THE SKIN AROUND HIS WRISTS HAD TO BE RAW and bloody, but he refused to stop trying to slip his bonds. It had been hours since they'd arrived at Camp Fortuna, and his efforts had dwindled as the pain increased to unbearable levels. Even if he didn't make it out of here, he needed to make sure Lorraine did. He wouldn't be able to live with himself if something happened to her.

When Anastasia had told them Harris was with Cassie, he'd been ready to jump in her car and go. Lorraine had put a steadying hand on his arm and begged him to stop and think. Why would Anastasia be so willing to switch sides, to work *with* them instead of *against* them?

But he hadn't wanted to hear it. He had to see Cassie with his own eyes. Had to hold her in his arms. Had to know she was real and alive and safe.

He'd told Lorraine to stay behind, but she'd refused. When they'd climbed into Anastasia's SUV, the woman had smiled at them from the rearview mirror and left the precinct parking lot like they were just a couple of friends going on a road trip.

He hadn't expected to arrive at Camp Fortuna.

And he certainly hadn't expected Ross and Jack Hughes to step out of the shadows and usher them into an abandoned cabin at gunpoint. Anastasia had left, and the two men had tied him and Lorraine to separate support beams with quick efficiency, refusing to answer his questions. In under ten minutes, they'd been locked away, their fates unknown.

They'd been here for hours now, sweating and bleeding and not knowing what would happen next.

"I'm sorry," Jason croaked, thumping his head back against the beam behind him.

"You said that already," Lorraine replied.

"I'm sorry for everything, Lorraine. I've been a terrible boss. And a terrible friend."

She was silent for so long, he almost wondered if she'd somehow walked away. "You've been grieving, Jason. I understand that."

The usual anger he felt at the idea that Cassie could be dead wasn't there. In its place was a pit of despair. He stood on the edge, looking down into nothingness. "That's no excuse. I shouldn't have taken my anger out on you. Or Harris."

"No, you shouldn't have. But I forgive you."

He chuckled. That sounded too good to be true. "Just like that?"

"Yeah, just like that." An answering thump told him that she'd leaned back against her own support beam. "I miss her, too. Nothing's been the same without her."

For the first time, Jason voiced the fear he'd felt since Anastasia had given him hope. "Do you think—" He broke off when his voice cracked, unsure how safe he was to get vulnerable. But he had to say this. "Do you think Anastasia was telling the truth? That she's alive? That Harris was with her?"

"I don't know. I want to believe her, but—"

Lorraine broke off mid-sentence. He expected her to keep talking after a few seconds, but she remained silent.

"Lorraine?" he prodded. "But what?"

"Do you hear that?"

He sat up a little straighter, straining his ears. "No, hear what?"

"Barking."

"Could be wild dogs around here," he said, but his heart threatened to thump right out of his chest.

"It's getting closer."

He could hear it now. They weren't the barks of an angry animal, defending himself or his meal. The sound was high-pitched and excited. Leaning forward, he ignored the bite of the ropes around his wrists, desperate to pinpoint where the barking was coming from.

It wasn't long before the barking was right outside the door of their abandoned cabin. Claws scratched at the wood, and he could hear voices on the other side. He was dizzy from the lack of oxygen to his brain, but he didn't dare to breathe. Didn't dare to hope.

"Okay, okay. Good job, buddy." The voice was sweet and loving. "You did it."

"Jason? Lorraine?" This one was all business. "You in there?"

"Yes!" Lorraine shouted. "We're here!"

"Are you alone?" Harris asked. There was no way it wasn't her. "You okay?"

"We're alone," Lorraine said. "Tied up, but okay."

The door swung open and light poured into the cabin, forcing Jason's eyes closed even as he fought to keep looking. Blinking away the bright spots in his vision, he saw Harris step into the room, her gun out as she swept the space, making sure there were no surprises hiding in wait for them. She looked how she always did, despite the red marks around her wrists.

Bear slipped by Lorraine and bounded over to Jason, shoving his warm, wet nose against his ear and dragging his tongue along the side of his face. Jason finally sucked in enough air to let it out in a surprised laugh, never so grateful to see the big dog in his life.

And then someone was shoving Bear out of the way and kneeling in front of Jason. She had auburn hair and the sweetest smile. Big eyes that roamed over his face, checking for injuries or maybe cataloguing all the minute differences in his appearance since the last time she saw him.

He couldn't ask if it was her. Couldn't dare to dream that this was real.

"Jason?" she said, placing her hands on his shoulders. "Are you okay? Are you hurt?"

Someone—Harris—cut him free of his bonds. His hands tingled as blood rushed back into his fingertips. They shook as he brought them up to cup her face, tears gathering in the corners of his eyes as he felt how warm and solid she was beneath his touch.

"Cassie?" he asked, voice shaking.

Tears streamed down her own face. "It's me. I'm here."

"You're here," he echoed.

She nodded. Then she caught sight of his injuries. "You're bleeding."

"I'm okay," he said, still marveling at her. "It doesn't even hurt."

And it didn't. Not anymore. Not when Cassie was here, so very alive and well.

43

CASSIE KEPT ONE ARM AROUND JASON'S WAIST AS SHE LED HIM BACK TO the main house.

He didn't need the support—the only injury he had were the cuts along his wrists—but she suspected he needed to touch her as much as she needed to touch him. He would glance her way and study her face, as though making sure that it was really her that he had his arm wrapped around. The haunted look in his eyes worried her.

After everything, she couldn't blame him for not trusting reality.

They hadn't had much of a chance to talk before they'd heard sirens wailing from the front of the property. As they made their way closer, Harris filled Jason and Lorraine in on everything that had happened since they'd parted ways. Cassie added in details where Harris didn't have them, but for the most part, she let her friend do the talking. She knew she'd be doing plenty of that soon as she slipped back into whatever was left of her old life.

A pair of police officers led Jack and Ross to their vehicles in handcuffs. Someone had done a quick patch job on Jack, but he still hobbled a bit as he walked. Omega had a fresh bandage around his torso. Although he still looked a bit pale and weary, he moved around with a bit more energy.

Spotting Cassie's raised brows, he walked over with a devious little smile. "They've got some great pain killers if anyone needs them."

Cassie laughed. "Feeling good, are you?"

His laughter joined hers. "Never better."

"Can we trust them?" Harris asked, nodding toward the new vehicles that had arrived in their absence. In addition to the police cars, there were a few nondescript vehicles that Cassie assumed belonged to some fellow federal agents. "I mean, how do we know they don't work for Apex?"

"I trust my team," Omega said, gesturing toward the men in suits instead of uniforms. "They hand-selected a few officers to pick up those two. Apex will undoubtedly try to stall this investigation every step of the way. They can slow us down, but they won't be able to stop us."

Cassie caught Jason and Lorraine's curious stares and cleared her throat. "By the way, this is—" She broke off when she realized she didn't know his real name. "This is Omega."

"Thomas." He reached out and shook Lorraine's hand, then Jason's. "Thomas Walsh. FBI. Counterintelligence. For what it's worth, I'm sorry you lot got wrapped up in all of this."

"Not sure if I should thank you," Jason said, "or hit you."

"I get that a lot," Thomas said with a solemn nod. "Though, I will warn you that my colleagues will arrest you for assaulting a federal agent."

"He saved my life," Cassie said, looking at Jason. "I wouldn't be here without him."

Jason shifted away from her, letting his arms fall free of her waist. Cassie felt cold in the absence of his body heat. She knew what was running through his head: Omega had been the one to keep her hidden for three months. He'd collected her when she'd broken into her own home after he'd refused to rescue Christina and her kids. He'd been willing to let Harris die if it meant Anastasia lost her leverage over them.

It was a struggle to reconcile the fact that Thomas, the man who now joked and smiled and laughed, was Omega. Cassie wouldn't forget those moments when he'd toed the line between enemy and ally, but at the end of the day, she was alive. And so were Harris and Jason and Lorraine.

"I have to live with all the decisions I made while undercover," Thomas said, the solemnity of his tone sounding more like Omega by the second. "Times when I should've acted and didn't. Other times when I wish I'd made a different choice. I have to live with all of them, the good and the bad, until the day I die. I'm not sorry that it led us here, to Apex's downfall, but I am sorry for how it's going to affect all of you."

He surveyed each person before he continued.

"Even if you never forgive me, I hope you can forgive Cassie. Every single choice she made was to keep you all safe."

Tears threatened to spill from Cassie's eyes. The tension in Jason's body softened but did not disappear. Harris had been all business since she'd seen Cassie in those woods, letting logic steer her every action instead of emotion. Even Lorraine looked at Cassie with a mixture of hurt and relief. It was going to take a long time to get back to where they were before Apex had upended their lives, but Cassie had to believe they would get there eventually.

"Speaking of Apex's downfall," Harris said, "what happens now? You have what you need, but how are you going to take down a network as large as theirs?"

"One step at a time," Thomas admitted. "First order of business is holding Jack Hughes accountable for his actions. That includes his knowledge of Douglas' crimes, as well as his involvement in Pearl Everly's disappearance."

"She's buried here," Cassie said. "Anastasia said she was under the newest cabin."

Thomas nodded his thanks. "We may have you come back and narrow the search, if you think that's something you'd be up for."

"Of course," Cassie replied. "I'd be happy to."

"What about Ross?" Harris asked. "He was as much of a pawn as anyone else."

"Something tells me he'll be more cooperative than his father," Thomas said, rubbing a hand along his jaw. "That'll help us out quite a bit, but Apex won't like it. We'll need to keep him and his family safe. The sooner the better."

"And what about the rest of it?" Cassie asked. "Five Winds and Zhang Wei, plus China's attempts to steal military technology? How will we hold everyone accountable?"

Thomas smiled at her, full of sympathy that bordered on pity. "Your job here is done, Cassie." His gaze moved from one person to the next before it landed on her again. "All of you go home. Rest up. Heal. It's over."

"It doesn't feel over," Jason said, rubbing a hand along his chin. "Not until they're all behind bars."

Thomas sighed, a familiar weariness seeping into his features. "Unfortunately, that's not altogether realistic. It must feel like we just dodged a doomsday scenario to you folks, but this wasn't my first rodeo. Probably won't be my last, either."

Thomas looked over their shoulders at the horizon.

"Every day, someone's trying to poke at our weak points to see where we might fold. There's a lot that goes on behind the scenes that the average American citizen remains blissfully unaware of. And trust me, it's better that way."

Cassie hated that his words rang true. She'd felt the same way about her abilities over the years. It was why she'd spent so long hiding them, only trusting a select few with her secrets. If people knew what life was like after death, they'd be looking for it around every corner. Not every person could live with that kind of knowledge.

"I went to a reporter," Jason admitted, avoiding Harris and Lorraine's sharp gazes. "She has enough information to know where to keep digging."

"Annette Campbell?" Thomas asked.

Jason looked a little surprised but nodded.

"She's been on our radar for a while." Thomas placed a hand on his side, grimacing a little as he shifted his weight. "Good reporter. We'll talk to her."

When Jason opened his mouth to argue, Thomas held up a hand. "As long as she doesn't interfere with any of our investigations or reveal any identities, we won't make her scrap the story. I'm not saying the public should be kept in the dark entirely. They should know what's already out there. We just don't want them afraid of their own shadows."

"Maybe they should be," Jason muttered.

"World wouldn't be a very nice place if that were true."

One of the other agents whistled, and when Thomas glanced over his shoulder, the woman waved him over.

"That's my cue," he said, turning back to the group. "I'd say it's been good meeting you, but I don't think this was fun for any of us."

"Will we see you again?" Cassie asked.

"I'm sure of it," he said, stepping forward and clasping her hand in a firm grip. "There's still a lot to do. Testimonies to give. Trials to attend. A body to exhume. Several to bury. I'll have a goddamn mountain of paperwork to get through but might be a good change of pace."

He chuckled. "We'll need the four of you to be available for a bit, but the hard part is over. Go home. Relax."

Cassie scoffed. She was ready to go home, but she doubted it would be relaxing.

After all, she had to figure out how to come back from the dead.

44

CASSIE LEANED BACK AGAINST THE COOL BRICK WALL INSIDE JASON'S office. One week had passed since the harrowing events at Camp Fortuna, but the feeling of being under a microscope hadn't dissipated. Her worries about Apex were still at the forefront of her mind, even though Omega—*Thomas*—promised the company had bigger problems to deal with than her.

But that's not what made her skin crawl as though she were under a hot spotlight.

No, that was from the constant glances she received wherever she went, whether it was to Harris' office or the grocery store, out for a walk with Bear or dinner with Lorraine. It seemed like everyone knew who she was now, and if they didn't, they at least recognized her picture from the news.

A few bold strangers had come up to her to ask if she was the woman who'd come back from the dead. It'd been jarring in the beginning. What do you say to a question like that? She had no interest in revealing her whole story to someone she didn't know, but it also made her feel *seen*.

The probing looks that really got to her were the ones from her friends and family. Once she'd finally made it back to her house, it had been next to impossible to pick up the phone and dial her sister and parents. After all, there was no gentle way to ease your loved ones into the kind of conversation she'd needed to have with them, and so she'd ripped the Band-Aid off as soon as possible.

All three of them had hopped on a plane and arrived in Savannah that night, unable to believe her story until they saw her with their own eyes. Of course, she didn't tell them every detail of the last few months, but she'd been upfront about the ongoing investigation into Apex Publicity.

It was strange seeing them here, both in Savannah but also in Jason's office. Harris had insisted on throwing a "Welcome Back from the Dead" party. Cassie had balked at the idea at first. But then Harris explained it could help get her through this transitionary period in her life. Everyone could come to the party, hear her story and get used to the idea she was alive, and then leave knowing she was working on getting back to normal.

The first hour of the party had been uncomfortable as she shared the highlights of the last few months, but once she stepped out of the spotlight and they all started mingling, she began to relax. It had been nice to see people from the museum, like her friend Magdalena and her old boss George. A few people from the precinct had also shown up. Danny Olson, who was still in charge of the cold case files, broke out into a wide grin when he'd seen her. Detective Stone, who'd moved to greener pastures outside Savannah but had come back at Harris' invitation, had shaken her hand with a solemn nod. She almost felt normal eating pizza and sharing a drink with everyone.

Almost.

She'd seen too much to feel like she belonged in this world, sipping a glass of wine and having a normal conversation with a group of her friends. It would get easier, but all she could think about now was Apex and whether it was really over.

The FBI kept her in the loop when they could. She'd returned to Camp Fortuna and helped them locate Pearl Everly's body, thanks to a little help from the girl's spectral form, and had given her full testimony to a pair of agents who'd shown up on her doorstep.

And, of course, there were hints of what was going on behind the scenes.

Some stories took less effort to decipher than others. Jack Hughes had been arrested and served his divorce papers on the same day. Information about Douglas and Pearl had become common knowledge, and Cassie was glad to see the people of Savannah honoring the lives of all the kids who'd become victims. The public believed Pearl had been just another target of the Ash Wednesday Killer, but considering her real murderer and Anastasia Bolton were both dead, there was no point in complicating the narrative with the truth. She was at peace now.

Cassie hoped the same could be said for Jett, Pearl's half-brother. His death had been chalked up to a home invasion, which Anastasia must've staged prior to tracking down Cassie in the park outside Nashville.

The other deaths—Ross' head of security, Sienna Vogel, and several Apex soldiers—were not a matter of public record. Anastasia made an easy scapegoat for Warden Wickham and Richard Blackwood's deaths, given their connection to Apex.

The other bits of information they'd come across would seem much more innocuous to most people. Only select circles felt the ripple effect of a Chinese tech giant losing multiple government contracts and flying back to his home country.

The information Chris had discovered was damning enough that Apex lost most of their clients, filed for bankruptcy and closed down shop. Most people didn't care that a handful of politicians and Hollywood bigshots lost their publicists, but it had put a smile on Cassie's face for an entire day. Thomas had shared that a few at the top had been arrested for crimes like insider trading, tax evasion, and fraud, but she didn't find any of that in the newspapers. The government didn't want the American people to know just how close Apex had come to rocking the country to the core, after all.

Taking a sip of her wine, Cassie realized she *could* live with that.

Like her, Thomas worked best from the shadows. Sometimes it was lonely, keeping secrets like this, but not everyone could handle the truth. If that was her burden to bear, then so be it.

Glancing around the room, Cassie caught Laura's eye and watched as her sister broke off from her conversation with Magdalena and Jason to head over to Cassie. There was a smile on her sister's face, but her eyes were full of concern. "You're doing an awful lot of deep thinking over here by yourself."

Cassie resisted rolling her eyes. Laura had been more than a little overbearing since Cassie had come back. Not that she'd ever blame her sister for that. If Laura turned up after being presumed dead for three months, Cassie would sleep on the floor of her bedroom every night for a year.

"I'm fine," Cassie said, trying and failing to keep the exasperation from her voice. "I promise."

"It's okay if you're not," Laura said. At the look Cassie gave her, she held up her hands. "Sorry, it's hard to turn the therapy brain off."

"I appreciate you," Cassie said, nudging her sister with her shoulder.

"Good." Laura looked out over the small crowd of people milling around. "Remember that when you hear what I'm about to tell you."

Cassie pushed off the wall, her heart speeding. "What is it?"

Laura bit her lip and searched Cassie's face, a strange mix of humor and anxiety in her gaze. "I'm moving back to Savannah."

Cassie shook her head. "No. You're not leaving your life in California because of me."

"I'm not," Laura said. When Cassie just stared at her, she rolled her eyes. "Okay, I am. But will you at least hear me out?"

"Will you stay in California if I refuse to?"

"No."

Cassie sighed. "Fine."

Laura looked away from Cassie, back to the other people in the room, but her gaze was distant. "I'm not going to lie and say the last three months weren't the most difficult of my life. I did a lot of introspection, and I realized I'm not happy with my life in California. I haven't been in a long time."

"And moving back to Savannah is going to fix that?"

"No," Laura said, turning her attention back to Cassie. "But I miss you. I miss Mom and Dad."

"Oh God—"

"They're staying in North Carolina, don't worry. Although they might visit more frequently."

"I'm not against that."

"And they feel better about staying *there* knowing I'll be *here* with you."

Cassie groaned. "You already talked to them about this?"

"Yes. I already made up my mind, Cassie."

"I don't want you to worry about me. I'm fine. I'll *be* fine."

"That's the thing," Laura said, her tone serious. "I *am* worried about you. I'm going to *continue* being worried about you, whether you tell me you're fine or not. Visiting you here and seeing you out in California have been some of the biggest highlights of the last few years. Being out West was new and exciting for a while, but I miss Savannah. I need a change of pace. And I'd really like your support."

Cassie took Laura's hand and squeezed. "Of course you have my support. I'd love for you to be closer so we can see each other more often. I just don't want you to uproot your entire life because of me."

"It's not just because of you. Maybe I won't stay forever, but for now, this feels like the right move."

Cassie searched her sister's face, looking for the answer to a question she wasn't sure she should ask. "Have you told Adelaide yet?"

Laura looked away, but she didn't pull her hand from Cassie's grasp. "No. We haven't really talked much. Not since, you know, I blamed her for your death and all."

"You should talk to her. I think she'll be excited to see you more, too."

Laura glanced back at her, eyebrows pinched in suspicion. "Things were complicated between us before you went missing. I'll be lucky if she wants to be friends after everything I said. I'm not looking for anything else."

Cassie wasn't sure that was entirely true, but she didn't say that out loud. "I think she'll forgive you. I think she'd love to be friends again."

Laura gave her a small smile and squeezed her hand before slipping free. "We'll talk more later, okay? I'm going to need your help finding an apartment."

"Okay. I guess it's the least I can do after pretending to be dead for a few months."

Laura's mouth pulled down into a frown, but Cassie could tell she was trying not to laugh. "Too soon, Cassie. Way too soon."

The smile on Cassie's face felt almost normal as she watched her sister rejoin the crowd. Eventually, she'd have to do the same, but before she could peel herself away from the wall, Jason tossed his empty beer bottle in the trash and made his way over.

"Hey," he said, leaving about a foot of space between them as he leaned against the wall beside her.

"Hey," she replied, hating the tension that filled the air around them.

"Looked like you and Laura were having a nice talk."

"She's moving to Savannah."

Jason's eyebrows rose in surprise. "Really?"

"Yeah. Needs a change of pace."

"I'm sure Harris will be excited to hear that."

Cassie grinned. "That's what I said. Laura thinks they'll be lucky to be friends after everything, but you should've seen her blush. There's still something there between them."

Instead of sharing in her excitement, Jason grew solemn next to her. "I'm glad she'll be here with you."

There was a sense of finality to Jason's words. They'd seen each other a few times over the last week, but between helping the FBI and visiting with her family, their time together had been limited. They'd talked about what happened, about how she'd stayed away to protect him. Jason had told her he understood, but he hadn't said he'd forgiven her. That would take time, she knew.

But the way he spoke now sounded like goodbye.

"Jason?" she asked, anxiety making his name come out in a whisper.

"I'm going home for a while. To New Orleans. I need to see my family. Spend some time with them."

"Okay." Emotion clogged her throat, nearly choking her. She was only able to get out one word. "When?"

"I'm leaving tonight." He checked his watch. "Probably going to head out in a few minutes."

Her heart felt like it was breaking in two, but she forced the next question out of her mouth. "For how long?"

"I'm not sure." Jason cleared his throat, looking anywhere but at her. "I won't be gone forever. Savannah is still my home. It's where I want to be."

He blinked rapidly, then rubbed the back of his neck. He wore a frown, and his brows were pinched together until his forehead was a mess of wrinkles.

He finally looked at her, his eyes wide and apologetic. "I just need some time away. To get my head back on straight."

Her heart cracked in two, splintering like Jason had taken an axe to it. But while her chest ached, her mind was calm. She understood why he needed this. But she couldn't bring herself to say it.

"Lorraine's going to keep an eye on the office for me. You're welcome to use it if you need to."

Again, she nodded. And again, she couldn't utter a single word.

Jason leaned in and placed a chaste kiss on her cheek. "Take care of yourself, Cassie."

"You too," she replied, but it was rote. Hollow.

With a final nod, Jason walked away.

45

Harris smiled up at the waitress when she dropped off their drinks—a domestic beer for her and a fruity cocktail for Cassie. The woman gave a polite nod and hustled over to the next table in the bar. It was a local joint, somewhere neither of them had been before, but the atmosphere was nice. The dim lighting helped it stay cool, and the rock music playing over the speakers was just loud enough to cover up individual conversations without having to yell at one another.

Harris took a sip from her beer, eyeing Cassie over her bottle. When she released the drink from her lips, she asked, "How've you been?"

"You saw me yesterday," Cassie said. "And the day before. And the day before that."

It was true. A few days ago, she'd thrown a "Welcome Back from the Dead" party for Cassie and spent every day before and after checking in. Sometimes it was a quick house call and others they went out for dinner. Tonight, it was to grab a quick drink. Harris knew she was being clingy, but something told her Cassie needed this as much as she did.

"Wow, can't a friend ask after your well-being, Cassie?" Harris smirked and pointed her beer bottle in her direction. "You know, you've changed since you came back to life."

Cassie laughed and then took a dainty sip from her cocktail. Harris knew she was using the moment to think about the answer to her question. Mentioning that Cassie had supposedly died and come back to life was their little joke. A way to make it feel like it wasn't that big of a deal.

It's true that Cassie *hadn't* changed. She was the same person she'd always been before she disappeared from Harris' life for three months. It was everything—and every*one*—else that seemed different. Harris wasn't sure if she envied Cassie for that, or if it made her even more worried.

"I'm good," Cassie said after a moment. "Things are still tough, you know? They will be for a while. But I've got my first therapy appointment soon." She took another sip of her cocktail, keeping her eyes on the liquid. "Should be an interesting one."

Harris snorted. "I don't think one hour will be long enough for you to even tell her what you've been through, let alone dissect it all."

"No, but I've got time. We'll get through it all eventually."

Harris pursed her lips. Cassie had been holding it together better than anyone. She kept a positive attitude, but a little of her light had dimmed.

Harris set her bottle on the table with a clink. "I talked to Laura today."

Cassie sat up a little straighter, her smile bright and wide. "You did?"

Harris stifled a laugh. She knew Cassie wanted nothing more than her and her sister to get together, but that ship had sailed. Still, she'd mentioned the conversation because she knew it would make Cassie happy.

"She apologized for blaming me for your death. I accepted, of course." Harris fiddled with the label on her beer bottle, not quite looking Cassie in the eye. "I missed talking to her."

"You'll get to talk to her a lot more when she moves back to Savannah," Cassie said, waggling her eyebrows.

"That's not for another month. Who knows what will happen between now and then?" Harris held up a finger. "And even if we do end up talking more once she's here, it doesn't mean anything. I'll be happy just knowing you two are spending more time together."

Cassie's smile turned soft. "Thank you. And obviously I don't want to put any pressure on your shoulders, so just know that I'll be happy with whatever happens too. I just love the idea of having my best friend and my sister by my side."

Harris snorted. "What happened to you not wanting Laura to move here because of you?"

"She said it's not *entirely* because of me. Besides, it'll be nice to have someone else around to spend time with. A good distraction."

Harris reached across the table and placed a hand on Cassie's forearm. "You haven't heard from Jason at all since he went back to New Orleans?"

She looked up at her friend and shook her head, her eyebrows turned down. "I didn't expect to. He was pretty clear he needed space. I don't blame him. I just..."

"Miss him?"

Cassie nodded, blinking rapidly to keep her tears at bay. "Yeah."

"I miss him too, the big idiot." A swell of gratitude filled her chest with warmth. "He was a pain in my ass while you were gone, but he never gave up on you. Never stopped fighting."

Cassie looked at her, a tear dripping down her cheek. She sniffled and wiped at her nose. "Then why'd he leave?"

Harris frowned. "He was different when you were gone. Angrier than I'd ever seen him. I don't think that anger went away when you came back the way he'd expected it to."

She paused, thinking through her next words.

"If I had to guess, I'd say he's probably afraid that he'll never go back to the way he was, and I don't think he wants you to see that side of him. It wasn't pretty."

"We could've worked through it together," Cassie said, swiping her tears away. "He didn't even give us that chance."

"I'm not saying I agree with what he did," Harris replied, "but I do understand. He might never have consciously gotten past the denial stage, but he grieved for you, Cassie. Your disappearance consumed every part of him, day and night." The table next to them erupted into laughter, and Harris had to wait until it died down before she could speak again. "I think a little space might be better for both of you. We all need to process what happened, and we're all going to do that in our own way. This is his."

Cassie let out a breath through her nose, leaning forward and taking a long sip of her drink. She sat back up. "I hate when you make sense."

"If that were true, you'd stop dragging me out all the time."

"You dragged *me* out! If I didn't know any better, I'd say you were the one who's lonely, Harris."

Harris matched her friend's scowl and tipped her beer back to cover up the jolt of pain that seared her chest. Harris didn't have too many people either. She had her colleagues, but she didn't spend time with any of them outside of work. She and Cassie would remain close, but there was no telling how Laura's presence in their lives might change their relationship. Jason was gone. Lorraine was the only one left. Harris adored her, but she was busy taking care of her mother and searching for a new job.

That sparked a new question in her mind, and Harris was glad to find a new topic to discuss.

"By the way—"

"Sorry to interrupt." Someone slid into view to stand next to their booth. "But I felt like I should come over and say hi."

Harris and Cassie looked up to see Annette Campbell, the reporter for the *Savannah Morning News*. She held a beer in her hand and her curly blonde hair was pulled back in a ponytail. Her gaze remained sharp despite the relaxation in her shoulders.

Annette laughed and held up one of her hands in surrender. "I promise I'm not here in an official capacity." Her gaze landed on Cassie. "Mostly I just wanted to say how happy I was to hear that, uh, the rumors of your demise were greatly exaggerated."

Cassie laughed. "Thank you, Annette. I appreciate that."

Annette nodded, then looked at Harris and tipped her head. "Assistant Chief."

"Annette," Harris said, fighting back a smile. They'd come a long way since the start of their antagonistic relationship, but she still liked to give the reporter a hard time. "Jason told me the two of you had a secret meeting. I keep expecting to see your byline under a headline about Apex, but so far, it's been quiet."

Annette frowned. "The Feds shut down my article. They've given me a list of items I can report on, but it's very, *very* short."

"I'm sorry," Cassie said, as though she were the one responsible for making that decision. "If you've done at least a little bit of research on the company, you'll know how slippery they can be. Agent Walsh doesn't want to take any chances."

"I don't like it, but I do understand." Annette studied Cassie for a moment. Harris had seen the look on Annette's face many times—calculating her best chance of getting something from the exchange.

Finally, the woman said, "There is a way you can make it up to me."

The glance Cassie shot to Harris was more like a cry for help. "I don't know if I'm going to like this."

Annette was serious as she gazed down at Cassie. "From what I've read and heard through the grapevine, I know how big of a deal this Apex Publicity story is. It's too bad that the public won't know about all the people who put their lives on the line to stop them from doing what they wanted to do."

She sighed. "It was the kind of story that could've taken my career to the next level. Hell, probably up through the next couple of levels."

Cassie looked torn. "I wish I could help, but—"

"I'm not asking for information you can't give me." Annette glanced at Harris, and she knew the reporter was thinking of their first meeting too. "I've learned that lesson, and the last thing I want to do is jeopardize this investigation or the lives of any people involved."

"Then what could you possibly want with me?" Cassie asked.

"As I was reading through everything Jason gave me, I started to notice some interesting patterns. If I didn't know the kind of person you are, or the company you keep, I would be questioning your sanity right now."

Harris and Cassie exchanged a glance but said nothing.

"The story about Apex would've been national news, but I realized there's a story a little closer to home that more people might be interested in."

Cassie paled, noticeable even in the dim lightning. "No one will believe you. You'll become a laughingstock if you write about me."

"Maybe." Annette shrugged. "Maybe not. I've talked to a few people already, and quite a few are willing to go to bat for you, Cassie. You've already got everyone's attention by coming back from the dead. Don't you want a chance to tell your story in your own words?"

Cassie opened her mouth, but nothing came out.

Annette slid a card from her pocket and placed it in the center of the table.

"Think about it. Give me a call if you want to talk about it some more."

Harris watched Annette disappear into the crowd before she turned back to Cassie. "Well, that was interesting."

"Yeah," Cassie said, picking the card up off the table. "That's one word for it."

Harris signaled for their waitress to bring them another round. Cassie looked a little lost as she stared down at the card in her hands.

"You thought about what you're going to do once things settle down?"

Cassie blew out a breath and tucked Annette's card into her purse. "Not sure. I'll always miss working at the museum, but I don't feel like I fit in that world anymore."

Harris shrugged. "You've always got a job as a consultant for the PD."

"Danny cornered me at the party, asking if I'd be interested in tackling any of the cold case files with him."

"That's one option."

Cassie eyed her. "You sound like you have other ideas."

"If you speak with Annette and she publishes that article about you, there will be a lot of people who know your name. Know what you do."

"That doesn't sound like a good thing to me."

"Depends on how you look at it. You've always loved helping people, Cassie. This could be a good way for you to do that."

Cassie looked at Harris like she'd grown two heads. "I can't believe you *want* me to talk to Annette."

"I want you to do whatever you're comfortable with," Harris said. "But I don't want you to be afraid to put yourself out there. At one point in time, you were afraid people would judge you for what you said you could do. But like Annette said, there's a lot of people who would go to bat for you. Maybe it's time to put your money where your mouth is."

"And what?" Cassie asked, searching Harris' face. "Become a paranormal investigator?"

Harris grinned.

Cassie leaned back, gulping down the rest of her cocktail, then wincing. All the alcohol must have settled on the bottom. "You've lost your mind."

"Maybe, but that doesn't mean it's a bad idea. Jason's not using his office space right now, you'll be able to drum up some business with Annette's article, and you can supplement your income by consulting with the department."

Cassie stared at her, slack-jawed. "How long have you been thinking about this?"

"About sixty seconds. But you've gotta admit it feels like a step in the right direction. It's time to put Apex behind you and move onto something new. Not everyone gets a second chance at life, you know."

"I think I'm on my third or fourth at this point."

The waitress arrived with their drinks and disappeared again just as quickly. Harris grabbed her bottle and held it aloft. "To the next chapter of our lives."

Cassie smiled, a little more brightness returning to her eyes. She held her cocktail up and clinked it against Harris' beer.

"To the next chapter."

Cassie Quinn returns in *Into the Light*! Pre-order your copy now: https://a.co/d/bSlmElX

Join the LT Ryan reader family & receive a free copy of the Cassie Quinn story, *Through the Veil*. Click the link below to get started: https://ltryan.com/cassie-quinn-newsletter-signup-1

THE CASSIE QUINN SERIES

Path of Bones

Whisper of Bones

Symphony of Bones

Etched in Shadow

Concealed in Shadow

Betrayed in Shadow

Born from Ashes

Return from Ashes

Risen from Ashes

Into the Light

ALSO BY L.T. RYAN

Find All of L.T. Ryan's Books on Amazon Today!

The Jack Noble Series

The Recruit (free)

The First Deception (Prequel 1)

Noble Beginnings

A Deadly Distance

Ripple Effect (Bear Logan)

Thin Line

Noble Intentions

When Dead in Greece

Noble Retribution

Noble Betrayal

Never Go Home

Beyond Betrayal (Clarissa Abbot)

Noble Judgment

Never Cry Mercy

Deadline

End Game

Noble Ultimatum

Noble Legend

Noble Revenge

Never Look Back

Bear Logan Series

Ripple Effect

Blowback

Take Down

Deep State

Bear & Mandy Logan Series

Close to Home

Under the Surface

The Last Stop

Over the Edge

Between the Lies

Caught in the Web

The Marked Daughter (Coming Soon)

Rachel Hatch Series

Drift

Downburst

Fever Burn

Smoke Signal

Firewalk

Whitewater

Aftershock

Whirlwind

Tsunami

Fastrope

Sidewinder

Redaction

Mirage

Faultline (Coming Soon)

Mitch Tanner Series

The Depth of Darkness

Into The Darkness

Deliver Us From Darkness

Cassie Quinn Series

Path of Bones

Whisper of Bones

Symphony of Bones

Etched in Shadow

Concealed in Shadow

Betrayed in Shadow

Born from Ashes

Return to Ashes

Risen from Ashes

Into the Light (Coming Soon)

Blake Brier Series

Unmasked

Unleashed

Uncharted

Drawpoint

Contrail

Detachment

Clear

Quarry

Dalton Savage Series

Savage Grounds

Scorched Earth

Cold Sky

The Frost Killer

Crimson Moon

Dust Devil (Coming Soon)

Maddie Castle Series

The Handler

Tracking Justice

Hunting Grounds

Vanished Trails

Smoldering Lies

Field of Bones

Beneath the Grove (Coming Soon)

Affliction Z Series

Affliction Z: Patient Zero

Affliction Z: Abandoned Hope

Affliction Z: Descended in Blood

Affliction Z : Fractured Part 1

Affliction Z: Fractured Part 2 (Fall 2021)

Alex Hayes Series

Trial By Fire (Prequel)

Fractured Verdict

11th Hour Witness

Buried Testimony

The Bishop's Recusal (Coming Soon)

Stella LaRosa Series

Black Rose

Red Ink

Black Gold

White Lies

Avril Dahl Series

Cold Reckoning

Cold Legacy

Cold Mercy (Coming Soon)

Savannah Shadows Series

Echoes of Guilt

The Silence Before

Dead Air (Coming Soon)

ABOUT THE AUTHOR

L.T. Ryan is a *Wall Street Journal & USA Today* bestselling author. The new age of publishing offered L.T. the opportunity to blend his passions for creating, marketing, and technology to reach audiences with his popular Jack Noble series.

Living in central Virginia with his wife, the youngest of his three daughters, and their three dogs, L.T. enjoys staring out his window at the trees and mountains while he should be writing, as well as reading, hiking, running, and playing with gadgets. See what he's up to at http://ltryan.com.

Social Medial Links:

- Facebook (L.T. Ryan): https://www.facebook.com/LTRyanAuthor

- Facebook (Jack Noble Page): https://www.facebook.com/JackNobleBooks/

- Twitter: https://twitter.com/LTRyanWrites

- Goodreads: http://www.goodreads.com/author/show/6151659.L_T_Ryan

K.M. Rought is a writer and editor hailing from Upstate New York. Through she graduated with a degree in Art History, she fell into a career of freelancing, fulfilling her childhood dream of being a published author.

Now residing in Ohio, K.M. spends her days writing, playing video games, and telling her cat that no, it's not time to eat yet. Her obsessions include foraging for mushrooms, buying neon green kitchenware, and reading every single book by Rick Riordan.

You can find her on Instagram @karenrought.

Made in the USA
Middletown, DE
11 August 2025